SUPERPOSITION

SUPERPOSITION
DAVID WALTON

an imprint of Prometheus Books
Amherst, NY

Published 2015 by Pyr®, an imprint of Prometheus Books

Cover design by Grace M. Conti-Zilsberger
Cover image © Media Bakery

This is a work of fiction. Characters, organizations, products, locales, and events portrayed in this novel either are products of the author's imagination or are used fictitiously.

Inquiries should be addressed to
Pyr
59 John Glenn Drive
Amherst, New York 14228
VOICE: 716–691–0133
FAX: 716–691–0137
WWW.PYRSF.COM

19 18 17 16 15   5 4 3 2 1

Library of Congress Cataloging-in-Publication Data

Walton, David, 1975-
    Superposition / by David Walton.
        pages ; cm
    ISBN 978-1-63388-012-2 (paperback) — ISBN 978-1-63388-013-9 (e-book)
    I. Title.

PS3623.A454S87 2015
813'.6—dc23

2014043772

Printed in the United States of America

To Miriam
because second is best

"Our imagination is stretched to the utmost, not, as in fiction, to imagine things which are not really there, but just to comprehend those things which are there."

—Richard Feynman,
1965 Winner of the Nobel Prize in Physics

CHAPTER 1
UP-SPIN

I should have known better than to let him in. Brian Vanderhall showed up on my doorstep in the falling snow wearing flip-flops, track shorts, and an old MIT T-shirt, the breath steaming from his mouth in little white gusts. It would have saved me a lot of trouble if I had slammed the door in his face, never mind the cold. Instead, like a fool, I stepped aside.

I had been in the basement working the heavy bag when the doorbell rang. A vee of sweat darkened my gray, sleeveless shirt, and my arms were slick with sweat.

"Jacob Kelley," he said. "Looking like a Neanderthal, as always."

"And you're as charming as ever," I said. "Where's your coat?"

He gave me a weak smile. "Close the door."

I peered out and saw nothing but snow and darkness. "Everything okay?"

"Just close it, will you?"

Brian Vanderhall had been a friend since college, probably my best friend through graduate school and all the drama surrounding our careers at the New Jersey Super Collider. He hadn't always been the most loyal of friends, and there were reasons I'd let him slide out of my life. Finding him unexpectedly at the door like that, I thought he would try to pull me into some kind of messy personal or financial problem, but I wasn't expecting disaster. I guess we never do.

Brian stamped snow off his flip-flops and kicked them into a corner. A blast of frigid air invaded the room's fireplace warmth as I pushed the door shut and relocked it. His face and hands were chapped red, and several days' worth of stubble covered his face. It had been two years since I had seen him in person, and he looked different, though I wasn't sure why. His hair was a bit longer, I thought, and the glasses might have been a new pair. Maybe he just looked older.

We climbed the three steps from the landing to the living room, where my daughter Claire sat curled by the fire doing her math homework, her blond hair spreading like a sunrise over her shoulders. I gave her a quick kiss on the forehead, and we rounded the corner into our kitchen.

The kitchen was the room that had sold Elena and me on this house. It was spacious and modern, with long countertops and a butcher-block island. Elena soon had us around the breakfast table with hot mugs: coffee for her and Brian and tea for me. I could hear Alessandra practicing her trumpet upstairs.

Brian cupped his hands around his mug and inhaled the steam. "Thank you," he said. "Really, I can't say how much."

Elena and I traded glances. She was small, athletic, and wore jeans and a health club sweatshirt. Her looks, as far as I was concerned, had only improved since she was twenty-two, when I'd spotted her running ahead of me in the Philadelphia marathon and I'd finished in record time just to keep her in sight.

"How are things at the NJSC?" she asked.

"Oh, you know, same old," Brian said distractedly. "Richardson is an ass, as always." He looked at me. "Things were never right after you left."

"Things were never right when I was there, either," I said. The New Jersey Super Collider was the largest particle accelerator in the world, built under the Pine Barrens at Lakehurst, not far from Princeton. Massively expensive, its construction far over budget, it had been condemned by many as the "Big Dig" of our generation, the protests compounded by the environmentalist outcry about long-term radioactive effects on the pine forest ecology. Despite all the objections, Richardson had managed to push it to completion. Once it was operational, the political feeding frenzy had increased, only instead of fighting about whether the accelerator should be built, they fought over who should be allowed to use it. There were some aspects of working there that I dearly missed. There were others that I didn't miss at all.

"I don't understand why you left," Brian said. "Nobody does. You've got a PhD from Princeton. You're a published physicist, top of your game, the next Wheeler maybe. How could you give it up for . . ." He waved his hand vaguely around the kitchen.

"I'm teaching physics at Swarthmore College," I said. "I love it there. I have some bright kids. And there's no politics, no squabbling over experiment time, no need to prove to strangers that my work is worthwhile in order to keep doing it."

That had been the last straw for me, when the appearance of our research to the outside world overcame the commitment to genuine discovery. There was such a pressure for our multibillion-dollar investment to produce new results that the value of the science itself was jeopardized. For the first time since Congress had canceled the Superconducting Super Collider in Texas in 1993, the United States was on the leading edge of particle physics. We could have finally overcome the infamous American nearsightedness where science was concerned. Instead, we spent so much effort trying to prove the value of the NJSC to taxpayers that we hardly got any value from it at all.

"You could at least have taught at Princeton," Brian said. "They would have found a place for you."

"I left to *avoid* politics," I said.

Brian shook his head. "You would have been something special. Remembered by the history books. And you threw it all away."

I sipped at my tea to mask the bunching in my muscles. "Just because a man is a talented pianist doesn't mean he has to choose music as his career," I said. "Just because a girl is a talented ice skater doesn't force her to choose the life of an Olympian." It felt like we were picking up the conversation right where we'd left it two years before. I was tired of it already.

He sipped his coffee, made a face. "That brilliant mind of yours is squandered helping mediocre students get a few science credits."

I half stood, my hands flat on the table, scraping the chair against the tile floor. Elena put a quick hand on my arm. "Look," I said. "Did you come here just to insult me, or did you have some other purpose?"

"Sorry, sorry," he said. "I know. Old habits and all that." He lifted the mug back to his mouth, but his hand shook, and some of the hot coffee spilled over the edge. He slammed the mug down, slopping more on the table, shouted a garbled expletive, and sucked at his hand.

"Here," Elena said. She ran a dish towel under cool water and handed it to him. He wrapped it around his hand, while I used another cloth to wipe away the coffee mess.

I realized then why Brian looked so different. He was scared. Not stressed—I had seen that before, when he had money problems or feared that one of the women in his life would find out what he was doing with the other. This was different. He was stealing glances at the windows and startling at sudden noises. He was like a squirrel on the road, poised to bolt to safety the moment he was sure which way the danger was coming from.

"Spit it out," I said. "What's wrong?"

"What do you mean?"

"You've never made a social call in your life. What do you want from us?"

He brushed a stray lock of hair out of his eyes, which promptly fell back down again. "I'm in a bit of trouble," he said.

"There's a shock. Is it the work or the women?"

Brian gave a bitter laugh. "I guess you could say both."

I drank the last of my tea and brought the mug over to the sink, where I washed it and set it on the drying rack. A holiday candle burning on the counter gave a sharp wintergreen smell to the air. "Keep talking."

"Have you kept up with the literature?" Brian asked, but we were interrupted by a wailing cry before I could answer. Sean, my son, catapulted into the room and crashed into me. At five years old, his only speed setting was full acceleration, and his only means of stopping was collision.

"Slow down," I said. "What's wrong?"

"Alessandra won't let me play," he said, still crying.

"She's practicing. Why don't you find your bugle?"

"It's broke. And she hit me!"

"Alessandra hit you?"

"In the head! With her trumpet!"

I looked at the spot and, sure enough, a small half-moon cut was swelling, clearly visible through his blond, short-cropped hair. I sighed. Another chapter in the ongoing drama of the Kelley children.

Alessandra flew around the corner a moment later. She was dark-haired, like her mother, but without Elena's easy-going patience. "It wasn't my fault," she said.

"Not your fault?" I said. "Look at that cut! You're fourteen, Alessandra, not seven. You have to find a better way of dealing with him than violence."

"I was just playing. He ran into it."

"You're seriously going to tell me he got that cut just running into you? That you were practicing, minding your own business, and he just crashed into your trumpet hard enough to leave that mark?"

She crossed her arms and gave me one of her ferocious, sullen glares.

"Don't look at me that way," I said. "You have to learn to keep that temper of yours under control."

"You mean like you did with that guy at the gym who insulted Mom?" Alessandra asked.

I felt my blood rising. "Don't push me, young lady. Fix your attitude right now and apologize to your brother."

Elena put a hand on my arm again. "We have a guest," she said. "You stay and talk; I'll bring the kids upstairs and deal with this." She rummaged in the freezer and pulled out a teddy bear icepack, which she pressed to Sean's head. "Upstairs for your pajamas," she said. She rotated Sean by his shoulders and pointed him in the right direction.

"Give me a moment to get the kids to bed, and then I'll be back," Elena said to Brian. "Help yourself to coffee; there should be another cup's worth in the pot."

I caught Brian staring at Sean's short arm, though he didn't say anything about it. It's what most adults did: they stole glances, with varying degrees of subtlety, but didn't ask. Sean had been born that way, his left arm half the normal length, with a tiny hand at the end of it that couldn't grasp anything very well.

I heard Alessandra still protesting her innocence as they climbed the stairs. Brian snickered. "Always the domestic, weren't you?" he said. "Diapers and runny noses." We'd been out of diapers for several years, but I didn't bother to point this out. I couldn't believe that even when he showed up at my house shaking in fear and asking for help, he could still manage to look down his nose at my family.

"Okay," I said. "Let's hear it."

Brian held my gaze for a beat. "You remember the nature-as-computer argument?"

"Sure. The idea that the whole universe is just one big quantum computer."

"All the information in the universe can be represented by a vast but finite number of bits, just a few for each particle: its type, its spin, its momentum, like that," Brian said.

"It always sounded like doublespeak to me," I said. "The universe is the universe. Calling it a computer doesn't provide any scientific insight."

Brian looked a little offended. "Yes, it does. You can simulate any real set of particle interactions with a quantum computer made up of the same number of particles, no matter how many particles and how complex the interaction."

So far, this didn't sound like anything to make anyone run out into the snow in flip-flops. It just sounded like wonky metaphysics. "Yeah? And I can simulate an apple with an apple. So what?"

"So, if you can simulate the universe with a quantum computer the same size as the universe, that means that the universe is indistinguishable from a quantum computer. For all practical purposes, it *is* a quantum computer."

"Which means . . ." I was starting to get it.

"Which means it's a computational device with a complexity factor far in excess of Pronsky's Threshold."

"Sufficient to generate consciousness," I said, letting my incredulity show in my voice.

"Right."

I couldn't help it. I laughed. "You're telling me, what? The universe is sentient?"

"Pieces of it."

"You're serious?"

Brian sat rigid in his chair, darting glances at the windows. He didn't have to answer. I knew he was serious. I just didn't know if he was crazy or not.

Just then, Claire came in and helped herself to Oreo cookies and a glass of milk. At sixteen, Claire generally chose her own bedtime. She sat down at the table, unscrewed a cookie, and dunked half of it.

I welcomed the distraction. "Claire, you remember Mr. Vanderhall?" I said.

"Sure, a little," she said. "Glad to meet you."

Brian's eyes focused, and he shook her hand. "My pleasure." He studied her face. "You've really grown up since I saw you last."

He was right—in the last few years, Claire's freckles had faded, and she'd traded girlish cuteness for a real beauty. Given Brian's reputation with women, though, I didn't like him noticing it. Besides, it wasn't just Claire's beauty that made her an impressive young woman.

"Claire's at the top of her class," I said. "National Merit semifinalist, too."

Claire rolled her eyes. "Dad."

Elena came back into the room. "Head upstairs, please," she said to Claire.

"I haven't finished my cookies."

"Take them upstairs with you. We need to speak with Mr. Vanderhall privately."

"Can I watch the stream before bed?"

"Fine. Just go upstairs."

She gave me a kiss, murmured a "G'night, Daddy," and went up.

Elena settled into the chair next to me with her mug of coffee, probably cold by now. "So, what's this all about?"

I rolled my eyes. "Brian was telling me how there are invisible fairies in the spaces between the atoms," I said.

He leaned forward. "They're real, Jacob."

"What are? The fairies?"

"Consciousnesses. Beings. Artificial intelligences, like in a computer, only the computer in this case is the whole universe."

"And you've seen them?"

"A lot more than that. They've talked to me. Taught me things." His expression was cryptic, a smile laced with uneasy fear. "It's probably easier if I show you." He leaned over and picked a gyroscope up off the floor. Sean must have left it there—he was forever leaving his toys about. The gyroscope had been a gift from me, like the microscope and chemistry set and electricity kit—all attempts to interest Sean in science. He had paid little attention to my explanations of angular momentum, but he did like to watch the gyroscope spin at odd angles, balanced on a wire or a pencil point. For the first day, at least. Ultimately it was no more to him than a glorified top. He had lost the string and moved on to other toys.

Brian held the gyroscope up like a magician displaying a coin that was about to disappear. I felt a strange internal tugging sensation and wondered what it meant. Nervousness? Did I really care that much about what this was all about?

He held the gyroscope upright on the tabletop. Without the string, there was no way to set the gyroscope spinning. When Brian let go of the wheel, however, it started spinning on its own. He removed his hand, and it kept going, precessing with a slight wobble, but otherwise stable. My practical mind looked immediately for the power source, thinking that he might have switched the gyroscope for one with an ingeniously hidden battery and motor, but as far as I could tell, it was the same steel and plastic model, simple and cheaply made. There was no room for a power source. Despite this, the gyroscope kept spinning.

Elena started to say something, but Brian held up his hand, and we kept watching. Two minutes went by, and it didn't slow down. Not even a string-pulled gyroscope went on for that long without losing momentum. Three minutes went by. Four.

Finally, Elena reached out and snatched the gyroscope, her fingers stopping the spinning wheel. Her breathing was hard, and her eyes bored into Brian's.

"Maybe it's better if you tell us," she said.

CHAPTER 2
DOWN-SPIN

"A ll rise!"

The court officer bellowed the phrase, which he'd probably been calling for most of his adult life. "Court is now in session for the People versus Jacob Kelley, the honorable Ann Roswell presiding."

The federal courthouse in Philadelphia was a beautiful building of stone pillars and balconies, only slightly marred by the more functional modern office buildings grafted onto the back. A similar fusion of old and new reigned indoors, with marble staircases adjoining handicapped-accessible elevators. Courtroom five, where the marshals had led me and then removed my handcuffs, was a high-ceilinged space with wood paneling, tall windows, and oil paintings on the wall. After months of procedure by lawyers on both sides, my trial for the murder of Brian Vanderhall was finally about to begin.

I missed Elena. I missed my children. I wished there was someone in the packed courtroom viewing area who was on my side. I was also tired of waiting, and I was glad it would soon be over, one way or another. It had been four months since Brian had first appeared at my front door in his flip-flops and ruined my life. Now, finally, we would see what a jury of my peers would think of my story.

My lawyer, Terry Sheppard, sat next to me at the defense table. He had a handlebar mustache and wore leather boots. He looked like he'd be more at home on a horse than in the courtroom, and the truth was, I had no idea if he was any good or not. I'd picked him because, of all the sharply dressed sharks that had paraded through the prison meeting room to show off their sleek folios and tailored suits, Terry Sheppard stood out. He didn't try to impress me with his resume or his Harvard vowels. He was simple; a straight shooter. I trusted him.

Judge Roswell was in her sixties, with a kind face and pleasant manner. I wanted to think that was a good sign, but I doubted it. Terry said Roswell had a reputation for being tough, and as a former prosecutor, she wasn't inclined to sympathize with the defense. For nearly an hour, she talked to the jury about their responsibilities, introduced the two sides in the courtroom, and explained to them that only what was spoken into the record by sworn witnesses—not the opening or closing arguments by counsel—was to be considered as evidence in their deliberations. She was articulate and engaging, but also severe in her warnings that they were to avoid the media in this highly-publicized case.

Finally, she addressed the prosecutor. "Mr. Haviland," she said. "Your opening statement."

David Haviland stood and faced the jury. Camera flies hovered not far from his face, and I wondered how he resisted the urge to swat at them. He was well-dressed, at ease in a suit, with the voice of a newscaster. Worse, he had the air of a principled man, a man who might have made a killing as a defense attorney but who had chosen to be a prosecutor out of a sense of conscience. I might have been impressed with him myself, if he weren't trying to get me sent away to prison for life.

"Ladies and gentlemen," he said, pivoting and raising his hands. "This case is about murder." The courtroom was packed with journalists and gawkers, but Haviland addressed himself to the jurors, not to the crowd. I studied them—six men and six women of a variety of ages and races—trying to gauge whether they were likely to be sympathetic or not. It was difficult to tell.

"Murder, pure and simple," Haviland continued. "The taking of another man's life. You have never met Brian Vanderhall, and now you will never get the chance, but let us not forget that he was a very real person. Just like your own husbands or fathers or sons. Was he a flawed person? Perhaps. Aren't we all? That doesn't mean that at thirty-eight years old, he deserved to have his life torn away from him.

"Mr. Sheppard is going to try to convince you that this case is about technology. He's going to make your mind spin with words like 'quarks' and 'leptons' and confuse the facts with expert testimony about science that only a few people in the world understand. It's nothing more than a conjuror's show, designed to distract you from the evidence. And the evidence, ladies and gentlemen, is very clear. The facts will show you that Mr. Jacob Kelley murdered Brian Vanderhall in cold blood." As he said my name, Haviland leveled an accusing finger at me. I wondered if they taught him to do that in law school, or whether he'd just picked it up from the movies.

"Your task, ladies and gentlemen, is to find the truth. In our great country, we don't believe the highly educated or the very rich are more qualified to find the truth than you are. Truth is something we can all recognize and understand. That's why we choose to put the safety of our homes and neighborhoods in your hands. We trust you to have the courage to convict Mr. Kelley"—the pointing finger again—"of the heinous crime of murder."

One juror's eyebrows furrowed slightly, and I thought Haviland might have gone a bit too far with the word *heinous*. If he wanted to project himself as a man of the people, he was going to have to keep his vocabulary down.

"You've all heard the term 'beyond reasonable doubt,'" Haviland continued conversationally, starting to pace a little and rub his chin. "I want to explain to you what that means. Sometimes people get the idea that you can't convict a man unless there is no possible way he could be innocent. That's not true. The word *reasonable* is crucial: Is it reasonable to think that Jacob Kelley is innocent? Given the amount of evidence that you will see, would that evidence be enough to convince you, as a reasonable person, to take action on an important matter in your own life? That's what the law means, and Judge Roswell will tell you the same thing. Even Mr.—"

"Excuse me, councilor," the judge interrupted. "You have a great deal of latitude in your opening statement, but I am going to ask you to refrain from giving my opinion, about which you can have little insight."

Haviland was instantly contrite. "My apologies, Your Honor."

"Members of the jury," the judge went on. "I will remind you that opening statements are not evidence, nor are they law. They are an opportunity for the councilors to introduce their cases to you, but you are not to hold their words as having any weight in this case. The witnesses they call will provide the evidence, and I will explain the law." She nodded at Haviland. "You may proceed."

"Thank you, Your Honor," Haviland said, although he looked like he'd swallowed something unpleasant.

He continued in the same vein, but with some of the wind taken out of his sails. I worked hard to maintain a grave demeanor. Terry, sitting next to me, apparently had no such scruples and leaned back with a wide grin on his face.

"Reasonable doubt," Haviland said. "Let's think about what it means in this case. Jacob Kelley held the gun. This we can prove. He was angry at Mr. Vanderhall and wanted revenge. This we will also prove. You will hear how Mr. Vanderhall attacked Mr. Kelley's wife. You will hear about Mr. Kelley's history of violence and rage, especially when those he loves are threatened. And finally, you will hear about how Mr. Kelley followed his victim to an underground bunker and there shot and killed him. I submit to you that there is no reasonable doubt in my mind, nor will there be in yours once the evidence is presented, that Jacob Kelley"—out came the pointing finger, yet again—"with full control of his senses, did intentionally and willfully take the life of a fellow human being."

Haviland sat down, nodding and looking pleased with himself. The gesture looked choreographed to me, and I hoped it did to the jurors as well.

"Thank you, Mr. Haviland," the judge said. "Mr. Sheppard?"

Terry rose to his feet ponderously, as if suffering from painful joints. "Mark this day on your calendar," he said. His voice had suddenly grown a Texas drawl that hadn't been there before. "This is the day when a defense attorney agreed with the prosecution. Everything Mr. Haviland said was correct."

He bent at the waist as if he were going to sit down. Despite my determination not to show my feelings in the courtroom, my jaw literally dropped open, and for a split second I thought that was all he was going to say. Then he straightened, and with a twinkle in his eye, he said, "Well, *almost* everything.

"The part about my client killing Mr. Vanderhall wasn't true, but we'll go into that in a bit. For the rest, Mr. Haviland pretty much nailed it. I *am* going to cover a lot of science in my side of the testimony, and some of it can get a bit complicated. The difference is that, unlike Mr. Haviland, I think you can handle it.

"Mr. Haviland seems to believe that you're not smart enough to understand science. He wants to spoon-feed you only the bits he thinks you can grasp. Personally, I find that kind of condescension offensive, but he's entitled to his opinions. What he's not entitled to do is withhold from you all the facts of the case. He's not entitled to decide that there are some facts you're not qualified to understand.

"Mr. Haviland apparently thinks that the world is divided into two kinds of people: those who can comprehend the really difficult things and those who can't. And he's already decided that you're in that second category. Well, I think that you can understand the evidence in this case. I'm going to give it all to you, not just the parts Mr. Haviland thinks you can follow.

"At the end of the day, I think you'll agree with me that not only is there reasonable doubt that my client was responsible for Mr. Vanderhall's death, but there is good reason to believe he had nothing to do with it at all."

CHAPTER 3
UP-SPIN

Elena clutched the gyroscope and stared Brian down. I couldn't think of any scientific explanation for what Brian had just done. A gyroscope stays upright because of its angular momentum. Ideally, it would never fall, since the torque that gravity supplies is not sufficient to offset its gyroscopic inertia. In real life, however, friction gradually erodes the rotation, causing it to precess more and more, until finally the rotation degrades and gravity takes hold.

This left one of two options. Either Brian had managed to eliminate any appreciable friction from our tabletop—not to mention air resistance—or he had a way to inject more energy into the system without touching the gyroscope, thus overcoming the effects of the friction. I couldn't think of any way he could do either of those things.

"Okay, I give up," I said. "How did you do it?"

Brian looked grave. "*They* showed me. The quantum intelligences."

"I see. The little fairies are spinning the gyroscope?" I tried not to let the cynicism creep into my voice, but it was hard.

"Of course not," he snapped. "It's ground state energy. The energy of a single particle's spin. It never stops. It's an infinite source of power."

I hesitated, finding it hard to believe, but at the same time hard to discount the evidence of the gyroscope. "So you took a feature of the quantum world and made it apply in the larger world," I said.

"Amazing, isn't it?" Brian said quietly. "Gonna change the world."

"If it were real, that would be a technology worth trillions of dollars," I said. "Is that why you're here? Are there people chasing you, trying to get this from you?"

"They're chasing me," he said, "but they're not people."

I threw up my hands. "You'd better start talking sense."

"One more example, then," he said. He reached under the table, and suddenly there was a Glock 46 in his hand, the barrel pointing at Elena.

I was on my feet in an instant, my chair toppling over behind me. I held my hands up, palms out. "Put it down," I said. "Brian, listen to me."

Elena stared into the gun's barrel, motionless, hardly breathing. "Don't do this," she whispered.

"It won't hurt you," Brian said. "The bullet will just diffract around you."

"You're talking crazy," I said. "Look at me." He didn't move. "Look at me!" I shouted. He looked. "It's a bullet, not an electron," I said. "If you pull the trigger, it will kill her. You don't want that."

He stood. "You won't believe me unless I show you."

I started to ease around the edge of the table toward him. "I do believe you," I said. "Let's just sit down, and you can tell us all about it."

"No, you don't. You call them fairies and make fun of me. But they're real, Jacob. I'm not going to hurt anybody. I just want to prove it to you."

"Point the gun somewhere else, then," I said. "Point it at me."

"It won't hurt her," he said, and pulled the trigger.

I grew up in South Philadelphia, no stranger to violence. My father was a petty thief and a drunk who died in prison before I was two. I had two uncles, my mother's brothers, who took an interest in my life. They were boxers, mostly the illegal, no-holds-barred type, and they taught me how to fight. I was red-haired and freckled in a mostly Italian neighborhood. I did well in school, though I tried to hide it. I learned early in life that on the street smart didn't matter for much. I was only as good as my fists.

Besides, it felt good to fight. I was angry all the time, angry at my mother for drinking instead of working, angry at the men she brought home, angry at my father for dying, angry at my teachers for telling me how much potential I had if I would only apply myself. Striking out with my fists relieved some of that pressure, put me in control. Nobody could tell Uncle Sean and Uncle Colin what to do, and I wanted to be just like them.

By the time I was thirteen, I was boxing in kids' leagues, but it was just a sport, with gloves and rules and manners. I was bigger than most kids my age by then, and I was constantly getting cited for punching too soon, or too late, or in the wrong part of the body. They weren't the rage-fueled battles that my uncles' matches were, the air thick with cigarette smoke and the smell of blood.

By that age, I knew my uncles were owned men. They were deeply in debt to bosses in suits who quietly ran the books and manipulated the outcomes. They couldn't stop fighting, not if they wanted to stay alive. Even so, I knew that was my future. It was the only thing that mattered that I was good at. One day, the bosses would own me, and I'd never get out either.

Then when I was fifteen, Uncle Sean was killed, and everything changed. An opponent kicked him repeatedly in the head when he was down, hard enough to push his brain stem out through the base of his skull. He died on the floor of the ring in vomit and sawdust. No one even called the hospital. The bosses disposed of his body quietly; I don't know how. I aged ten years that month, and suddenly the thought of staying in that neighborhood and that life was unbearable.

I stopped boxing and threw myself into my school work. I didn't know much about life outside of South Philly, but I knew the only way out of that neighborhood was to go to college, and the only way to go to college was to get a scholarship to pay my way. My mind had always held on to concepts like a magnet, but before, it didn't seem to matter. Now it was everything.

For three years, I studied harder than I had ever worked at anything, not because I liked school, but because it was my way out. I was angrier than ever, but I learned how to keep it in check—too many fights in school would ruin my chances. Every night, I pounded the speed bag in my basement until my hands bled.

Physics came as a complete surprise. It was simple and beautiful. It explained the world in clear lines of power, motion, and speed. It wasn't the violence of it that attracted me; it was the unequivocal nature of it. So much of the rest of my life was complicated. Physics was simple. It was how the world ought to be.

We'd been learning about Einstein, a relative nobody who, in his spare time as a patent clerk, came up with four papers that turned the world upside down. I thought if he could do that, then I could at least get myself out of Philadelphia. In the spring of my junior year, I applied to Princeton, Berkeley, and MIT. I was lucky enough to match perfect grades with a political academic environment that made it desirable to accept applicants from low-income neighborhoods. I was accepted, with full-ride scholarships, to all three.

By then, Uncle Colin was in prison, and my mother hardly knew I was alive. I left them behind without looking back, packed most of what I owned in an old suitcase of my father's, and took the bus to Boston, Massachusetts.

MIT was mostly what I expected—it seemed like everyone I met was either a rich American kid with a home in the Hamptons and a chalet in the Alps, or else the favored, oldest son of a politically connected family in Korea or China or Vietnam. Nobody's background was anything like mine, and it was hard to make friends. But the physics! Everything I loved about it was right there, codified in perfect, uncluttered symbols. Torque and inertia, linear motion and angular displacement, force equals mass times acceleration, decisive action with equal and opposite reaction. It made sense. It meant the world made sense.

The professors treated us like we were the cream of the new generation. There was a spirit of excitement at MIT, no matter where you were from, a sense that we were at the center of the scientific world, a specially chosen elite, given this great opportunity to study with the best in the field. I'd never felt that way before, and I soaked it up. I loved physics more every day.

The anger receded into the background, like a pit bull chained in the shadows. I still worked out with the bags in the gym, but I didn't talk much about my background. I wanted to leave it behind. I was a scientist now, someone who believed in the inherent order of the universe. The chaos was behind me.

The gun went off with a deafening blast. The coffee mug Elena was holding exploded into shards. I didn't think; I just reacted. I leaned toward Brian, pivoting my hips and throwing my weight into a right cross as hard as I knew how. The punch knocked him backward, sending him sprawling in a jumble on the floor. I looked at Elena.

She still sat at the table, eyes wide and mouth slightly parted, her face ashen. Her mug lay shattered in front of her in a pool of coffee.

"Are you hurt? Elena!" My ears were ringing; I could hardly hear the sound of my own voice. I rushed to her side. She was still sitting in the chair, breathing, stunned but apparently unharmed. I couldn't believe it. I thought at first the bullet must have deflected off of her coffee mug, but no—in the wall behind her, following a direct line through the middle of her chest, there was a hole punched into the drywall. The bullet had gone straight through her.

"Call 911," I said.

She didn't move.

"Elena!"

She jolted, as if startled awake, and fished the phone out of her pocket to make the call. Brian hadn't moved from the floor. He was still breathing, but the punch had dazed him.

"Yes," Elena said into the phone. "Someone . . . a . . . a man just fired a gun at me in my house."

Brian stirred and looked at Elena. His eyes focused suddenly, and he shook his head. "What are you doing? Are you calling the police? Don't do that." He looked at me. A trickle of blood was running out of his left nostril. "Please!" he said. "Look at her—she's not hurt! The bullet diffracted around her, just like I told you! I was just showing you." He stood shakily to his feet.

"Right here in the kitchen," Elena said. "Please hurry."

"Please, put the phone down," Brian said.

I stepped between them. "Get out of my house."

"Jacob," he said, his voice pleading. "I need your help."

I advanced on him, fists raised, heedless of the gun he still held in one hand. He turned and started yanking on the door that led to the backyard. It didn't budge. He fumbled at the lock. I didn't help him. It was all I could do not to hit him again. Finally, he managed to turn it and yanked the door open. With one last backward look of reproach, he ran out barefoot into the snow.

The stairs thundered with descending feet, and Claire, Alessandra, and Sean burst into the room, all talking at once.

"What was that sound?" Claire asked.

"Did he shoot a gun at you?" Sean asked, eyes wide.

"It's all right," I said. "He's gone now. Go and get dressed. The police are coming, and I'm sure they'll want to talk to you, too."

Elena was shaking. I put my arms around her, and she clung to me. I felt her slim neck and delicate bones and stroked her hair and thought about what might have happened. About what my life would be like if she were dead. I felt the pit bull in the shadows, tugging at its chain, wanting to get free. I wanted to hurt someone. I had it under control, for the moment, but I knew that if Brian came to my house again, that control wouldn't last.

Elena didn't let go, and neither did I, and we stood that way until the police arrived.

CHAPTER 4
DOWN-SPIN

The prosecution's first witness was Officer Richard Peyton, a big guy with a thick neck, red blotches on his face, and blond hair cropped so close to his scalp that you almost couldn't see his receding hairline. He climbed the short stairs to the witness box, stiff in a freshly cleaned and pressed uniform and holding his cap, which he set on the rail next to him.

The court officer held out a Bible, and Peyton placed his hand on it. "Do you swear to tell the truth, the whole truth, and nothing but the truth, so help you God?" The officer rattled it off like it was one multisyllable word.

"I do," Peyton said.

Haviland advanced. "Officer Peyton, what is your profession?"

"I'm an officer for the Media Police Department."

"How many years have you been a police officer?"

"Eight years, give or take."

Next to me, Terry Sheppard slouched, apparently bored with the witness, and played with the end of his mustache. I figured it was a pose, meant to communicate to the jury a contempt for the witness, but I wasn't sure. He did this all the time. He might actually be bored.

"Do you remember where you were the evening of December second?" Haviland asked.

"Yes, I do. I was cruising the downtown Media area when I got a call from the dispatcher to Woodview Lane, possible armed assault," Peyton said.

"And you went to the scene as ordered?"

"Yes, I did."

"Were you the only one there?"

"No, my partner, Officer Jimenez, was in the car with me, also Officers Esposito and Ashford arrived on the scene in their car approximately five minutes after we did."

"And what did you find when you got there?"

"We found Mr. and Mrs. Kelley, the owners of the house, along with their three children. Mr. Kelley claimed Brian Vanderhall had discharged a firearm at his wife."

"Was there evidence of that?"

"Yes, sir. There was a bullet hole in the kitchen wall, and a shattered coffee mug with gunshot residue consistent with a firearm discharge about five feet away."

"And can you identify Mr. Kelley? Is he in the courtroom today?"

"Sure." Peyton pointed at me. A lot of people were doing that today. "That's him, right there."

"Let the court records show that the witness identified the defendant, Jacob Kelley," Haviland said. "Thank you, Officer. How did Mr. Kelley seem to you?"

"I'm sorry?"

"How did he seem to be feeling?" Haviland asked. "Was he happy, sad, angry, annoyed, amused?"

"Objection!" Terry called out. He stressed the first syllable, as if this were the twentieth objection he'd made, and he was growing weary of the prosecutor's games. "What is the relevance of this line of questioning to the murder?"

"I'm trying to establish motive," Haviland said. This incident occurred the day before, and is crucial for demonstrating the defendant's state of mind."

"Overruled," Judge Roswell said. "You may answer the question, Officer Peyton."

"He was angry," Peyton said. "Blazing mad. Some guy just took a shot at his wife. I'd be angry, too."

"Angry enough to kill?" Haviland asked.

"Objection!" Terry said.

But Haviland waved it away. "I withdraw the question," he said.

I was having trouble staying in my seat and listening to all this. My muscles kept clenching and unclenching, just like they used to do when I had to sit and listen to a scientist lie through his teeth about the worthlessness of some competing experiment in an attempt to raise the value of his own research. I felt so powerless: unable to explain, unable to speak up or do anything at all. All my life, I had hated that feeling of helplessness and vulnerability. I wasn't sure how I was going to stand it for several days of trial.

"What time did you come to the house?" Haviland asked.

"At 8:25 in the evening."

"How can you be certain?"

"The time was recorded in my report of the incident, which I reviewed before coming here today."

Haviland reached under the prosecution table and pulled out a giant interactive whiteboard that showed a line with dates and times marked. A rectangle marked "Next" appeared on the bottom right corner of the board, and when Haviland touched it, a box appeared over 8:25 PM on December 2, which read "Police arrive at Kelley home."

"Is this time correct?" Haviland asked.

"Yes, it is," Peyton said.

Haviland spun briefly to give the jury and the audience a good look, then leaned it against the table. "So you came to the house and found evidence of firearm violence and a very angry Jacob Kelley," he said. "What did you do next?"

"I called it in, and they started a manhunt for Brian Vanderhall. We put an APB out on his car and searched the neighborhood, but we didn't find him," Peyton said.

"You didn't find him? Was this a halfhearted search?"

"No, sir. We went house to house for blocks in every direction, knocking on doors and searching yards. We alerted the departments in surrounding towns, as well as the New Jersey State Police. Nobody saw him."

"How long did the search continue?"

"Until his dead body was found."

"And in all that searching, did Mr. Kelley mention to you that there was a secret bunker, hidden underground, in which he and Mr. Vanderhall used to perform scientific experiments?"

"No, he did not."

"He didn't suggest to you that Vanderhall might be hiding down there, evading capture?"

"No, sir," Peyton said.

"Why do you think that is?"

"Objection," Terry said. "He's asking the witness to speculate."

"Sustained," Roswell said.

Haviland shrugged. "One final question. What time did the police leave the Kelley home that night?"

"At 10:55," Peyton said.

Haviland picked up his whiteboard and pressed the "Next" square again, causing a new box to appear over 10:55, which read "Police leave Kelley home."

"Is this correct?" he asked.

"Yes, it is."

"No further questions, Your Honor."

Haviland sat down. Terry leaped to his feet and practically ran to the lectern, where he threw down his notes. The pose of yawning indifference had disappeared in a moment. He glanced at me briefly, and his eyes were ablaze.

"Mr. Peyton," he said in the same strident tone I used to use to call one of my children to task when they misbehaved.

"Officer," Peyton corrected.

"Ah yes. An officer of the law. Keeper of the truth. Mr. Peyton, in your eight years as a police officer, how many times have you been called to a scene of violence in someone's home?"

Peyton made a huffing noise. "I don't know. Hundreds."

Terry held up a sheaf of papers. "According to police records, over five hundred times?"

"I would believe that, though I don't keep track," Peyton said.

"And how many of those incidents have involved one or more angry persons?"

Peyton gave him a strange look. "I'm sorry?"

"Come on, Mr. Peyton. In how many of those incidents of violence in the home did you encounter someone who was, if I may quote you, 'blazing mad'?"

"Most of them, I guess," Peyton said.

"And how many of them resulted in someone's death?"

"Not many."

Terry held up the papers. "Fifteen?"

Peyton was getting a bit irritated. "It could be. I don't remember the exact number."

"So is it safe to say," Terry said, "in your expert opinion as a police officer, that when someone is angry, it doesn't necessarily mean he will kill someone?"

"No, it doesn't."

"Mr. Peyton, when you encounter a man who you believe is a danger to himself or other people, what do you do?"

"We take him into custody."

"Would you include in your report your belief that you feared that person would do violence to others?"

"Yes."

"Did you take Jacob Kelley into custody that night?"

"No."

"Did you include in your report that you feared he would do violence to others?"

"No."

"Why not?"

"I didn't believe him to be a threat, sir."

"So in your professional opinion, as a police officer on the scene at the time, Mr. Kelley gave no indication of being angry enough to murder someone."

"That's not something you can tell just by looking at someone," Peyton said.

"But at the time, you did not think he was angry enough to commit murder."

He didn't want to answer the question. Peyton knew his main purpose on the stand was to introduce a motive for murder. "I wasn't certain one way or another," he said. "At that time, he had not committed a crime."

Terry wasn't going to let him off the hook. "According to your report, however, you had no reason, at the time, to believe that he would commit a crime, correct?"

Peyton took a deep breath and let it out. "That's correct."

Terry smiled. "Thank you. No more questions, Your Honor."

CHAPTER 5
UP-SPIN

The police interviewed me, Elena, and each of the kids individually, although the kids had seen nothing and had little to say. The questions were polite, though repetitive, and I told them the truth about everything, except that I left out the spinning gyroscope and the apparent diffraction of the bullet. When the police finally left, it was nearly eleven o'clock, and we were all exhausted.

Sean was practically asleep on his feet, so I picked him up and carried him to his room. His bed was set on a loft over a desk and play area, both of which were scattered with Legos, action figures, and plastic dinosaurs. On the desk, a set of green plastic army men that had been mine when I was young lay in various fallen poses in a field littered with spent rubber band ammunition. Because of his short arm, he had learned to fire by holding one end of the rubber band in his teeth while stretching it forward with a finger on his right hand.

"Did you really punch that guy in the face?" Sean mumbled.

"Yes, I did," I said.

"Awesome," he said.

I thought more of an explanation was probably required—about when it was and was not appropriate to hit other people—but it wasn't the time. I gave him a quick kiss and turned out the light.

"The nightlight!" he said.

I flipped it on and slipped out of the room.

"Daddy! My music!"

Sighing, I went back in and turned on the soft music he always fell asleep to.

"My drink," he said.

"Not tonight," I told him. "It's late. Go to sleep." I kissed him once more and stroked his hair, thinking of Brian and the gun and the police. Someday, Sean would be strong enough to take care of himself, but as a child, he was so helpless. He relied on me, trusted me implicitly to take care of him. He was asleep by the time I left the room.

Elena was in the shower, and Claire's room was dark, but the lights were still on in Alessandra's room. I peeked in and saw her lying on her bed.

"Lights out," I said.

No response.

"Sweetheart, it's late. Time to go to sleep."

Still no response. Her eyes gave a telltale twitch, and I realized that she was eyejacked, her vision overlaid by the icons and images of a shared network. Sometimes I think the technology was invented as a means to ignore parents and teachers while appearing to pay perfect attention. She could trade video clips or stills of what her eyes were seeing with similar viewfeeds from other people. At this moment, she might be looking at a school friend's new shoes or following the drama of a family argument in China, while half a dozen strangers were looking at me. It was disconcerting to think that I might be parenting to an audience, but it was the culture of my children's generation, and I didn't feel I could keep them out of it entirely, much as I might wish to.

I spotted her phone in its cradle on her dresser and leaned over to punch the disconnect button. Alessandra's eyelids closed, fluttered, and then sprang open again. She sprang to her feet, her face a mask of fury. "Dad! You could kill me doing that!"

"It won't kill you."

"You're supposed to bring me out gradually. Do you want to leave me brain-dead and drooling?"

"Don't be ridiculous."

"At least when I'm dead, you'll still have Claire."

I didn't want to get dragged down that rabbit hole. "Time for bed, Alessandra."

She crossed her arms and gave me a belligerent look.

"Good night," I said, and turned off the lights.

Elena had finished her shower. I brushed my teeth in the bathroom, thinking about Brian's endlessly spinning gyroscope and the bullet that had apparently passed through—or diffracted around—Elena. In the quantum world—among particles smaller than an atom—such oddities were commonplace. Spinning particles had a ground state energy, a rate of spin that couldn't go any slower. And all particles, whether they had mass or not, had a wavelength and could diffract like light. But such things only worked on the subatomic scale, not with gyroscopes and bullets.

The subatomic world was a weird and wonderful one, a world where common sense broke down. It took me until my second year at MIT to really come to terms with it, to realize that the beautiful world of cause and effect I had fallen in love with in my high school physics class was a sham. Lurking deep inside the stable laws of Newtonian physics was the ambiguous world of the subatomic, where probability reigned. Not the probability of ignorance, like a coin flip, where if you knew enough about the force of the flip and the rotation and the wind and the air pressure and the scars on the referee's finger, you could predict the outcome. No, at the bottom of everything was a *fundamental* probability, an unknowable, unpredictable creation and an annihilation of particles with no rhyme or reason to it. The real world, the quantum world, was dark and terrifying and didn't make any sense at all.

Here's the problem: Every particle in the universe is also a wave. It's not like a marble or a stone, with a clearly defined position, diameter, and velocity. It might be either here or there. It might be moving slow or fast. It might have a lot of energy or a little. It isn't just that you don't know. The particle itself hasn't decided. It's in an indeterminate state, smeared out over a region of space. Since even the smallest everyday objects are composed of billions of particles, the uncertainty usually averages itself out in the larger world. But it's there.

I resisted it for a while. Like most physicists, I went through a phase where I believed we just didn't understand enough. That behind the exploding chaos of trillions of particles spontaneously transforming into other particles was a set of rules to predict it. Einstein himself had clung to that view until he died. Eventually, though, I came not just to accept the truth, but to love it. The world might be chaotic and unpredictable at its root, but it could be controlled. The random firing of particles could be mastered and made to keep order, to follow Newton's laws in aggregate, to bend to the will of mathematics and technology. In the end, the chaos didn't win.

Which was why what Brian had showed us was so disturbing to me. He had found a way to let the chaos out. I believed him when he said it would change the world. Whether it would change the world for the better, however, was harder to predict.

A sharp knock on the wall snapped my attention back to the present. "What are you doing in there?" Elena called from the bedroom.

I realized I'd been brushing my teeth for far longer than was practically necessary. I spit and rinsed my mouth, then headed back into our bedroom, but no one was there.

"Elena?" I said.

The door shut with a bang behind me, revealing Elena hiding behind the door, wearing one of my T-shirts. It was long enough on her to serve as a nightgown, but only just. She wrapped her arms around my neck and planted a long kiss on my mouth. I returned the kiss eagerly, delighted but surprised. Elena was a morning person, generally, and it had been a long day.

"Seriously?" I asked. "You're not tired?"

"Mmm," she said. "I've been wanting to do this ever since you punched Brian in the face."

"That's me, your big protector," I said.

She reached an exploratory hand up the inside of my thigh, and her eyes sparkled. "Yeah, you could say that." She took a few steps back and made sure I was looking. She has this thing she does where she crosses her arms, takes hold of the bottom of her shirt, and pulls it over her head in one lightning-fast move. She knows I like it, and it's gotten to be a thing with us, kind of a secret signal, where she'll catch my eye—in, say, a crowded room—and she'll subtly cross her arms and finger the hem of her shirt. She did it now, and I grinned at her.

"You are so hot," I said.

"How hot?" she asked, still toying with the hem of the shirt.

"Ionizing radiation hot," I said. "Neutral pion decay hot."

Elena snorted. "You're such a romantic," she said. Then she pulled off the T-shirt, and we both stopped talking for a while.

Afterward, Elena settled in with a computer on her lap to work on our finances a little before bed. Despite my background in math, I'm no good with a budget, and she's always managed the money side of things. I lay on my back, staring at the ceiling, tired but wide awake, still unable to put the day's events out of my mind.

Brian's research at NJSC had to do with quantum computing, a concept that was getting close enough to reality that large manufacturers were starting to invest heavily in it. It was just the sort of thing the NJSC was willing to prioritize: promises of breakthroughs right around the corner that would benefit everybody, with significant grant money available to be claimed. What was lacking to make it a reality was the ability to connect quantum effects to large mechanical objects (large in this context meaning at least ten micrometers across) without storing those objects at near absolute zero. Any warmer and the natural vibrations of the atoms in the material tended to drown out any quantum effects.

We knew it was possible, because birds did it. When photons struck their eyes, entangled electrons were scattered and forced to spin in different ways depending on the Earth's magnetic field. The change in electron spin subtly changed the chemical state of the molecules, which in turn altered the flow of cellular signals through the bird's eye. The result was that the bird could actually see the magnetic field, and thus know which way was north, regardless of where it was or what the weather was like. The bird's eyes weren't cryogenic, though. So we knew it could be done.

It seemed that Brian must somehow have succeeded, far beyond anyone's expectations, and found a way to have quantum properties affect the everyday world. An electron never stops spinning; it's a perpetual motion machine, moving endlessly without any loss of energy. A particle fired at an atom might have a wavelength larger than an atom; it has a pretty good chance of passing right through it without hitting it. To apply these principles to gyroscopes and bullets was crazy, though. A bullet is made up of *trillions* of atoms, and although it did technically have a wavelength, it was something like ten to the minus thirty-four meters long, so it shouldn't be able to diffract around anything.

"It's eating you up inside, isn't it?" Elena said.

I sighed and nodded. "It bothers me. It shouldn't be possible, and if it is possible . . ."

Elena finished my thought. "Then the world isn't as stable as you want it to be."

She was right. To Elena, it didn't make any difference if the world was made of quarks or superstrings or tiny elves. She cared about her children and her husband and exercise and eating well and whether Penn State beat Purdue. But it made a difference to me. I needed to know if the world was inherently predictable or chaotic, whether the random outcome of trillions of probabilistic encounters ultimately resulted in order that I could control.

Elena sighed. "I think you should take Marek with you."

"What?"

"When you go out to the NJSC tomorrow. Take Marek with you."

I pushed up on one elbow. "Who says I'm going to the NJSC?"

Elena gave me a look. "What have we just been talking about? Go find out what Brian was researching; get it settled it in your mind."

"I can't leave you alone here. What if Brian comes back?"

"There are police swarming around this whole neighborhood." As if to emphasize her words, we heard a helicopter chattering overhead. "He's no secret agent. They'll find him soon enough."

"Since I left Philly, I've only punched another person three times. Two of those times, it was Brian," I said.

"I'll be fine," she said. "I don't need you hovering around protecting me. He's not going to come back and shoot me again." I leaned over and kissed her on the mouth. She punched me good-naturedly. "We already did that, you great brute. Go to sleep."

"Thank you," I said.

"I know how it is with you," she said. "You get something stuck in your mind, and you can't let it go. Better just to go get it settled."

I fell back onto my pillows, feeling suddenly exhausted.

"And Jacob?" she said.

"Mmm . . . yes?"

"Don't do anything stupid."

CHAPTER 6
DOWN-SPIN

The wooden spectator benches in courtroom five were hard and low and looked like they dated from Colonial times. Despite this, the crowds who gathered to see me humiliated had not abated, though they did tend to fidget in the uncomfortable seats as the afternoon wore on.

"Officer Lin, what is your profession?" Haviland asked, in a ringing voice that suggested that her profession would be the key to the whole case.

Brittany Lin was a pretty, dark-haired, Asian policewoman in a smart jacket and skirt and glasses like flat ovals. She was fit and athletic, and I guessed her age at about forty. "I'm a senior forensic analyst with the New Jersey State Police," she said. Her voice was low pitched and no-nonsense.

"And your time in that position?"

"I've been a police officer for fourteen years and a forensic specialist for ten of those years."

"Then it's safe to say you are an expert in your field."

"I know my business, Mr. Haviland."

Haviland went on to establish her certifications as an investigator and the status granted her as an expert witness in various other courts. She had led the forensic team that had processed the crime scene in the underground bunker.

"At the time you were called to the scene, were you aware that police had been searching for Mr. Vanderhall?"

"Yes, sir."

"Why didn't the police find him?"

"The bunker was two hundred feet underground, in a supposedly abandoned experiment room. No one even knew to look for him there."

"Except for Jacob Kelley?"

"Objection," Terry said. "Assumes facts not in evidence."

"Sustained," Judge Roswell said. "Mr. Haviland, please limit your questions to those about which the witness can have knowledge."

"I apologize, Your Honor," Haviland said. "Ms. Lin, what did you find when you entered the bunker?"

"I found a dead male, mid to late thirties, with a gunshot wound to the chest as the apparent cause of death. The victim had been dead approximately twelve hours," Lin said.

Haviland made a note on his legal pad, as if this was a new piece of information he needed to write down. "How was time of death established?"

"The level of decomposition, given the warm temperature in the bunker and the mass of the victim, limits the time to no more than twelve hours, while the presence of firmly established livor mortis suggests at least that long."

"What time was this analysis made?"

"At four o'clock in the afternoon on December third, placing the death at approximately four o'clock in the morning."

Haviland held up his giant whiteboard timeline. "Permission to approach the witness, Your Honor?"

"Granted," the judge said.

Haviland handed a huge red marker to the witness. "Ms. Lin, can you indicate for us on this timeline, using a red X, when the victim died?"

She complied, vigorously marking the spot as if she were etching it in blood. Haviland held it up again so the jury could see, then rotated it to include the audience. "Four AM on December third. Is that correct?" he said.

"Yes."

"So, approximately eight hours after Mr. Vanderhall ran away from the Kelley residence, and five hours after the police finished questioning the family?"

"Objection," Terry said. "Asked and answered."

"Sustained, Mr. Haviland. Let's move along." Judge Roswell said.

"Yes, Your Honor." Haviland flipped to another page in his notes. "Was any suicide note found on the premises?" he asked.

"No sir, there was not," Lin said.

"Were Mr. Vanderhall's injuries consistent with a theory of suicide?"

"No sir. Suicide was not a serious consideration."

"Why not?"

Lin smiled condescendingly. "Mr. Vanderhall was shot in the middle of the chest from a distance of at least three feet. The insubstantial amount of gunshot residue found on his skin and clothing rules out the possibility that he was any nearer to the gun when it was fired. Besides which, he was then shot two more times while he was lying on the floor."

"He was shot a total of three times? Was one shot not enough to kill him?"

"No sir, it would have been enough. The first shot passed through Mr. Vanderhall's heart, almost certainly killing him before either of the other two shots was fired."

"In your expert opinion, what do those extra shots suggest?"

"It's what we call overkill. One shot might indicate an accident or a thoughtless action taken in a moment of passion. Multiple, unnecessary shots suggest that the murder was intentional. They suggest that the first shot, while sufficient to cause death, was not sufficient to complete the emotional experience. It means that this killer wanted to be very, very certain that Mr. Vanderhall was dead."

CHAPTER 7
UP-SPIN

M arek Svoboda was my brother-in-law, married to Elena's sister Ava. He was Romanian, a carpenter by trade, and a genius with crown molding. He had immigrated to the States ten years earlier, when the Russo-Turkish war over the Balkans in the twenties had devastated his country's economy. The retirement of the Baby Boomer generation had caused a serious shortage of working-age people in the United States, and Marek had taken advantage of the immigration incentives the United States was offering at the time. For years, he worked in construction, sending most of his paycheck back to his family in Romania, until he discovered that his wife had married another man and kept it a secret so Marek would keep sending her money. Now he was married to Ava, and he didn't send his salary anywhere if he could help it.

He was nearly as big as I was and more densely muscled. He'd helped me with a lot of carpentry work at our house over the years and had come to be a good friend.

"How far away is it?" he asked. I was driving; he was picking the music. At the moment it was some kind of Latin/Slavic fusion rock that sounded like a family of cats caught on a firing range.

"Not far now," I said. It had been nothing but pine forest on either side of us for miles. The New Jersey Pine Barrens covered over a million acres, and every acre of it looked pretty much the same. For large portions of it, there wasn't even any cellular phone coverage. It was considered an International Biosphere Reserve by the United Nations and protected from most development. Despite this, we were actually driving over the particle accelerator, which ran underneath the trees, a huge ring buried two hundred feet beneath the surface and stretching thirty miles in circumference.

I had spent most of the trip trying to explain to Marek how it worked. "It's like a big racetrack," I said. "We use thousands of magnets to get little particles zipping around at the speed of light and then, bang! They smash into each other."

"Little?" Marek held up his thumb and forefinger with only a small space between them. "Like this big?"

"Um . . ." I grinned. "Actually, you could line up a few million subatomic particles between your fingers right now."

Marek took being off by six orders of magnitude in stride. "And you shoot them as fast as light?"

"Well, it's more like 0.999999 times the speed of light, but close enough."

"So, millions of dollars, to smash little bits together," Marek said.

"Actually, it's more than ten *billion* dollars. But yeah, pretty much."

Marek's eyebrows knitted together as if in pain. "And the point is?"

Marek had a thing about money. He complained about every dollar of taxes he had to pay and raged about government waste, seeing his own salary being spent on things he didn't care about. He always thought products were overpriced, though math wasn't his strong suit. He would drive ten minutes out of his way to save two cents on a gallon of gas.

"It's trying to answer some of the deepest questions we have about the universe," I said. "Questions like, 'Where does mass comes from?' and 'Why can't we see most of the matter in the world?' and 'What happened during the first few fractions of a second of the beginning of the universe?'"

The endless trees finally gave way to housing developments and strip malls. A sign with a picture of the Hindenburg said, "Welcome to Lakehurst, Airship Capital of the World." In the distance, a jet took off from McGuire Air Force base.

Marek frowned. "You are trying to find God?"

I shook my head, ready to correct him, but Marek's family had been Orthodox for centuries, their faith surviving even through the Communist regime. As far as I knew, Marek himself never went to church, but religion was a fundamental part of his ethnic and family identity. "Something like that," I said instead.

The buildings of the NJSC loomed ahead of us, twelve of them in all, dominated by the silver-domed Feynman Center. I had called ahead and arranged with Jean Massey, a friend from the days when I'd worked there, to get us in. We entered through the employee gate, and security waved me through when I showed my ID. I turned left beyond the Einstein Building onto Strange Street, and parked in front of the Dirac Building, where I had worked with Brian before I left. I turned off the car but made no move to get out.

"Are you okay?" Marek asked.

"Fine," I said. "Just some people in there I haven't seen for a while."

We got out of the car. The doors all required card readers to get in, but I called Jean and she buzzed us through.

The girl at the front desk said, "Hey, are you guys from the police?"

"Not hardly," said Jean, coming around the corner. She handed each of us a visitor's badge.

"Jeannie," I said. "Good to see you."

We shook hands, and she gave me a quick peck on the cheek. Jean Massey was about thirty-five, thin as a rake, with big glasses and flyaway brown hair that already showed streaks of gray. She was about the most brilliant person I remembered working with in my old career, though she was so unassuming you could miss her at a party. We walked through the building toward Brian's office, things looking pretty much as I remembered them.

"How are you?" I asked. "How's Nick?" Shortly before I had left the NJSC, Jean had married a young genetics professor from Princeton. The office staff had oohed and aahed over her wedding dress and all the plans, and everyone seemed to think it was a match made in heaven. I was a bit afraid to ask, given how quickly marriages sometimes fell apart, but Jean just smiled.

"Doing fine," she said.

"And did I hear you had a baby?"

"Yeah, that's right."

"I'm sorry, I forget. Girl or a boy?"

"A girl. Chance."

"Chance?"

She answered wearily, as if tired of explaining. "That's her name."

I didn't mention that Elena used to have a cat named Chance. It had been run over by a car shortly after we started dating, to Elena's great distress. I didn't mention that either. "Um, that's cool, actually," I said. "Sounds like a quantum thing. Or a genetics thing, maybe. Or both."

She brightened a little. "Yeah. That and Nick likes to play the slots in Atlantic City."

"Well, come on," I said. "Don't you have any pictures to show off? What does this quantum baby look like?"

We reached Brian's office and stepped inside. Jean pursed her lips. "I don't want to be rude," she said, "but I'm going to have to run and leave you to it. I have a panel review meeting in about an hour, and I'm not quite ready for it."

"Sure," I said. "Good luck."

She gave us a tired smile. "Thanks. Good luck yourself. You'll need it to find anything in here."

I looked around the office. The desk surfaces were cluttered with papers, sandwich wrappers, empty soda cans, and office supplies, with half a dozen smartpads scattered amidst the debris. There wasn't much else. His office was sparsely decorated: a few diplomas, badly mounted and hanging askew, but no artwork, no photographs, and none of the squirrely knickknacks that covered most people's desks. The smartpads might contain something interesting about his research, but they were likely to be encrypted.

"Has he said anything to you about what he's been working on lately?" I asked.

Jean shook her head. "You know how Brian is about people stealing his ideas. Lately, he's been even worse."

"Secretive?"

"Ridiculously so. People have been making complaints. That's just not how science is done anymore, with one maverick genius locking himself in a room and coming out twenty years later with a breakthrough. There's process, teamwork, accountability. Anyway, good luck."

She stepped out, closing the door. The motion revealed Brian's leather jacket hanging from a hook. I thought of what he'd been wearing when he showed up at my house and picked up the jacket. I felt around, and in one of the pockets I found an envelope. The words "Jacob Kelley" were penned on it in Brian's handwriting.

I tore it open and pulled out a single sheet of folded smartpaper. The only words were a single line of printed text: "What is your favorite number?"

Marek looked over my shoulder. "What's that, some kind of password request?"

I smiled. "Something like that. You have a pen?"

Marek fished a Bic pen out of his pocket, and I wrote "137.036" on the paper. When I stopped, the printing disappeared and was replaced by a longer message:

> *Dear Jacob:*
>
> *I wanted to come and tell you about all this in person, but I didn't have the nerve. I think it's for the best this way. You're smart; you'll figure it out, and maybe someday you'll join me.*
>
> *Say goodbye to Cathie for me.*
>
> *Brian*

I showed the letter to Marek.

"I thought he did come see you in person," Marek said.

"Yeah. I don't know what he means. Maybe he changed his mind after he wrote this." I replaced the jacket on the hook on the back of the door, and a small mirror to one side caught my eye. Something about the light reflected from it seemed wrong. Marek moved in front of it, and his reflection flitted across the mirror in the opposite direction of his movement. Definitely odd. I stepped in front of it, so I could see my own reflection, and saw right away that my hair was parted on the wrong side. It was like looking at a photograph of myself instead of a reflection. I raised my hand, and the wrong hand went up. This wasn't really a mirror.

"What's going on with this?" I asked. I reached out to lift it off the wall. My reversed reflection in the mirror did the same, though with the wrong hand. I looked in my face, only there was something wrong, so horribly wrong that for a split second I couldn't figure out what it was. My eyes were missing. In their place, there was only a smooth expanse of skin, unbroken, with not even a cavity where the eyes should have been.

It was like when a child in a crowded room reaches up and grasps, with easy familiarity, her father's hand, only to discover that it is not her father after all but a complete stranger. A moment of calm reassurance is transformed into a moment of horror as she realizes that, not only is she holding the hand of a man she doesn't know, but she has no idea where her father is.

I jerked away from the mirror, letting it fall back against the wall, and touched my eyes. The reflection in the mirror was normal again, too. "Did you see that?" I asked.

Marek peered in the mirror, then back at me. "See what?"

"Come on," I said. "Time to go."

"Where are we going?"

"To say goodbye to Cathie, like the letter says."

"Who's Cathie? Someone who works here?"

"Cathie's not a who," I said. "She's a what."

Underneath the Feynman Center were several levels of subbasement and the main access to the collider ring. The badges Jean had given us granted access to the elevator that descended into the collider tunnel itself. The tunnel was a huge concrete borehole similar in size to a highway tunnel—the same kind of earth-borer machines had been used to dig it out—except that this one was thirty miles long and ran in an ellipse. A large portion of the space was taken up by the particle ring itself—in which the subatomic particles orbited—and the huge electromagnets that straddled it, along with their entourage of other coolant pipes and snaking electrical cables.

There was a pedestrian path, about fifteen feet wide. Scientists who had to get from place to place along the ring usually rode bicycles, but there were a few golf carts used for VIP tours or maintenance runs. The whole thirty-mile track had to be checked regularly for cracking concrete, for rats or other animals that might chew on the cables, for signs of shifts in the bedrock that might cause problems, or any other potential problems with the machinery. We took one of the golf carts and headed out.

CATHIE was the Controlled Acceleration and Temperature Heavy Ion Experiment, a brainchild of Brian's and mine when I was still working at the NJSC, but one that had never been fully funded. We had pushed it far enough that an underground bunker along the path of the collider ring had been dug to house it, but the project had been scuttled in favor of an experiment controlled by another colleague who was poor at experimentation but gifted at playing the game of politics. It had been the beginning of the end for me, to see our financing and most of our equipment taken away. The bunker had remained a concrete shell, emptied of its scientific apparatus, but Brian's letter suggested there was something there he had wanted me to see.

SUPERPOSITION

Fifteen minutes later, we reached it and parked the golf cart. The door into the bunker was closed and had a warning sign indicating it was not in use, but I tried the handle and the door opened. There was a bad smell, but it wasn't strong, and the implications didn't dawn on me at first. Inside, we saw half a dozen card tables stacked with scientific equipment and strewn with paper cups and food wrappers. Black and blue cables snaked across the floor and tangled around the table legs. Instead of overhead fluorescents, the room was lit by a half-dozen yard-sale lamps. Was this an approved project? It didn't look like it. There were thousands of dollars' worth of instruments here, though; I had no idea how Brian could have purchased or stolen this much. He must have used the maintenance elevator access from the pine forest above to get it all down here secretly.

This was not the CATHIE experiment. As collider experiments go, CATHIE was a small one, but it would still have involved dozens of collaborating scientists and months of installation of a set of barrel-shaped detectors around a section of the ring. In fact, none of the instruments here was connected to the accelerator at all that I could see, except that Brian had tapped into the ring's power lines. He had been using this underground bunker, not for its proximity to the accelerator, but because of its secrecy. What he was studying was something else entirely.

It wasn't until I walked around one of the card tables that I saw him. He was lying on the concrete floor in a dark puddle, one leg crumpled under him at an odd angle, his chest a bloody ruin. It was Brian Vanderhall.

CHAPTER 8
DOWN-SPIN

J udge Roswell called a short recess, after which Haviland continued his questioning of Officer Brittany Lin. Lin gazed straight at him with a confident expression as she answered, only occasionally looking to the jury when clarifying a word or technical term. She was a well-rehearsed and experienced witness.

"In the course of your investigation of the underground bunker, did you check for fingerprints?" Haviland asked.

"Yes, I did."

"Can you share with us your findings?"

"Yes. Aside from those fingerprints that matched the victim, there were fingerprints found on a pair of microscopes and on a length of steel pipe. One of the microscopes had been badly damaged, possibly by being struck with the pipe."

"And were these fingerprints matched to a person?"

"Yes. They were Jacob Kelley's."

"Could the fingerprints have been left from some previous visit that Mr. Kelley made to the bunker, sometime before the murder?"

"Yes, theoretically they could have, but given their clarity, it is unlikely they were there for many days. Also, the fingerprint evidence is consistent with other indicators we have that Kelley was at the scene at the time the murder took place."

"What evidence is that?"

"A pair of size twelve New Balance athletic shoes left footprints in the victim's blood. Bloody tracks from those shoes were found in a clear path leaving the bunker, then traveling up the stairs of a maintenance exit leading to the forest."

"And were these shoes identified?" Haviland asked.

"Yes. Jacob Kelley was still wearing them several hours later, when he was apprehended by police."

Haviland shuffled his notes to let this revelation sink in before continuing. "One more question, Officer. Did you examine the door that led to this secret underground bunker?"

"Yes, sir," Lin said.

"Can you tell us your findings?"

"The door had been fitted with a fingerprint recognition lock."

"Could you explain to the jury what a fingerprint recognition lock is meant to do?"

Lin faced the jury and shrugged in a way that communicated that of course they all knew what it was already. "It's meant to permit entry only to certain, designated people, based on their fingerprints."

"Just entry? Does that mean anyone could lock it?"

"No, I'm sorry. The lock is an electromagnetic bolt that can only be activated or deactivated by the designated person. To be locked, the door must be closed, and the lock can only be engaged by a person whose fingerprints are recognized."

"It can't be locked by an approved person when the door is opened, and then closed by someone else?"

"No. The mechanism can only be activated when the door is closed."

"So the person who locked and closed the door must have been one of the people whose fingerprints were programmed into the locking mechanism."

"Correct."

"Had the lock been reprogrammed since Mr. Vanderhall's death?"

"No. The internal computer logs clearly showed the lock programming had not been changed in years."

"How many people was this lock programmed to allow to enter the room or lock it?"

"Two."

"Who was the first?"

"The deceased, Mr. Brian Vanderhall."

"And the second?"

She nodded toward me. "The accused, Mr. Jacob Kelley."

CHAPTER 9

UP-SPIN

He was dead. Brian was dead. I felt for a pulse, though there could hardly be any doubt. His skin was cold. There was a lot of blood on the floor. I realized it was on my shoes and backed hastily away.

A Glock 46 lay tossed on the floor in a corner. I was pretty sure it was Brian's gun, the same one he had fired at Elena.

Marek had his phone out, but he shook his head. "No reception." There were call stations every mile along the tunnel, so we would have to drive to one of those to call the police.

My hands were shaking. I was trying to look anywhere but at the body. A pair of microscopes on a central table drew my attention. It occurred to me that whatever Brian had been studying was probably what got him killed. I peered into one of them. I couldn't see anything.

"Shouldn't we go?" Marek asked.

"We can't help him now," I said. "And there's something here he wanted me to see. I just want to take a look, before the police come and trample everything."

I searched for an electrical box, found it under the table among the snaking cables, and switched it on. Equipment hummed as it came to life and cooling fans spun up. I fitted my eye back into the microscope's eyepiece and adjusted the focus. A digital readout told me the magnification and scale. The object in the scope was a tiny piezoelectric resonator, barely more than a micrometer in length, but gigantic compared to the size of an electron or any other particle in the quantum world. It took me a little tinkering to figure out the setup, but once I did I was able to send a tiny pulse of energy and set the resonator oscillating.

It was what we'd been working toward for years—a relatively "large" object displaying quantum effects. Considering that the resonator was not cryogenically cooled, this was a remarkable scientific feat all on its own. But there was another microscope. I switched eyepieces, already knowing what I would find. A second resonator, vibrating much like the first . . . except that it was not connected to the electrical source. I checked the computer readout and saw that the frequency and direction of the oscillation was the same as the first one. The two microscopes were right next to each other, but as far as the quantum world was concerned, it might as well be on the other side of the world.

"Um . . . Jacob?" Marek said.

My eye was still pasted to the microscope. "This is incredible. He's actually demonstrated entanglement on a macro scale." It was more than incredible. My mind was soaring with visions of ansibles and faster-than-light communication. It was the biggest discovery of the century. Why had it not been accomplished in the open, with journal publication and world fame? Why was Brian hiding underground in the bunker of an abandoned collider experiment?

"Jacob? Are you seeing this?" Marek asked.

I pulled away, a little annoyed to be interrupted, but my annoyance disappeared as soon as I saw what Marek was talking about. All around the makeshift lab, objects were now spinning. Soda cans rotated rapidly where they stood; ballpoint pens spun on their ends or on their sides; a coin twirled on a tabletop as if flicked. The swivel chair behind me whirled crazily. Marek was standing against the wall, his eyes wide. "What's happening?" he asked.

"I don't know." I walked around the objects, peering at them from all sides. I gingerly tapped a Coke can, which dipped and then sprang right back up again like a gyroscope would. I went back to the microscope table and reached out to switch off the power, but as I did so, I caught sight of my reflection in a mirror on the wall. The mirror was the same as the one in Brian's office, a cheap plastic variety with a gold-painted frame. It was a reverse image, the same as in his office, with one difference. The objects that were spinning on my side of the mirror weren't spinning on the other side.

Impossible. I thought about what I was looking at. Millions of photons were striking the glass, knocking electrons into higher energy states, being absorbed and then emitted back again. Despite the fact that in most mirrors the light appeared to travel in straight lines, bouncing off the surface with an angle of incidence equal to the angle of reflection, I knew that wasn't really what happened. Individual photons actually took a myriad of possible paths—all possible paths, in fact—from the source to the mirror, and then from the mirror to my eye. It was just the averaging out of probability waves that made it appear to reflect in straight lines. In *this* mirror, however, the probability waves averaged out to show me a reverse image, as if the light was coming from behind the mirror instead of in front of it.

Hesitantly, I shifted my position so that I could see my own reflection, and once again, my image in the mirror had no eyes, just blank skin where the eyes should be. I felt my own eyes, and they were normal. The mirror figure did the same, touching the skin over its grotesquely missing eyes. I eased backward, reaching for the power switch again, only it was gone. Completely gone. I looked in the mirror, and there it was, just as it should have been. I was getting scared. Something was happening here that went way beyond the usual study of quantum effects. Something Brian had discovered that had terrified him and sent him running to knock on my door.

I was just thinking of running myself when the man with no eyes came out of the mirror. He didn't step or climb through, as if the mirror were a window. He refracted through as beams of light, and as he did, his face split and angled as if seen through beveled glass. He was bright, brighter than the haphazard lighting in the room warranted. In the same moment that he appeared in the room, all the rotating objects froze, balanced where they stood as if captured in a photograph.

The lighting on him seemed wrong, and he moved his head from side to side as if he were seeing something else. Was he really standing there with us, or was he in some other room, in some other universe? Did he even know he was here? That question was quickly answered when he reached out and demolished a nearby computer screen. He touched it lightly with the back of a finger, as if stroking a lover's face, but at his touch, the screen shattered, sending glass shards raining down on the desk.

I froze, too, my body disobeying my panicked signals to fight or flee.

"Where did that thing come from?" Marek shouted, backing up toward the door.

The man with no eyes had my basic height and weight and shape, but he was put together wrong, his ears a bit too small and mismatched, his jaw too big, his arms not quite connected right. His joints bent a bit too easily and in the wrong ways, as if someone who wasn't quite sure how a human was supposed to work had put one together from spare parts.

He didn't bother to walk around objects; the tables and wires and equipment seemed to bend around him instead, like light through a lens. He reached one of the microscopes and casually destroyed it, crumpling the metal like it was paper, looking on with an unreadable expression. This was something other, something alien, an intelligence that had no relation to humanity or the world I knew and understood. It was an enemy, and I knew how to deal with an enemy.

I sidestepped to the corner and picked up the Glock. I wasn't a marksman, but I'd been around enough firearms in my youth to know how to use it. I set my legs, raised the Glock with two hands, and fired. The gun exploded, deafening in the enclosed space, and a cloud of concrete dust erupted from the wall behind the man. He swiveled his head toward me, apparently unharmed. I fired a few more bullets through him, but they passed through without harm just like before.

The man with no eyes stood between me and the door. I cast about for another weapon and spotted a steel pipe lying on the floor. I shoved the Glock into my pocket and picked up the pipe. The man advanced. I swung the pipe in an overhand motion, like an ax, putting the muscles of my back and shoulders behind the swing. Just before the blow struck, the man blurred into a thousand dim copies of himself. My pipe passed right through the blur without slowing down and hit the concrete floor with a jarring crash. The pipe rang with the impact. The blur coalesced into a single man again, about three feet away from where he had started.

Marek, seeing I was trapped, advanced with his fists raised. We hit him together, Marek delivering a right hook and my pipe swinging down from above. The man blurred again, but this time the blur was made of alternating spots of dark and light, the brightest in the middle, with larger darker spots on either side, and brighter spots again beyond that. I recognized it immediately, and my mouth dropped open. It was a double-interference pattern, classically used to demonstrate the wave nature of light. This creature had its own wave pattern, something that had never been demonstrated in any object larger than a nanometer.

But this was no particle. This was a thing with intelligence and purpose, inscrutable as that purpose might be. It coalesced again into a single figure where the brightest part of its waveform had been. I started to raise my pipe again, but the pipe glowed briefly and then flared out in all directions. It disintegrated in my hand, flowing away as light. I wondered how much radiation had just passed through my body, but I had more immediate concerns.

Marek and I ran for the door, but neither of us made it. As soon as I tried to step over one of the blue cables on the floor, I was thrown off my feet by a bright flash and a deafening crack. I hit the ground hard, moaning, surrounded by wispy smoke and the smell of burnt fabric.

I looked up and saw Marek on the ground, looking similarly dazed. I tentatively reached out a finger, inching it out over the wire. Nothing happened. As I leaned forward, though, I could feel a buzzing sensation at the back of my neck. I drew quickly back.

Marek looked ready to run for the door again. "Don't try it," I said. "The air above the cables is electrified."

The cables spread out across the floor, crossing each other frequently. I was trapped on one small piece of floor, Marek on another. We were completely helpless.

"This is crazy," Marek said. "How did your friend walk through here when the power was on?"

I made a wry face. "I don't think the wires normally do this." A moment ago, I had crossed them without difficulty.

The man with no eyes strolled forward, in no apparent hurry. He stepped between us, blocking my view of Marek. I couldn't tell what he was doing.

Then I heard horrible, wet, tearing sounds, and Marek started to scream.

CHAPTER 10
DOWN-SPIN

E ven though I was on trial in Philadelphia, the prisons were so overcrowded that I was incarcerated in the George W. Hill Correctional
Facility in Thornton, a forty-five minute drive by van to and from
the courthouse. My cellmate was a big nineteen-year-old accused of car
theft and multiple counts of battery, who was still waiting for his trial
to start. We hadn't had any problems, but I was pretty sure I could take
him in a fight if I had to. Youth and strength don't mean all that much if
you haven't been trained how to use them. I was lucky, if you could call
it that, to have only one cellmate— the prison was so crowded that many
cells had three, even though they were only built for two. If I was convicted, I would be moved to a different, higher security prison. I wasn't
even sure where, but I guessed it would probably be worse than this place.

I jumped at the chance to meet with Terry whenever I could, if for no
other reason than to get out of my cell. The prison meeting room had a
futuristic look, like a plastic prison onboard a space station. Three of the
four walls were transparent, with metal cage wire braided through the
material. Through them you could see other defendants talking to their
lawyers, like an infinite progression seen through a pair of facing mirrors.
The table was a thin, silver-colored slab on a central post, surrounded by
six yellow chairs that were bolted to the floor. I liked to imagine it was
to keep them from floating around in microgravity, though more likely
it was to prevent inmates from using them to club their lawyers to death.

"Haviland's scoring points with that big interactive whiteboard of
his," I said after Terry arrived. "It looks like a string of facts. I got angry
with Brian at time A, and then I killed him at time B. Case closed."

An armed guard stood just outside, able to see everything that happened in the room, but—supposedly—unable to hear through the sound-proof glass.

"That's not true," Terry said. "Don't undersell the jurors; they can tell the difference between graphics and evidence."

"Can they?" I asked. "Then I guess they'll just focus on the finger-prints and the blood on my shoes. Innocent for sure." I was out of my cell but still feeling helpless. Nothing I could do would change the outcome of this. All I could do was watch. "One of these days," I said, "I'm going to just get up and punch Haviland in the head."

"You know you can't do that." Terry looked at his watch. We were just waiting, talking idly, but of course he was still billing by the quarter hour.

"I know," I said. "I understand, believe me. But you have to under-stand me, too. I hate just sitting by and watching while other people determine my fate. It makes me feel like hitting something."

The guard opened the door, and Jean Massey came in, breathing hard. "Sorry I'm late," she said. "It was murder finding parking." She gave an embarrassed chuckle and glanced at me nervously. "In a manner of speaking."

Jean was our expert witness. Obviously, I couldn't do it, and we needed someone who could explain the science of the case to the jury. I had given Terry a list of colleagues from the NJSC who could effectively speak about quantum concepts, and Jean was the only one who had said yes. She wasn't ideal, since she was a friend, and thus could be consid-ered less than objective, but she was willing, and she knew what she was talking about, and that counted for a lot.

We had gone over her testimony before, but Terry still had a ten-dency to forget key components of the science, or else refer to it using language that made no sense, betraying his lack of basic understanding. That wasn't necessarily a bad thing—the jurors would be in the same boat, and seeing that he didn't understand it either would help them connect with him and his questions. But he had to understand it well enough to get the questions right.

"So, tell me about these resonators again," Terry said. "I'm having trouble remembering why two spinning doodads smaller than a clipped fingernail are so important."

The question seemed to spark Jeannie's enthusiasm. "One word," she said. "Superposition. Let's try explaining it another way. Do you have a coin?"

Terry rummaged around in his pockets. "Somewhere around here, I think." Ever since the United States had pulled coins out of circulation, leaving the dollar bill as the lowest legal denomination, metal coins were getting harder to find. Ask my daughters what a nickel or a dime was and they probably wouldn't know. Finally, Terry came up with an old, blackened penny. "I keep it for luck," he said.

Jean flipped the coin up with her thumb, let it fall on the tabletop, and slapped it flat. With her hand still covering it, she asked, "Which side is up?"

"I don't know," Terry said, playing along.

"So, at this point, it could be in either of two states, heads or tails, right?"

"No," Terry said. "It's only in one state. I just don't know which one it is."

Jean grinned. "A true lawyer talking. And as far as the coin is concerned, I'd have to agree with you. But in the quantum world—if this were an electron with two possible spin states, say, instead of a coin—it no longer holds. The electron is actually in both states at the same time. It's not until you look at it"—she lifted her hand, revealing the head of Abraham Lincoln, barely visible through the grime—"that it resolves into a single state."

"That's just silly," Terry said. "If you can't see it, how do you know it's not already in one of those states, just like the coin?"

Jean and I traded a look. "Here we go," I said.

Jean took a deep breath. "Okay. New example. Imagine there's a tennis ball bouncing back and forth between these two walls. It never slows down or falls; it just keeps bouncing back and forth endlessly."

"Okay," Terry said.

"We turn off the lights, and you pull out your camera and take a flash picture. What do you see?"

"A green dot, in the air, somewhere between the walls."

"Is it any more likely to be in one place than another?"

"Not if it's moving at a constant speed, and assuming the impact with the walls doesn't slow it down."

My respect for Terry increased the more time I spent with him. All his answers were precise, and he seemed ready to sit there all day until he understood what Jean was talking about. He could have been a scientist. Though I suppose if he'd gone that route, he wouldn't be able to bill four hundred dollars an hour.

"Let's say you take a thousand pictures, or a million, and merge them together," Jean said. "What would you see?"

"A set of green dots stretching from wall to wall," Terry said. "A solid green line, if I took enough pictures."

"Right. So now we'll step into the quantum world. Say this was an electron instead of a tennis ball, though any particle would do. When you look at your million pictures, what you will see is a pattern where some areas have the usual number of green dots, some areas have twice as many dots, and some areas have no green dots at all."

Terry gave her a skeptical look. "None?"

"None."

"So no matter how many pictures I took, I would never catch the ball in those spots."

"The ball never is in those spots."

"So how does it get from wall to wall?"

I laughed, enjoying his consternation. I could tell he thought he was missing something, but he wasn't. The truth is, everyone is confused by quantum physics, no matter how much they've studied it. We learn all the technical jargon, and we can do all the math, but nobody really understands it, because it defies all common sense. "It gets worse," I said. "Trust me, it gets a lot worse."

"Let's say you don't believe this is actually possible," Jean said, "so you hire one of your interns to hold a tennis racket in the path of the ball, right at one of those blank spots where the ball never appears in your pictures."

"In the dark," Terry said.

"Yes."

"And I take some more pictures. Let me guess: the ball keeps bouncing back and forth against the walls, as if the racket wasn't there."

"You've got it," Jean said.

"You should have been a physicist," I said.

"Okay, so what really happens? Does the tennis ball—the electron— fly right through? Or go around? I'm losing the thread here."

I stepped in. "The point is, electrons and protons and neutrons are very different than tennis balls. The tennis ball is made out of them, but they're not the same thing at all. The electron isn't bouncing back and forth, not really. It exists everywhere between the two barriers at the same time, at some probability. This is the probability wave—the chance that it will be in any given spot when you look at it. The tennis ball has a probability wave, too, only its wave averages out to be consistent with how we experience the world. The electron's probability wave doesn't make any normal sense at all."

"That's the concept of superposition," Jean said. "Being in more than one place, or more than one state, at the same time. You can overlay multiple probability waves on this poor electron, like overlapping wakes from two different boats on the ocean, changing the probability that it will or will not be in any given place."

"So, the coin?" Terry said. "You were explaining why it wasn't really heads or tails until I looked at it."

"Right," Jean said. "Just like the tennis ball. It's everywhere at once along its path, with varying probability, until the moment at which you take a picture. Then the universe rolls a giant pair of dice, and bam—the tennis ball is *there*. That's not how it works with tennis balls. Tennis balls really are in one place at one time, whether you're looking at them or not. But an electron isn't. It's smeared out over a whole area, with a certain probability. Or, like the coin, one of its characteristics—heads or tails, or which way it's spinning—is similarly smeared."

She waited. Terry nodded, but whether it was because he understood or because he'd given up, I wasn't certain.

"Now, entanglement"—Jean cracked her knuckles loudly—"this is where we really start to blow your mind."

She moved to flip the coin again, but she was interrupted by a tinny orchestral version of "The Hall of the Mountain King" coming from somewhere under the table. "Excuse me," she said.

She lifted her purse, a massive black handbag that could have stored a collapsible tent and still had room for a sleeping bag, and began rummaging through it, trying to home in on the song, which was steadily increasing in volume. Finally, she found it, glanced at the display, then flipped it open and held it up to her ear. "I'm busy, Nick." She retreated to a corner of the tiny room, facing away from us to imply some measure of privacy.

"Is this all for real?" Terry said.

"It's how the world works," I said. "Everything you do, every day, is governed by this science. It doesn't usually matter to you, and it's operating on such a small scale that you never see it. But the reason you can see me right now is because the electrons in my face can absorb and then emit photons, which the electrons in your retina can absorb in turn. There are trillions of particles being annihilated and created in your cells every minute, allowing the electrical interaction necessary for their survival. So yeah, it's for real."

"But the whole bit about the coin being both heads and tails, until you look at it? It sounds ridiculous. How can my looking at something affect what it is?"

"In the macro world, not so much," I said. "But you have to remember that in an electron's world, a single photon is a pretty big deal. 'Getting looked at' to an electron means getting whacked by a photon. At that small a scale, looking at something *does* affect what it is."

"I can't talk right now, okay?" Jean said. "I'll be there when I can. This is important." A pause. "If that were true, you wouldn't be doing this to me. Yeah, okay. Bye."

She shut the phone with a snap and tossed it back into her cavernous bag.

"Sorry," she said.

"Do you need to go?" I asked. "We could try this again later." Terry looked sour at the suggestion, but I ignored him.

"No, it's nothing," Jean said, sounding irritated. "I'm staying here as long as I need to, and Nick can just . . . forget it. Let's get back to work. Where did I put that coin?"

She found the penny, flipped it, and covered it again. "Okay. This is an electron's spin state. As we said before, at this moment, since we haven't looked at it, it's *both* heads and tails. Undetermined. Or, for the electron, both up and down. You with me so far?"

Terry gave an uncertain nod.

"Let's say that, without looking at the coin, I make a wax impression of both sides. I give one impression to Jacob"—she mimed handing me something which I pretended to take without looking at it—"and I put one in my pocket. Now, which do I have in my pocket, heads or tails?"

"Both at the same time," Terry said. "With some probability wave."

"What about him?"

"Same thing."

"Very good! He can be taught." She stood and walked over to the corner of the transparent room. "I take my wax impression to Paris. Jacob takes his to Seattle."

"Why can't I go to Paris?" I asked.

"You'll be lucky just to get out of jail," she reminded me.

"Good point. Seattle it is."

"Now, I pull out my wax impression and look at it." She pretended to do so. "It's tails. The probability wave collapses. Now what about his?"

Terry shrugged. "It collapses too?"

"Yes. By looking at my wax impression, I caused his to become heads, from the other side of the world. I sent information around the world faster than the speed of light."

Terry was shaking his head. "This is ridiculous," he said. "You didn't change anything. It was heads to begin with."

"No," Jean said firmly. "Remember the tennis balls. This is the quantum world. These are particles, not coins."

He kept shaking his head, sadly. "That may be. But I don't know how you expect me to convince a jury."

Jean made an aggravated huff. "I'm doing the best I can here. Tennis balls, coins—these are everyday objects. If we use subatomic examples, it'll only get worse."

"They just need to get the idea that something can be in two states at once," I said. "They don't have to understand it entirely, but they have to believe it as a thoroughly tested and noncontroversial finding of modern science. So how do we do that? Quote Einstein? Cite polls of leading scientists?"

"None of that matters to a jury," Terry said. He pointed at Jean. "What matters is her. If she can sell it, and not let Haviland talk her in circles or undermine her credibility, then they'll accept it as fact. So let's do our role playing again. I'll be Haviland on cross-examination. Act naturally, take your time, don't try to anticipate my questions, and especially—especially!—only answer the exact question I've asked."

Jean ran a hand through her hair and grimaced. "I'm going to be here all night again, aren't I?"

"Probably," Terry said.

CHAPTER 11
UP-SPIN

Marek's scream pierced the air. More than anything, I wanted to see what was happening to him, but once I did see, I almost wished I couldn't. Marek was in pieces on the ground. His arms and legs and hands and fingers had been torn apart. Incredibly, there was no blood. It was like an old Saturday morning cartoon where the hapless villain is shredded in a propeller or flattened under a steam roller, but he gets up, shakes it off, and is as good as new.

In fact, as I watched, the man with no eyes put Marek back together again, piece by piece. He did it with meticulous care, as if assembling a model airplane, pausing to peer—with no eyes—at the result. It was almost as if the man wanted to see how a human being was assembled. I reached out tentatively and realized that the air above the cables was no longer electrified. Perhaps the thing could only perform one miracle at a time—or was just distracted. I stayed where I was, however, afraid to move lest it disappear and leave Marek spread out in pieces on the floor. Though how Marek could possibly survive the encounter, I didn't know. Finally, when the man finished the last piece of his gruesome puzzle, he stepped back as if to admire his handiwork. Marek opened his eyes. Incredibly, he seemed alive and perfectly whole. He felt his head, his arms, his legs. He said something that sounded like *varcolac* and crossed himself.

The man with no eyes still stood between us and the door we had come through, blocking our exit, but there was another way out of the bunker, an emergency exit with stairs up to the outside. All the experiment rooms were reachable through maintenance access doors all along the ring, deep in the Pine Barrens. They couldn't be entered without an access card or key, but they allowed easy exit in case of emergency.

"Can you run?" I asked.

"I think so," Marek said.

"Follow me, then," I said.

Marek took a careful step backward. The man with no eyes seemed to regard him, but made no move. Marek took another step.

"Now!" We bolted for the emergency exit, not looking back to see if the man with no eyes was coming after us. There was a service elevator, but there was no time to punch the button and wait. We used the stairs instead.

We took them two at a time. Twenty flights later, breathing hard, we broke out into the pine forest. I still didn't know if we were being followed, but we didn't stop to find out. After a few moments to catch our breath, we struck out running along the overgrown path toward the road.

In a short dirt driveway, perhaps a hundred feet off the road and obscured by brush, we found a battered Toyota Viva, a car that I recognized at once.

"This is Brian's car," I said. "He must have parked here and snuck down the maintenance access."

"How did he get in?" Marek asked.

"They don't monitor them," I said. "They're pretty remote. When I was working here, Brian and I rigged this one so we could go in and out without triggering the alarm." That was back when we were installing equipment for CATHIE and had every expectation of long and fruitful study. We sometimes got claustrophobic in our buried, underground bunker, and it was good to be able to come up for fresh, pine-scented air and occasionally, depending on the weather and how late we were working, a narrow view of the stars overhead.

We looked in the car. The keys were in the ignition. I tried my phone and still got no service. "Looks like we'll need to borrow his car," I said.

I climbed into the driver's seat, and Marek got in the other side. I turned the key, and the engine started easily. I got the car turned around, and it rumbled over the uneven dirt toward the road. When we pulled out onto the highway with a scrape of gravel under the wheels, I let out a long breath.

"It didn't hurt at all," Marek said. He seemed to be embarrassed that he'd lost his nerve. "It was just . . ."

"The most terrifying thing I've ever seen," I said.

Marek held his hand up to the light, flexing his fingers. He said something in Romanian that sounded like a curse.

"What?"

"This finger," he said. "When I was young, a teenager, there was an accident. My hand was crushed under a heavy beam. Several bones broke, but we were poor, and I was strong and proud. I never saw a doctor. But this finger . . ."

He flexed it again, and I remembered that it had always been stiff, the bones fused together in a slightly bent position. Now he was bending and unbending that finger along with all the others.

"It is not possible," Marek said.

"That's not the only impossible thing we just saw," I said. "That guy took you apart and put you back together again. Seriously, no pain? You're not just showing me how tough you are?"

Marek gave me a look. "I was screaming like a baby."

He wiggled his finger some more. I supposed that technically, that thing had healed Marek, but I wasn't ready to consider it a miracle. I wasn't at all sure that healing had been its purpose. It had looked more like an engineer taking a machine apart and putting it back together again to see what was inside.

"Better try the police again," I said.

Marek tapped some buttons on his phone, but shook his head. "No bars."

I wasn't too surprised. "We can't be that far out," I said. "Shouldn't take more than a few minutes to get in range of a tower."

Pine trees were whizzing by on both sides. The road was narrow and straight, with no other cars in sight. I pushed down on the gas and reflexively checked my rearview mirror for flashing lights, though at that point, a cop car would have been welcome. As I did, I noticed an old brown blanket draped over some junk in the backseat. The blanket moved suddenly, rearing up to fill my view. It fell away to reveal a man, lights flashing where his eyes should be.

Marek shouted. I slammed on the brakes and swerved, sending the car into the opposite lane. I spun the steering wheel hard the other way, adrenaline pumping through my veins, but we were moving too fast. Instead of righting itself, the car skidded sideways off the road and smashed into a tree. My head smacked into the steering wheel, but we didn't hit hard enough to set off the air bags.

I felt stunned and dizzy, but I fumbled with my seatbelt clasp, afraid to look back, expecting at any moment to be grabbed from behind. My hands were shaking; I couldn't find the button. Finally, I found it and the seatbelt popped open. I reached for the door and scrambled out. Marek was already out on the other side, and we ran for the trees.

I risked a backward glance and saw the man just getting out of the car behind us. Using the door. I stopped. The man climbing awkwardly out of the car wasn't the creature that had chased us in the bunker. What had seemed to be missing eyes had in fact been reflections from a pair of glasses. His clothes were wrinkled and his hair was tousled from sleep, and he moved like his body hurt from a night spent sleeping in the back seat of a car. It was Brian Vanderhall.

I advanced on him, feeling both foolish and furious. "What's going on here?" I asked. I was more angry than astonished. This was a trick, some kind of small-minded, immature trick of Brian's to get him out of some trouble or other, probably with a woman. He had somehow faked his own death, but the trick had gone sour, and now he and everyone around him were going to take the fall. It was typical Brian.

Brian lifted his hands as if to ward off a blow, then seemed to recognize me. "Jacob?" He blew out a breath of relief. "I thought you were car thieves. What are you doing here?"

"What am *I* doing here?" I barely knew where to start. "You're supposed to be dead!"

Marek came up behind me. "This is Brian?" he asked.

"Yes. Are you okay?" My head was ringing from the impact, and I'd have a bit of a bruise over one eye, but no real injuries.

"Fine, I think," Marek said.

Brian was wearing the same shorts and T-shirt as the day before, and one side of his face had a pattern pressed into it from where he'd been sleeping against the car upholstery. He looked worried and confused. "How did you find me?" he asked.

"By running up the stairs to get away from that thing with no eyes, who nearly killed us by doing impossible things, which I hope you are about to explain to me."

Brian's eyes went large and wild. "You went down there? Is it following you?"

"Of course I went down there! You nearly got me killed."

"Us killed," Marek said.

"Tell me you didn't turn the power on," Brian said.

"Of course, I turned it on. You told me to go down there and look around. So you'd better start telling us what's happening."

"I don't know what's happening," Brian said. "I didn't tell you anything. Trust me, I wouldn't have told you to turn the power on down there."

"I don't trust you as far as I can separate a pair of quarks," I said. "Tell me what you do know." I was angry enough to get back in the car and leave him there. I'd seen his corpse on his floor of the bunker, and if that had just been some kind of elaborate hoax, I wasn't finding it very funny. I remembered that I still had Brian's Glock in my pocket, but I decided not to give it back to him quite yet.

I examined the car. The brakes had taken most of our forward momentum, so the hood of the car was only slightly staved in, and none of the glass was broken.

Brian rocked from foot to foot. His skin was peppered with goose bumps. The snow hadn't lasted, but it was still pretty cold outside. "Can we get back in the car?" he asked. "I'm cold."

"Fine," I said, disgusted.

He climbed in the backseat again and wrapped himself with the blanket. Marek got in the passenger's side, and I took the driver's seat and tried the ignition. Nothing. I tried three more times, and finally the engine sputtered and caught. I backed the car away from the tree and, after spinning my tires a bit, got it back onto the road and moving forward again. I continued toward Lakehurst, though at a more careful speed. I tried my phone again. There was still no reception, but at this point, it wasn't clear what I would tell the police anyway.

"Start talking," I said.

"Okay," Brian said. "You remember the nature-as-computer argument?"

I rolled my eyes. "Yes. We had this conversation already."

"We did?"

I glanced back at him in the rearview mirror. He was wrapped up in the brown blanket so that only his eyes were showing, like an animal in a cave. "Yes. At my house. So was that thing in the bunker one of the quantum intelligences you were talking about? The oh-so-friendly fairies who gave you their technology?"

Brian looked puzzled. "When was I at your house?" he asked.

I was getting irritated. I was getting tired of being pushed around, and I wanted some answers. "You were at my house last night. You fired a gun at my wife, and I punched you. You seriously don't remember that?"

Brian looked blank. "I haven't been to your house in years. I wanted to come, to tell you everything, but I didn't."

"Okay," I said. "Something is seriously wrong with you."

"You're right about the quantum intelligences," Brian said. "Though I don't know how you know. They're formed from the interactions of the subatomic world, life springing out of complexity. That's what you saw."

"I know what I saw," Marek said. "It was a *varcolac*. My grandmother saw one when she was a girl."

"What's a varcolac?" I asked, mauling the pronunciation.

"A demon. A monster. They live on the other side of the world," Marek said.

"New Zealanders live on the other side of the world," Brian said.

"No, not like that. On the other earth, the mirror world, on the other side of ours. There are the gentle folk, the *blajini*, who fast all year and benefit humankind, though they don't understand us. Then there are the *varcolaci*, who devour and kill."

I raised my eyebrows. "You think the thing we saw in the bunker was a monster from some kind of Romanian myth?"

"Some say they are the souls of unbaptized children," Marek said. "Others say they are the spirits of those who drowned after Moses commanded the Red Sea to flow back over their heads. But they exist."

"So . . . Egyptian monsters from a Romanian myth about a Jewish fable," Brian said. He gave a derisive laugh. "Listen to me. This isn't story time. We're talking about self-aware intelligences generated from the complexity of particle interaction on a large scale."

Marek twisted around in his seat to face Brian. "You think using scientific words changes what it is?"

"I'm talking about something physical, not a spirit."

"I hear what you're saying. You're saying that if a thing is complicated enough, it will be conscious," Marek said.

"Pretty much," Brian said. "If it's a network, like a brain or computer, with a means of passing information. People tend to romanticize consciousness, as if it's something spiritual. It's just a word we use to describe complexity."

Marek looked at me. "This is why I hate scientists," he said.

I grinned. "I'm a scientist."

"Not like that. Why is calling them *quantum intelligences* any better than calling them *varcolaci?*"

"Look, I'll step you through it," Brian said. "Is a toaster conscious?"

"No," Marek said.

"Why not?"

"It's a machine. It does what it was built to do," Marek said.

"What about one of those automated lawn mowers or vacuum cleaners? We say things like, 'It tried to go around the tree, but it got confused.' Doesn't that indicate a consciousness? That it consciously intends to mow the lawn?"

"It's still just a machine. It follows its programming," Marek said.

"What about a dog? Is it conscious? Does it *intend* to get in the lawnmower's way, or chase the cat, or shed on the carpet? Or is it just following its programming?"

"A dog is conscious, I think," Marek said.

"Or do we just say that, because the dog's programming is more complex, and we can't always predict it?" Brian asked. "What about you? I grant you the label of *conscious* because I ascribe intent and unpredictability to your actions, but when it comes down to it, you're just following your programming, too. *Consciousness* is just when that programming becomes complex enough to warrant using a certain vocabulary."

Marek's hand darted into the backseat, quick as a snake, and grabbed Brian by the neck, just under his chin. I could only see him through the mirror, but I could tell Brian hadn't seen it coming. His mouth slammed shut and his eyes bulged.

"Is it just my programming if I break your neck?" Marek asked.

I knew Marek well enough by now to know that he wouldn't really do it, but Brian didn't. "There's no need for that," he croaked.

Marek made a deep sound in his throat that eventually became recognizable as a chuckle. He let go of Brian's throat and began to laugh heartily. Brian laughed, too, though not very convincingly, and rubbed at his throat.

"Free will is real," Marek said. "I can choose to break your neck if I wish."

"Science says not," Brian said. "Everything you do is just the accumulated result of a series of probabilistic outcomes."

"But I can decide. I haven't decided yet, but really, it could go either way," Marek said.

The superior grin flashed back onto Brian's face. "In fact, it goes both ways. Every decision you make is made the other way by another version of you in a parallel universe."

"We don't really know that," I put in.

"It's basic mathematics," Brian said, pouting now that I hadn't backed him up. "Say the number of particles making up the Earth and its environment in space is N. Each particle can only have a finite set of values—position, velocity, spin, etc.—so the number of possible states that a set of N particles can be in is another number, M. M is staggeringly large, but finite. In an infinite universe—which ours assuredly is, or is so vast as to make the difference unimportant—those M states will all occur, and all be repeated, again and again. Not to mention all of the other infinitely sized bubble universes. Everything you do is being repeated by someone exactly like you—millions of yous, in fact—in every possible slight variation."

Marek made a disgusted look. "A person is not the same as a toaster. If you don't know that, your science is worth nothing."

Brian held his hands protectively over his throat, but he kept talking. "We want to believe we're special. But every great scientific discovery in the past has had to break us of the idea of how special and different we are as humans. Copernicus made us give up the idea that the Earth was the center of the universe. Darwin made us give up the idea that humans are greater than animals. Einstein made us realize that even our perspective on motion and time is not absolute.

"Quantum mechanics is the worst, though. It undermines our sense of purpose. It tells us that everything is driven by probabilities, the random dice roll of a billion particles. Every decision you think you make is in fact a rolling probability wave, the result of a giant quantum computer that's calculating you and everything else. Worse, the opposite of every decision you make is probably being made by a parallel you in another universe. Einstein didn't want to believe it either, but science doesn't lie."

"If that's what science gives you, what good is it?" Marek asked. "You can talk professor as much as you like, but there was a varcolac in that bunker, and you let it out."

"And more to the point," I said, "that varcolac tried to kill us."

"You're not seriously going to call it that," Brian said. "They're not spirits. They're physical creatures, the same as we are. Although their 'bodies' are composed as much of photons as they are of other particles. I think they've been around a lot longer than we have, maybe even from the first few seconds of the big bang."

"Well then," I said slowly, "we can probably call them sprites or faeries or angels or demons or varcolacs, and not be wrong. Most primitive cultures have animistic belief systems. Maybe they're based on something real: other beings that live in the fabric of the universe."

"Call them what they are," Brian said. "They're quantum intelligences. And I doubt anyone else has seen them before. Before I contacted them, I don't think they were any more aware of our existence than we were of theirs."

"How did you even know they were there?"

"I didn't. You saw my resonators?" When I nodded, Brian grinned like a proud little boy with a model airplane. "That's where it started. That was the beginning. Normal human interactions are no more noticeable to them than the rotation of the Earth is to us. They speak in entangle-

ment and probabilities and weak and strong forces. When I communicated quantum effects over a distance, however—when I could turn them
on and off with a switch and see the results, it was like picking up radio
waves from a distant galaxy, or . . . or, I don't know, a UFO landing on
their front lawn. They suddenly knew that someone else was out there,
someone with the intelligence to communicate and respond.

"It was nothing that made sense at first. I would charge the resonator,
and it would spin, sometimes one way, sometimes another, sometimes
fast, sometimes slow. It was a complex probability wave, but I made
enough observations that I knew what it was. I couldn't predict any one
measurement, as you might expect, but I could predict the distribution
of any hundred. Then, inexplicably, it deviated."

"Interference from another wave pattern," I said.

"Yes, but this time, the pattern wasn't predictable. The oscillating
frequency kept getting higher. Finally, I got a look at the values . . ."

"Prime numbers," Marek said, jumping back into the conversation.
"They were a list of primes."

Brian looked startled. "How did you know?"

Marek rolled his eyes. "That is what the aliens always send, don't
they? In all the books and movies. Primes don't occur in nature, so if you
get primes, you know it's from something intelligent."

"I don't know if they did it on purpose to communicate or not, but
there it was. I fed the numbers back into the system—I flipped my switch
twice, then three times, then five, etcetera. I barely left the bunker, not to
sleep, not to eat. We followed primes with natural ratios like pi and the
golden mean, and then more complex mathematics. I programmed my
smartpad to control the switch, and soon we had a language of sorts going,
based entirely on math. I told them about us—our chemical makeup, our
genetics. They sent me formulas to describe what they are—it was fasci-
nating! Soon they were feeding me formulas that I implemented in meta-
circuitry on my pad, and that's when things really started to happen.

Through the resonators, we broke the barrier between the macro and sub-atomic worlds. When we dream of tapping the quantum realm, we think of making faster computers to play video games, but there's so much more that's possible. It'll revolutionize everything, what we think of ourselves, what it means to be human. There's almost nothing they *can't* do."

I thought about how that thing in the bunker had behaved, and a chill went up my spine. "And now they know we're here."

Brian didn't pick up on my tone. "It's amazing. For more than a century, we've looked for aliens in distant galaxies, but they were here all along, right among us. *Through* us even, in the very molecules that make up our air and food and our own bodies. Another whole civilization, living on Earth—or in the Earth, I should say. The surfaces of things aren't as important to them as they are to us, and things like gravity and electricity are just one more kind of particle interaction.

His eyes glistened. "They told me they could make me just like them. I was going to have all their power, live an immortal life across the universes . . ."

"Okay," Marek said. "We get it. They're great and all. Practically gods. So how come you're sleeping in the backseat of your car at the same time as you're lying dead on your bunker floor?"

"As I'm what?" Brian asked.

"A bloody corpse with a hole in your chest," I said.

"What are you talking about?" Brian asked.

"Look," I said. "This is not a thought experiment. You pulled me into this, and I have a right to know what's going on."

"I've been telling you," Brian said.

I braked hard and pulled off the road. I jammed the gearshift into park, and then turned around to face him.

"You're saying you don't know about the body."

"What body?"

"Or the letter. There was a letter for me in your office."

"The letter I sent you?" he asked.

"Sent me? I found an envelope with my name on it in your jacket pocket in your office. It told me to go look in the bunker."

Brian shook his head. "I mailed that letter to you," he said. "I sent it yesterday."

I pulled the letter out of my pocket and waved it in his face. "If you mailed it yesterday, how did I pull it out of your jacket pocket today?"

"I don't know! What body are you talking about?"

"You are, as we speak, lying dead in the CATHIE bunker with a bullet hole in your chest," I said.

Brian's face got very pale, and that look of terror came back into his eyes. "Oh, no."

"Explain to me how that's possible," I said.

Brian stared at me as if he didn't understand the words. His jaw flapped like a fish on a hook. His gaze, which had been staring off into the distance at some bright, imagined future, suddenly snapped into focus. He began shaking violently. "No, it can't be," he said.

"What?"

"Give me the letter," he said. "Did you get through the passwords?"

"Passwords, plural?" I said.

Brian used his finger to scribble "137.036" on the page, and the letter reappeared. "I told you to 'say goodbye to Cathie,'" Brian said. "The second password is the date they shut our program down." He traced some more numbers.

"And I was supposed to figure that out?" I asked. "I thought you wanted me to go look in the bunker."

Brian showed me the paper. It was now filled with tiny programming circuits, connected with a tangle of colored lines. I knew if I touched any one of the circuits, it would expand to show me more circuitry inside. The paper was humming. I could feel a strange internal tugging sensation, just as I had felt when Brian had made the gyroscope spin.

"You programmed all this?" I asked.

"Most of it."

"What it doing?"

"It's a Higgs projector," he said. "It's locally altering the Higgs field."

"Oh, come on," I said.

"I'm serious."

"What, you figured out how to isolate the Higgs field in your office, with an Erector set and some Play-Doh? A project like that would be a billion-dollar operation, if it were even possible."

"I didn't. *They* did. They gave me the equations for the core modules; I just wrote wrappers to interface with them."

"What's a Higgs field?" Marek asked.

"It's an invisible field, uniform throughout the universe, that gives our universe its physical qualities, including the idea of matter itself," I said. "The theory is that the big bang produced not just one universe, but countless, frothing up out of the early expansion like so many bubbles. Each universe could have a different Higgs field, stronger or weaker than ours, and thus have a different set of basic constants. That means it could have a different set of fundamental particles, and thus a different periodic table, and, obviously, an entirely different structure," I said.

"So, the varcolac told you all this?" Marek asked.

"The quantum intelligences," Brian said. "I think maybe they *are* the Higgs field, or it's part of them somehow. They . . ." He trailed off, his eyes wide, staring at something behind me.

I turned. Through the windshield, I could see it coming. The varcolac strode through the trees as if they weren't there, heading right toward us.

I yanked the gearshift into reverse and hit the accelerator. The car lunged backward and smashed into a tree. I turned the wheel and shifted into drive, but the rear wheels just spun, throwing up loose dirt. I revved the engine frantically, but it was no good. "Out of the car!" I shouted. Marek was already out his side and running. I pushed my door open and ran the other way, not much caring if Brian followed or not.

I was fast and in shape; Brian was not. I heard him scream, and, despite my desire to put as much distance between myself and the varcolac as possible, I turned around. He was frantically doing something on the smartpaper as the varcolac bore down on him.

I heard a deep thrum, like a bass woofer turned up loud, and the varcolac disintegrated. Brian dropped to his knees, breathing hard. "That was close."

"What did you do?" I asked.

"It's tied to the collider," Brian said. "It feeds off the exotic particles the collider produces, and it draws a tremendous amount of power from it to maintain its physical manifestation. I altered the Higgs field locally to eliminate those particles."

Brian touched a few spots on the paper. The thrum stopped and the tugging sensation in my chest subsided.

"Shouldn't you leave that on?" I asked.

"It's gone now," Brian said. "It won't come back unless . . ." He stopped with a strangled choke as the varcolac reappeared less than a foot in front of him. Brian shrieked and dropped to his knees. He held the letter out in a shaking hand. "Take it!" he said. "Just take it!"

The varcolac bent and touched Brian. Brian's eyes unfocused, and his body glowed. Tiny particles lifted from his body, like sand in a windstorm, flowing from him into the varcolac. As we watched, Brian disintegrated completely and flowed into the varcolac itself. Horribly, the varcolac's jumbled features took on a little of Brian's appearance. The varcolac now held the smartpaper in its hand. A moment later, the paper burst into violent flame and was gone.

The varcolac turned toward us. We stood frozen, watching it. It took a step forward, then turned on its heel and disappeared. It didn't just vanish: it *turned*, like it was walking around a corner, only into some other dimension of space that I couldn't see. It might still have been quite close, for all I knew, invisible, watching us and getting ready to pounce, but if so, there was nothing I could do about it. For now, as far as I could tell, the varcolac was gone.

Marek ran up to me. "You all right?"

"Yeah."

"Let's get out of here," I said. I ran to the car and climbed in.

Marek climbed in next to me, but I had the car in gear and was pulling out before he had the door closed.

"Where are we going?" he asked.

I stomped on the accelerator, pulling us into a tight U-turn. "There are two of those letters," I said.

"What?"

"There were two Brians," I said. I squealed the tires pulling onto the road and did a U-turn, heading away from the NJSC, back toward home. "Two Brians, two letters. I don't know exactly how, but it's true. The Brian we found dead was the one who visited my house and left the letter in his jacket pocket. The Brian we just saw sent the same letter to me via FedEx."

"Which means . . . ?" Marek asked.

"It looked to me like the varcolac was after that letter," I said. "It killed Brian for it. The other version of the letter, however—the one that went out via FedEx was probably delivered today."

I heard Marek's quick intake of breath. "So if it wants the other letter, too, and knows how to find it, that would lead the varcolac . . ."

I leaned my weight on the accelerator, rocketing the car through a red light. ". . . straight to my house."

CHAPTER 12
DOWN-SPIN

D avid Haviland was apparently a morning person. He greeted the judge and the jury with a cheerful smile. I had barely slept, and, next to me, Terry didn't look much better. He was clutching a paper cup of coffee like it was a life raft.

"The People call Officer Brandon McBride to the stand," Haviland said.

McBride was a big man gone to fat, with thinning gray hair and the hint of jowls forming in his cheeks. He was wearing a tie that seemed too tight for the folds of his neck.

"Officer McBride," Haviland said. "How long have you been with the Media police force?"

"Thirty-seven years." McBride emphasized each word, apparently proud of his length of service.

"And what is your current title?"

"I'm a senior evidence technician."

"And what does that role entail?"

"We receive thousands of items ranging in size from hair samples to vehicles, and we track and store the items and release them as appropriate. Mostly my job is to ensure that the integrity of the chain of evidence is preserved. We store the items and make sure that nothing is tampered with and there is a clear chain of custody for any item from the place where it was confiscated to its appearance in trial."

"On December third, did your office receive into custody a weapon taken from Jacob Kelley when he was arrested?"

"Yes, we did," McBride said.

"How can you be sure?" Haviland asked.

"I reviewed the record this morning in preparation for this trial."

Haviland looked at the judge. "Permission to approach the witness, Your Honor?"

"Granted."

Haviland handed McBride a paper-clipped sheaf of papers. "This document is presented to the record as Exhibit A1. Officer, can you identify the document for the court?"

"This is the evidence register for December third."

"Is this the same record you reviewed in preparation for the trial?"

"Yes."

"Could you please summarize the entry for the court?"

"It says that a Glock 46 nine millimeter with black polymer grips and a scratched barrel was confiscated from the Kelley residence at three PM." McBride flipped through the pages. "There are photographs of both sides of the weapon."

"Do you receive many weapons?"

"Quite a few," McBride said.

"How could you be sure that a particular weapon was the one received from the Kelley residence?"

"The weapon is tagged with the evidence ID number and stored in a secure compartment. Anyone removing or returning it must sign in and out under the supervision of an evidence clerk, who also signs his or her name."

"Is that record part of the documentation in front of you?" Haviland asked.

"It is."

"Did anyone sign this weapon in or out on December third or fourth?"

"I signed the weapon in for the first time on December third, once I received it from Officer Carter, then I signed it out again on December fourth."

"And why did you sign it out?"

"Our office received a bulletin that the New Jersey State Police wanted Jacob Kelley in relation to a gunshot murder."

"And when you signed it out, what did you do?"

"I called Jersey to let them know, and then I personally walked the weapon over to ballistics to get it test-fired."

"Why did you do that?"

McBride smiled ruefully. "Well, I walked it over myself because I wanted to get some credit for making the connection. They can compare the bullet they test-fire to the slug they retrieve from the crime scene, see, and they can tell if it was fired by the same weapon."

Haviland lifted a plastic-wrapped handgun, and I recognized the Glock. "The prosecution would like to enter Exhibit A2 into evidence. Permission to approach?"

The judge nodded.

"Officer McBride," Haviland continued, "is this the firearm you brought to ballistics?"

McBride examined it carefully. "Yes, it is."

"And did you establish that it was the murder weapon?"

"Yes, sir. We test-fired it in our forensics lab, and we were able to match the rifling marks under a comparison microscope." He turned toward the jury. "Rifling marks on a bullet are left by the barrel of the firearm. Each one is unique, like a fingerprint. Two bullets fired from the same firearm will leave the same marks."

"So the gun that the police found in Jacob Kelley's possession on December third at Mr. Kelley's house was the same gun that was used to kill Brian Vanderhall?"

"Absolutely."

"Could there have been a mistake? Could this gun have gotten mixed up with a different one?"

McBride looked affronted. "This is my job," he said. "This is what I do every day. The chain of evidence is properly documented, and the firearm was under the proper security from the moment it was received. There is no doubt whatsoever."

Haviland produced another plastic bag, entered it into the record, and showed it to McBride. "Can you tell us what this is, Officer?"

"Those are Mr. Kelley's shoes, recovered by Officer Carter when he arrested Mr. Kelley and submitted to me at the same time as the firearm."

"Can you tell us what you found on the shoes?" Haviland asked.

"The soles of the shoes were covered in human blood," McBride said.

"And did you work with the New Jersey State Police in relation to this evidence as well?"

"Yes. They sent us images of the footprints they found at the murder scene, which we were able to match with these shoes. Also, DNA analysis of the blood confirmed that it was Brian Vanderhall's."

"Was there any other analysis performed on evidence taken when Mr. Kelley was arrested?" Haviland asked.

"Yes, we did a GSR test on Mr. Kelley's hands," McBride said. He turned toward the jury again, and it was clear that he had explained this to juries many times in thirty-seven years. "GSR stands for gunshot residue, the small, burnt particulates which fly out of a firearm when it's discharged and stick to surrounding objects within three to five feet away. The closer an object is to the firearm, the greater the residue. A shooter will have a high concentration on his hand and sleeve, as well as smaller amounts on his face and clothing.

"When a suspected shooter is arrested, the arresting officer uses a kit with small adhesive-coated metal discs. He presses one of the discs to each of the suspect's hands and seals the discs in a labeled plastic tube that comes in the kit. Back at the lab, we remove the discs and examine the particulates under a scanning electron microscope."

"And when you examined the discs collected from Mr. Kelley?" Haviland asked.

"We discovered large concentrations of lead, barium, and antimony on both hands, consistent with firearm discharge," McBride said.

"Could those particulates have gotten on his hands just by standing in the room when the gun was fired?"

"No. The concentrations were too large. Mr. Kelley held and discharged a firearm, probably several times."

Haviland bowed his head slightly. "No further questions, Your Honor."

CHAPTER 13
UP-SPIN

We tore across the bridge into Pennsylvania. I blew a dozen street lights getting to Media, with one hand on the wheel and the other calling Elena's number over and over again, but getting no answer. I swerved into my driveway, hardly slowing down. The front door was standing open. Heart hammering, I tumbled out of the car and raced inside, knowing before I got there that we were too late.

I saw Elena immediately. She lay crumpled just inside the door, eyes staring at the ceiling. She wore her brown suede coat, as if she had been about to leave the house. Her purse was still over her shoulder, and her keys lay on the floor not far from her outstretched hand.

I bellowed and threw myself on her and clutched at her hair. She had beautiful hair, full and black and slightly curled. A scream was sounding in my head, a long, drawn-out, high-pitched noise like boiling water, that drove away thought and reason. I started to shake her. I had to wake her up. I had her by the shoulders, and I realized that the high-pitched noise was actually coming out of my mouth while I yanked her up and down.

Strong hands closed around my wrists. I tried to fight, but Marek pulled me up away from her, and I let him do it.

"She was coming to see me," I said. "She was coming to New Jersey to be with me." The realization that Elena was not the only person who lived here suddenly penetrated the fog of my brain. Where were my children?

We searched the house, the choking dread thick in my throat. I thought I might throw up. It felt wrong to just leave Elena lying in the entryway. My brain started manufacturing reasons why I needed to stay downstairs, or even leave the house, rather than search from room to room for my kids.

I found Claire in our bedroom, sitting up against a pile of pillows. The stream was still projecting, a show about the real-life exploits of a famous actress, but I barely noticed it. Her face was a twisted into an expression of terror, as if she had seen her death coming just before it arrived.

I heard Marek call my name and followed his voice into Sean's room. There was Sean, on the floor next to a half-finished Lego spaceship, his longer arm bent awkwardly under him. Hundreds of Lego blocks surrounded him, like a shroud draped across the carpet, and I had a quick memory flash of helping him build a miniature Lego version of the NJSC.

There was something wrong with his body. Everything seemed wrong—in fact, seemed utterly impossible—and my brain kept trying to invent ways for it all to be a lie. The walls seemed to press in and then out, making the things around me grow huge and then shrink away into the distance, like someone else's story in a sad documentary. Out of this haze, however, a fairly rational part of my brain was insisting that something really was wrong with his body.

I took a step closer, crunching Lego bricks under my feet, and stared. His face seemed wrong. It was Sean, my son, no question of that, but . . . what was different? Was it just death that caused his face to look like that? Finally, I noticed the obvious. His longer arm was on the wrong side. The arm tucked under him was his *left* arm, and his *right* arm was now the short one, just visible beyond the special, shortened sleeve that Elena sewed for all of his winter clothes. Once I saw that, I noticed the other things on the wrong side: a mole on his neck, the part in his hair.

"He's backwards," I said.

Marek grabbed my bicep, probably expecting another violent outburst.

"No, look at him," I said. "He's the reverse of himself. His short arm is on the wrong side."

Marek's forehead wrinkled and he bent to look more closely. "Was it on the left?" he asked. He obviously didn't remember, and I was starting to doubt it myself. I knew it had been on the left, knew it as well as I knew my own name, but everything was so surreal, I wouldn't have been surprised if someone told me I had that wrong, too.

I pulled out of his grip and ran back to my bedroom. At the sight of my beautiful Claire lying dead, my vision blurred and my stomach clenched, but I fought through it and made myself actually look at her. Gorgeous blond hair flowing over her shoulders. Elegant young body just beginning to grow to adulthood. All the experiences she would never have, all the joys she would never know, crammed themselves into my brain so that I couldn't think, could hardly swallow the bile rising in my throat, but I made myself look. The T-shirt she was wearing had an image of a pop superstar singing on a stage surrounded by lights and the members of her band. It also featured the singer's name, DELIA SHARP, blazoned across the top. The letters were printed backwards.

Marek saw it, too. "It was not made like this?"

"No."

"What is going on?"

"I don't know."

We heard a noise from downstairs, a crashing sound, and then a girl's scream. I had only one daughter left. Alessandra.

I raced downstairs and there she was, still very much alive, but she wasn't the only one in the room. The varcolac stood next to her, gripping her impassively by the wrist. She struggled and twisted to get free, but it held her there with no apparent effort, as if made from steel. In her pinioned hand she held a letter. Even from where I stood, I could see that the address was in Brian's handwriting.

The varcolac pulled the letter out of her hand. It turned its head toward us as we entered the room, its features all wrong, like the bones in its face had been broken, staring at me with that utterly blank yet hungry expression. It stood on top of Elena's body, and for that alone I would have gladly torn it to shreds. In one of its hands, the letter burned briefly and then disintegrated. Its other hand still held tightly to Alessandra.

"Let her go," I said.

The varcolac stared placidly at me. There was intelligence there, but no emotion, like an auctioneer valuating items for sale.

"Alessandra," I said. "I'm going to distract it. If you can, pull your hands away." Her eyes were round and frightened. She nodded.

I slipped my keys from my pocket, took careful aim, and hurled them at the varcolac's face. It blurred, as it had done before, a waveform of probabilities, and reconverged a foot to the right, with the hand that had been gripping Alessandra now holding the keys. It opened its hand slightly and regarded them eyelessly, its head cocked like a bird's. Satisfied with whatever it saw, it squeezed, crushing the keys to powder, and opened its hand again, letting the steel filings drift to the floor.

"Slowly," I said to Alessandra. "Back up, but not fast." Without taking my eyes from the varcolac, I pulled two glass candle holders from the mantel and hefted one. I didn't have to hurt it, just distract it long enough for Alessandra to get away. "When you get the chance, run out of the house and just keep running, as fast as you can. Don't look back. We'll come find you."

She took another step, and the varcolac's head swiveled toward her. "Hey!" I said, and hurled the candle holders in quick succession. The varcolac caught both of them, but this time, instead of destroying them, it awkwardly threw them back. They crashed into the wall on either side of me.

Alessandra kept backing up toward the kitchen. Marek beckoned to her and held out his hand. I cast about for something else to throw and saw the poker and shovel in their stand by the fireplace. It was a gas fireplace, so they were just for decoration, but they were just what I needed. I snatched them up.

"Get her out of here!" I shouted to Marek. "Both of you, run now!" Marek grabbed Alessandra's arm, and they sprinted around the corner and out the back. I hurled the poker, javelin style. I'm strong, and it flew straight and hard, but the varcolac caught it effortlessly.

It wasn't graceful. Its body jerked backward with the impact, and at first, when I saw half the length of the poker protruding from its chest, I thought I had impaled it. No such luck. It twisted its hand, snapping the iron bar like a stick, and pulled the remaining half out of its chest with no ill effects. It showed no menace on its face, no anger, only curiosity, like a tourist experiencing a strange new country. The two lengths of iron clattered on the floor.

My mind raced. This thing had killed Elena and Claire and Sean and Brian, and it would kill the rest of us if I couldn't figure out some way to stop it. If Brian had been right, however, it had no true body that we would recognize, just a mind formed from the complexity of particle interactions. The body I could see was somehow formed by it in imitation of us. I didn't know if it could die. I didn't even know what it wanted.

As I was thinking this, the varcolac advanced. I ran, heading the same way Marek and Alessandra had, out the back door. I heard sirens, and a police cruiser pulled up against the front curb. There were no bushes on that side of the house, and they could see me. Two policemen spilled out of the car and shouted for me to stop. I kept running.

I climbed the fence into my neighbor's yard and out toward the next street, but another police cruiser pulled up, lights flashing, and blocked my way. I turned back to see the first two cops clearing the fence and coming after me, their hands on their holsters.

"Stay right where you are. Put your hands behind your head," one of them shouted.

It wouldn't help Alessandra if I got myself shot. I put my hands on my head, but I didn't lace them together. I held my body loose, ready for action.

One of the cops pulled handcuffs off his belt. He was a light-skinned African-American man with a livid scar on one side of his face where his ear used to be. "Jacob Kelley?" he said.

"Yes."

"You are under arrest for the murder of Brian Vanderhall. Anything you say can be used against you . . ." He rattled off my rights.

My mind raced. Murder? They must have found Brian's body. I realized how bad things looked for me—I had left his body lying in the bunker. I had Brian's gun in my pocket, and Brian's car was parked in my driveway. They would find the bodies of my wife and children inside, which I also couldn't explain. My story wouldn't convince anyone. It wouldn't even have convinced me a few days earlier.

Time slowed like we were underwater. My muscles tightened, and I felt the familiar buzz of a boxing match before a punch is thrown, when you can't quite believe you are actually going to walk into that ring and let a very strong, very fast man try to beat you to a pulp while you try to do the same to him. I couldn't let them take me. I had to find Alessandra and make sure she was all right.

My cell phone rang. The cops jumped at the sound, and I took advantage of their moment of distraction. I ran toward the closer one, maybe three steps away, and hit him in the face with a two-punch combination that knocked him flat. He never saw it coming. When you're boxing, you learn that if you telegraph your punches, they never land. You have to go from nothing to full acceleration with no chance for your opponent to react. The other cop tried to get his gun out, but the whole advantage of having a handgun is that you can shoot people when they're too far away to reach you. He was too close, and I dropped him with a single knockout punch before his gun even cleared his holster.

Of course, there were two more cops from the other car. One aimed his weapon and shouted at me not to move. I turned to run anyway, and the cop fired. I had expected a few more warnings before he actually fired in a suburban neighborhood, and I threw myself to the ground. I heard more shouting and another shot, and I risked lifting my head a fraction to look.

The varcolac was tearing the police car apart. The cops were firing at it, now, and as I watched the varcolac split itself into two, then three, then four duplicate versions of itself, each with same clumsy, conglomerate look, as if put together with written instructions by someone who had never actually seen a person. They pulled the metal frame away like it was tissue paper. The cops fired shot after shot into them with no effect.

I jumped to my feet and ran back toward my own house, climbing the fence again and racing across the yard. I climbed into Brian's car, turned the key, and pulled out over the grass, across my neighbors' yard, and into the street. I felt a pang of guilt for leaving the policemen to fend for themselves, but really, what could I do for them? The best course of action was escape. It was the only way I had any hope of finding out what these things really were and how to stop them from killing anyone else.

Once I was a block away, I pulled out my phone and checked the number to see who had called with such good timing. It was Elena's cell number. It gave me a rush of adrenaline to see it, before I realized that Alessandra must have gotten a hold of Elena's phone and called to tell me where she was. I started dialing back, but before I finished, I spotted her and Marek not far ahead. They climbed into the car. Alessandra's eyes were wild.

I looked at her face, and suddenly all the horror of the last half hour came crashing in on me. Elena, Claire, Sean, all dead. I grabbed her hand and squeezed it, tight. She started to cry.

"We're going to find a safe place to go," I said. "I won't leave you. I promise."

We drove. After ten minutes with no flashing lights in my mirrors, my heart rate slowed. I figured the varcolac and its duplicates must have killed the cops. I wasn't glad about it, but it gave us a chance to get away.

There was only one person I could turn to now, though I hated to ask him: my Uncle Colin. I navigated back roads, staying off the highways, driving automatically. I was boiling with rage. The dead faces of my wife and children kept floating in front of my eyes. If Brian had been alive, I would have gladly killed him. I wanted to kill him, to take his letter and all his selfish foolishness and shove it down his throat until he choked.

I wanted it all to be his fault, but I couldn't help thinking that it was my fault, too. I had failed them. I should have been there. I should have stayed at home and protected them instead of chasing after Brian. After a while, I just wanted to shut down, to stop thinking altogether. We approached an overpass, and I wondered what it would be like to just step on the gas and plow headfirst into the concrete wall.

But I couldn't. I still had a daughter, and she needed me. She would need my comfort, but first, she needed me to make her safe. I looked in the rearview mirror at Alessandra, now wrapped in the brown blanket and staring silently out the window. She was all I had now.

CHAPTER 14
DOWN-SPIN

"The People call Officer Moses Carter to the stand," Haviland said.

Carter was a light-skinned man with African features and a missing ear, probably in his late forties. He took the stand at a slow, deliberate pace. I got the impression that his lack of speed wasn't illness or injury related; he was just an unhurried man.

"Mr. Carter, can you please tell the court what you saw when you arrived at 58 Woodview Lane on December third?" Haviland asked.

Carter had a deep voice. "I saw Mr. Kelley running out of his house."

"For the record, do you see Mr. Kelley in the courtroom today?"

He nodded in my direction. "That man at the other table right there."

"Let the court records show that the witness identified the defendant, Jacob Kelley. Mr. Carter, can you tell us what happened next?"

"I pulled my cruiser in front of the driveway, to block any cars from getting out. My partner and I got out and approached Mr. Kelley."

"Were your guns drawn?"

"No sir, but we were ready to draw them at need."

"Why?"

"We were there to arrest him for murder," Carter said in the same measured way. "He comes running out of his front door, looking crazed, of course we're going to be ready."

"So what happened?"

"We tell him to put his hands on his head, which he does. My partner keeps ready with his weapon, and I take out my handcuffs. I tell him we're arresting him and read him his rights, and he lets me put the cuffs on, nice and easy. He has a gun in his pocket, which I take away from him, and all the while, he's talking crazy about how his wife and kids are dead. We figure, he shot the guy in New Jersey, and now he's come home and popped the family, too. So the other crew holds him, and I go inside and check it out."

"And what did you find?"

Carter shrugged. "Nothing. No bodies, no blood. I went back out and asked him where he stashed the bodies, and he says his wife was right inside the door, and how could I have missed her? So we figure he's nuts, and we book him and take him in."

I listened impassively, trying not to show my annoyance. If only I had run out the back door when the varcolac came for me instead of the front, I would have gotten away. I wouldn't be sitting here, day after day, listening to all these people accuse me of something I never did.

"Did he say anything in the car on the way to the station?" Haviland asked.

Carter nodded. "Yes, he did."

"And did you advise him that he did not have to speak without the presence of a lawyer, and that anything he said could be used against him in court?"

"I did."

"And he chose to speak anyway?"

"Yes."

"And what did he say?"

"He said, 'This is all Brian's fault.'"

"Did he elaborate as to whether he was talking about Brian Vander-hall or some other Brian?"

"No sir, he did not."

CHAPTER 15

UP-SPIN

olin's life had been turned upside down by Uncle Sean's violent death, just as mine had, though in a very different way. Instead of heading off to college, Colin had gotten meaner, more aggressive, more likely to kick an opponent when he was down. The bruiser who killed Uncle Sean in the ring eventually turned up dead in an alley. Colin told me he wasn't involved, but to this day I don't know if I believe him. Three days after I started college, though, he was busted for illegal possession of a firearm and spent a year in the pen.

The day he got out of prison, a bullet to the knee ended his boxing career forever. The details of how it happened were murky. He called me at MIT and told me he'd found Jesus and was turning his life around and leaving boxing behind. I asked him how that was possible, knowing that the underground boxing rings didn't easily let their boxers go, and he told me about his knee. That was twenty years ago, and I still don't know if he pulled the trigger himself.

Colin never left South Philadelphia. I took Passyunk Avenue to get to his place, past the rows of gentlemen's clubs and adult bookstores that in the bright of the day were empty and dark. I'd read an article recently that claimed that, according to the author's calculations, the sexual exploitation industry had surpassed the oil and gas industry as the largest grossing business in the world. In this part of town, it certainly looked like it, though of course most such business was conducted across the net and included men of every level of education and culture. Here on the street, there were just no pretensions.

The growing population of South Philadelphia was trapped: Center City to the North, the airport to the South, and the river and the wetlands preserve to the East and West. There was no room to grow, no place to go, and nothing to promote new development or new jobs. The neighborhoods, which had been poor when I lived there, had been sliding downhill ever since.

Colin was the founder of a Christian outreach complex called Salt and Light, located only a few blocks from where I grew up. He'd acquired one of the old stone churches that dotted the Philadelphia landscape, as well as the two row houses directly behind it, and had knocked holes in the connecting walls to join all three buildings into a warren of confusing turns and passageways.

Most of the space was used by a tiny Christian school aimed at teaching the gospel message to underprivileged youth, with about forty kids total in kindergarten through twelfth grade. Besides the school, there was a pregnancy center, a soup kitchen, and an evangelical chapel with daily services. The school charged students a nominal tuition—if they could afford it— which wasn't nearly enough to cover operating expenses or pay any salaries, and none of the other ministries brought in any money at all. My uncle, and the others who worked there with him, were entirely supported by the donations of the generous. I saw Colin as little as possible, but I sent a substantial donation every year. A kind of guilt offering, I suppose.

He welcomed Marek, Alessandra, and me into his tiny office, shook Marek's hand, and gave me a crushing bear hug. He was still strong, though his muscles were less defined and his skin had dulled to a leathery gray, his tattoos stretched and faded. Instead of hugging Alessandra, he crouched down to look up into her face. She stared at the floor, unresponsive. Colin stood, his smile vanishing. "What happened?"

I told him the whole story. He canceled classes and shooed away volunteers who came to his door with questions or problems. He didn't comment until I had told him everything, as much of it as I understood.

"The police must have found Brian's body in the bunker," I said. "They think I murdered him."

"So you're being chased by both the police and this demon," Colin said.

"Don't mock me," I said. "It's real."

"I'm not mocking," Colin said. "I believe you. You can't stay here, though."

"You're kicking us out?"

"Not exactly. I'm your one living relative. The cops will come here eventually, and they'll turn the place upside down looking for you. Don't worry, though; I have a safe house. We'll hide you there."

"A safe house? What are you, a drug runner?" I knew I was being rude, but I hated having to come here for help, and I hated Colin to see my failure. It wasn't Colin's fault, but I wanted to take it out it on him anyway.

Colin gave a tight smile. "This is a sanctuary. You're hardly the first person to come here with crimes on his record, deserved or not. We walk a fine line, but we need the trust of the street, or we'll never help anyone in this neighborhood."

The safe house turned out to be a grand name for the basement of another church. "I mostly use it for women who need to get away from their boyfriends or husbands," Colin said. "Or occasionally a guy borrows money from the wrong people and needs a little more time to pay it back."

It was past midnight by the time we got there. There were two twin beds in the room, a beat-up dresser, and industrial gray carpet with various stains. Alessandra lay down on one of them, curled up, and faced the wall. Colin pulled a blanket over her that was either blue or green, but old enough that it was hard to tell. Marek, Colin, and I climbed back up the stairs to the sanctuary, which was old as well, with threadbare uphol-stery on scratched pews, and a stained glass window that might have been beautiful before the outside was boarded over to prevent breakage.

"Alessandra hasn't said a word," I said, dropping into one of the pews. "She won't talk to me; she won't answer questions. She was there when"—I swallowed—"when it happened. I think she might blame me. For not being there to stop it."

"Don't push her," Colin said. "Grief takes time. Sometimes a lot of time. Blaming you, if that's even what she's doing, is a natural part of the process. As is blaming herself."

"Thanks for the tip, Father," I said. I couldn't help it. Colin's conversion had always seemed like a charade to me. I remembered every cruel thing he ever did, every person he bullied, how he treated his girlfriends, and every nasty word he ever said to me, so it was hard for me to take him seriously as a saint. He just seemed like a hypocrite to me, even though I knew full well that he wasn't, which made me feel even worse and increased the sense that he was looking down his holy nose at my choices.

"You can stay here as long as you need," he said, ignoring my remark. "Until you can get things cleared up."

I was still feeling belligerent. "Did you believe any of the story I told you?"

"Every word. Was it true?"

"Of course it was. But really? You're telling me you believe all that stuff about an alien creature?"

"Yes, I believe you."

"Doesn't the existence of another intelligent race undermine your faith?"

Colin sat sideways on the pew in front of me and propped his feet up. "Not a bit."

"I thought man was supposed to be unique. Created in the image of God."

Colin shrugged. "A lot of people might have trouble with the idea, I suppose, but there is some precedent."

"Precedent? For alien creatures?"

"Not aliens, exactly, but the angels in Scripture are a race of intelligent beings unique from man. They're not physical beings, but they can take different forms, and speak, and make their own choices. Some of them chose to follow God, and others—the ones we know as demons—rejected him, but they're both the same race. The same species, if you will. Unlike humans, though, they don't get a second chance. There's no redemption for them, no sacrifice to atone for their sins. No Christ comes to their race to take their due punishment."

I stole a glance at Marek, who had wandered across the room and was peering at the images on the stained glass. "So you think these quantum creatures are demons?" I asked.

"Not necessarily. I don't know what they are. I'm just saying, there's a precedent for a created race of intelligent beings that God deals with in a different way than he deals with us."

"This is ridiculous." I gripped the pew in front of me, wishing I could tear it apart or throw it across the room. My voice rose. "You're ridiculous. Sitting around talking about elves and gremlins as if any of this made any sense. This is all some crazy trick. If there is a God, he's probably laughing his head off right now."

Colin put his hand on mine. I shook it off and shoved him. "And don't give me some sanctimonious babble about God's ways being higher than ours. If this is the real world, and not somebody's messed up idea of a practical joke, then it was created by a sadist."

Marek came up behind me while I was talking and put a strong hand on my shoulder. It was just the excuse I needed. I whirled and threw a punch at his face. He was ready for it and twisted, letting the blow glance of his shoulder, and then wrapped his arms around me. I grappled with him, shouting, and we both fell on the floor. We rolled around, wrestling and punching each other at close quarters, while Colin sat by and did nothing to intervene, until I lay panting on my back and the tears came. My body shook with sobs, and I lay there on the floor, letting them come.

When they finally subsided, Marek gave me a hand and hauled me to my feet.

I dropped back into the pew, still breathing hard, and looked at Marek and Colin. Neither man said anything.

"What do I do now?" I asked finally. "My wife and children are dead. I can't go home. I can't go back to work. If I turned myself in, I'd never be able to explain my actions to the police."

"Not all of your children are dead," Colin said.

Any response I might have made was cut short by a scream from the basement.

I jumped up so fast I bashed my hip against the pew in front of me, but I still beat Colin down the stairs. Alessandra was sitting up in bed, clutching the old blanket, her face white.

"What happened? What did you see?"

"A face," she said. "In the mirror."

I swiveled and saw a battered shaving mirror hanging from a nail in the wall. "Whose face?"

"It was him. That man."

"No eyes?" I asked.

She nodded. I put my arm around her, but she remained stiff, her muscles tensed for flight.

"It's okay," I said, although I knew it wasn't.

"Miss Alessandra," Colin said formally. "Can I get you a Coke?"

"No."

Marek quietly turned the mirror around to face the wall.

"Can you tell us what you saw at your house?" Colin asked.

Alessandra pulled her knees up under her chin.

"I know you saw your mother and sister and brother die," he persisted. "It's hard to talk about. But we want to protect you, and we want to protect ourselves, and the best way for us to do that is to know exactly what happened."

She didn't answer.

"Let it go," I said.

Colin shrugged. "There are two kinds of people. Those who get up and fight, and those who just lie down and accept whatever happens to them."

I stood at that, ready to throw another punch, but Colin held up a hand, palm raised, and shook his head.

Alessandra glared at him. "I can hear you, you know."

"So what?" Colin said. "You won't do anything about it. You're the lying down kind; I can see that."

"My mother just died. You're supposed to be nice to me."

"Why?"

She made a noise of disgust. "I thought you were a priest."

"I'm not. I don't hear confessions, and I don't preach sermons. I'm more of a missionary to my own tribe."

"I don't need your help."

Colin sat at the foot of the bed. "If my mother was murdered, I'd be angry. I'd make sure the person who did it didn't escape. I'd find him and . . ." He trailed off and looked at her expectantly.

She couldn't help herself. "And what?"

"Turn him over to the police, probably. Or maybe kill him; I don't know. It depends. But I wouldn't leave it alone. I wouldn't say, hey, it doesn't matter, these things just happen. I'd do something about it."

"I'm fourteen years old!"

Colin crossed his fingers on his lap. "I killed a person for the first time when I was fourteen."

She gaped at him. I gaped, too. I had never heard that before. Was it true? Or was he saying it just to get a reaction?

"You did not," Alessandra said.

"I did." Colin smiled sadly. "It was a terrible thing. But you listen to me." His smile disappeared and he bored into her with his clear, blue eyes. "You're only a victim if you believe you are. You can do anything at fourteen."

"What do you know?" she screamed at him. She lashed out with her feet, kicking him in the side. "Shut up, just shut up!"

"I know that you can tell your father what you saw. I know you can remember every detail of how this creature moved and reacted. You know what it said, or what it seemed to be after, or what it could do and couldn't do, and you can tell your father, and he can figure out what this thing is and how to stop it before it kills again. I know you can do that."

She stood, shaking with rage, her lower lip trembling. "How do you know? You don't know me."

"Because you're a fighter. Unlike your sister Claire, who had everything she ever wanted, you had to make your own place. You fight, just like your father, just like me. I know. I can see it in your eyes. So tell us what happened."

"I ran," she said, her voice on the edge of tears. "I ran away and left them all, okay? They needed me, and all I thought about was myself." She bit her bottom lip.

"Keep going," Colin said. "Why did you run? What did you see? You can tell us."

"I can do better than that," she said. She yanked her phone from her pocket and hurled it at me. I caught it, by reflex, before it hit me in the face. "It's all there," she said, and began to cry. "Everything."

To my surprise, Colin had a pair of eyejack lenses, which he popped out and washed and let me borrow. I wasn't used to them, and they made my eyes water, but with some copious blinking I could stand to look around. After a few more minutes of fiddling, I even managed to get them synched to Alessandra's phone, and a menu appeared in thin air, like a scroll unrolling two feet in front of me and hovering there. I turned, and the menu moved as well, a bit disconcertingly, since there was no other indication that it wasn't a real, physical object. I reached out, almost expecting to feel real paper, but my hand passed through it.

"It's a bit easier if you sit down," Colin advised.

I did so, and only then realized how dizzy I was. Besides keeping teenagers connected to their friends, this technology was frequently used in business circles for virtual meetings that appeared to be face-to-face. The lenses might project the image of a coworker or customer into an empty chair at my table, as if he had come to visit, when in fact he was in San Francisco or Seoul or Jakarta. I actually had a pair of lenses at home that had come with my phone, but I had only tried them once before. I found the experience of seeing something that wasn't there a bit unnerving.

With a little practice, I could navigate the menu by centering my focus on a selection and blinking, though I had a tendency to blink unintentionally and choose the wrong option. I accessed the history of what Alessandra had seen—there were quite a large number of files available, but she kept them well organized, and I cycled through the video until I found the time in question. At first, it started playing in a two-dimensional rectangle about two feet in front of me, as if I were watching the stream. I selected full-screen mode instead, and I was suddenly immersed.

I was back in my house, in the living room, looking at a fashion magazine. It wasn't like watching a movie on the stream. The picture flicked around as Alessandra moved her eyes. My instinct was to turn my head and look around, but of course, that did nothing but make me feel lightheaded. What was recorded was only what Alessandra herself had seen. I couldn't change the viewing angle. Colin fitted earbuds into my ears, and I could hear as well.

"Alessandra! Put that down, and go tell your sister and brother to come get their shoes and coats on." It was Elena's voice.

The view changed as Alessandra looked up, and there was Elena, vibrant and beautiful and alive. She was just pulling the brown suede coat on over her green sweater. Her forehead was tight with worry and stress. I wanted to reach out and hold her hand, to whisk her away from there and protect her this time. A hard ball formed in my throat and my eyes stung. I coughed violently and shook my head to clear it.

"Where are we going?" Alessandra asked.

"You know that man who was here last night? The police just called and said they found him dead at the NJSC."

"Wow, like he was murdered?"

"That's what they say," Elena said tightly.

"Is that why the police called? To find Dad?"

"Yes, now please! Go get Claire and Sean."

"Why do I have to come?" Alessandra asked.

"Because I'm not leaving you here when I don't know what will happen, or how long I'll be. We should stay together."

"Why don't you just call him?"

"I have been calling, but he hasn't picked up. I called the NJSC, and they don't know where he is either. I don't want to sit here wondering. We're going."

"Are they going to arrest Dad?" Alessandra asked. "Did Dad kill the man?"

"Alessandra!"

"Well, did he?"

"Of course not," Elena said. She grabbed her purse from the easy chair and rummaged through it. Now go get Claire and Sean and tell them to meet me in the car." Elena took out her keys, swung the purse over her shoulder, and turned the handle to the front door. I wanted to shout, to warn her, but of course, she couldn't hear me. I wasn't really there. I watched mutely as she swung the door open. The varcolac was standing there.

Elena had never been one to scream. She stepped back and tried to shut the door again, but the varcolac walked through it as if it were air. It was followed by lighter, more shadowy versions of itself, like the interference pattern we had seen before, but these quickly merged into the one figure.

"Alessandra, call 911," Elena said in a sharp voice, which she kept admirably under control. "Right now."

The perspective changed as Alessandra jumped to her feet. An option scroll sprang into view in her vision. Much more rapidly than I could have done, she manipulated the options to control her phone and dialed the emergency number.

Elena took another step back. "Leave this house, or I'll call my husband."

The varcolac cocked its head, reached out, and put its hand through Elena's chest. It didn't break the skin; it just passed right through, like it had with the door. For a split second, she gasped, and her eyes flew wide, then her face crumpled and she collapsed. Alessandra screamed. I shouted and stood up, nearly stumbling over the chair. I felt Colin steadying me.

The varcolac leaned over Elena and peered at her, sniffing. Alessandra screamed again, and the varcolac looked at her, swiveling its head as quick as a bird. She ran, stumbling, into the kitchen, around the table, and out the back door. With one backward glance to make sure he wasn't following her, she crossed the back yard and climbed over the neighbor's fence. I kept expecting her to turn around, to go back to the house. I figured the varcolac must have gone upstairs to kill Claire and Sean, and then Alessandra went back and saw my car and went inside, and that's when the varcolac got hold of her. But it didn't happen. She kept running through the streets and crying until she saw Marek run along beside her, and then I pulled up in my car and they both climbed inside.

The dizziness was getting to me. I blinked the display off, pushed past Colin, and ran to the bathroom, just in time to throw up in the toilet. I'd barely eaten all day, so it wasn't much, but it made my throat burn. I realized I was shaking.

Colin came up behind me and helped me to my feet. He found paper towels under the sink and let me wipe and wash out my mouth before leading me back into the basement room. Alessandra was lying on her back on the bed, staring at the ceiling.

"Now you know," she said bitterly. "I ran away and left them all to die."

"You couldn't have saved them," I said. "You were right to run. But I need to know something: did you go back to the house at all?"

She glanced at me, suspicious. "You know I didn't. I saw Mom fall, and I ran. I didn't know if she was dead or what; I just ran away."

"I saw you, in the house. After Marek and I found Claire and Sean, we went back downstairs and saw you." I looked to Marek for confirmation, and he nodded.

"That's true," he said. "You were there."

She sat up. "Alive?"

I nodded. "Alive. The thing that killed Mom had a hold of you, and I distracted it, and you ran away."

Colin looked more worried now than he had since we arrived. "And did you see that just now? When you watched the recording?"

I shook my head. "No. And that wasn't the only strange thing. Alessandra, tell me—are you right-handed or left-handed?"

She looked at me like I'd gone mad, and I didn't blame her. "I'm right-handed, as you well know."

"Raise your right hand."

"What's wrong with you?"

"Please, Alessandra. Just do it. Raise your right hand."

Slowly, skeptically, she raised her left hand.

"You're not messing with me now, right? That's your right hand?"

Colin intervened. "What are you doing, Jacob?"

"Everyone, raise your right hand," I said. The four of us were in a circle now, the three men standing, and Alessandra sitting on the bed.

Marek and Colin and I raised our right hands. Alessandra raised her left.

We all looked at each other.

"What's going on here?" Colin asked.

"The rest of the family," I said, hardly able to keep my voice under control. "Elena and Claire and Sean. They might still be alive."

We talked around the events of the day for hours, but came to no real resolution. Alessandra fell asleep on the bed with the old, blue-green blanket wrapped around her.

"One of you must be mistaken," Colin said. "She couldn't have both come back to the house and *not* come back to the house. Either the two of you didn't see what you thought you saw, or she's blocking the experience from her memory."

"The recording backs up her story," Marek pointed out.

"True," I said. "But maybe you're wrong. Maybe she could do both."

Colin's raised eyebrow showed what he thought about that suggestion. "Let's keep our considerations to the physically possible, okay?"

I couldn't resist the shot. "Funny to hear you say that, of all people."

"Just because I believe in the miraculous doesn't mean—"

I waved away his explanation. "This *is* physically possible. We've already seen that the man with no eyes exhibits quantum probability waves. What if Alessandra was caught up in that probability wave? What if she briefly experienced superposition, like a subatomic particle, and existed as a set of possibilities, rather than a single reality? She was terrified, but at the same time she wanted to protect her siblings. She both ran away and she stayed, both at once. Both of those possibilities were in evidence."

Colin looked at me skeptically over his glasses. "In evidence. You're telling me there were two Alessandras running around your house and neighborhood."

"Not two girls, exactly," I said. "Two possibilities, momentarily unresolved. We say an electron orbits an atomic nucleus, like the Earth around the sun, but it doesn't really. It's part of a waveform, a probabilistic cloud that exists at every point around the nucleus at the same time, with some probability. Similarly, a particle can have an up spin or a down spin, but until it resolves, it has both—it's in quantum space, spinning both ways at once. For Alessandra, I think the wave resolved once I picked her up in the car, or maybe slightly before that. The two versions didn't deviate all that much."

"That's the most ridiculous theory I ever heard," Colin said.

"Wait," I said. "This is the important part. If Alessandra could split, then why not Elena and the others? They were about to leave the house. What if one version of them *did* leave the house, before the varcolac arrived, and thus weren't killed?"

"This is wishful thinking," Colin said. "Don't do this to yourself."

"It makes sense," I said. "The varcolac wouldn't arrive at a single, discrete point in time and space, like we would. Its arrival would be smeared over a range of times and places, with some probability."

"You're losing me," Colin said.

"Me, too," Marek said.

I growled, angry at them. Why couldn't they understand? "When you go somewhere, you arrive at one time," I said. "At five o'clock, say. But a varcolac doesn't. It arrives at 4:45 and 4:46 and 4:47, through to 5:15, and may eventually resolve to only one of those arrival times, though some have a higher probability than others. That means it arrived both before *and* after they left the house. They became entangled with its probability wave and split, one version of each of them heading off in the car to the NJSC, oblivious, while the other versions were caught and killed."

Silence. "Well," I said. "What do you think?"

"A lot of crazy things have happened today," Marek said. "Sure. I believe you."

Colin yawned. "It's two-thirty in the morning," he said. "Could we figure out what universe we're living in tomorrow?"

I apologized and let him go. I didn't know how I was going to sleep, though. I was buzzing. They were out there somewhere, alive. Tomorrow, I would find them.

Colin left us with a promise to bring us breakfast in the morning. I tried to convince Marek to take the other bed, but he insisted on the floor. The bed springs were old and creaked loudly, but as soon as I lay down, exhaustion took over, and I knew I was going to sleep after all. With a last nervous glance at the backward mirror, I closed my eyes. I dreamed of an endless hall of mirrors and of Elena, always just glimpsed in a reflection, but never there when I turned around.

I woke to Colin shaking me, his eyes wide. "Jacob. Jacob! Wake up. You have to see this."

I groaned and sat up, slowly registering the unfamiliar surroundings and remembering the horror of the day before. "Why couldn't you have let me sleep?"

"Look." He thrust a piece of smartpaper into my hand. It was a news feed, and I read the headline.

SWARTHMORE PROFESSOR ARRESTED
FOR MURDER OF QUANTUM SCIENTIST

I scanned the article and saw my name and an old picture of me. According to the article, I had been arrested for the murder of Brian Vanderhall, who had been found shot to death in his office at the New Jersey Super Collider. There was nothing about the deaths of my family, just that I had been picked up at my home, and the police were making no further comment.

"Why would they lie about that?" I asked. "You'd think they'd want people to know they were looking for me."

"Maybe they aren't."

"What do you mean, they aren't? I'm a murder suspect; of course they're looking for me."

Colin smacked me on the side of the head. "Wake up. You were the one going on last night about being in two places at once. Why should you be any different?"

CHAPTER 16
DOWN-SPIN

"T

he People call Sheila Singer to the stand," Haviland announced.

Terry cursed and started rummaging through his papers in a way that did not inspire confidence. "Your Honor," he said, still rummaging. "I have no knowledge of this witness."

Haviland's smile grew brighter. "Her name was provided to the defense weeks ago, in the discovery process. She works at the New Jersey Super Collider."

Probably twenty percent of the NJSC's three thousand employees had been on the prosecution's list of possible witnesses. Terry had made me go through them all and identify all those I knew, had ever worked with, or had seen during the events of last December third. It was a standard lawyer trick, apparently, to drown the opposition with irrelevant entries in order to hide the ones that really mattered.

"What is her relevance to this case?" Terry snapped.

"I hope her testimony will make that plain." Haviland was positively beaming now.

"There's nothing irregular here, Mr. Sheppard," Judge Roswell said. "The name is on the list. You may proceed, Mr. Haviland."

Terry glared at me, but I shrugged. I had no idea who Sheila Singer was, and when she took the stand, I was even more confused. She was twenty-something, slender, with a low-cut, turquoise blouse and a short, black skirt that revealed legs a half mile long. If I'd seen her before, I would have remembered. She flashed a brilliant smile at the jury.

"Ms. Singer, please state your name for the record." She did so, and he asked her to tell the court what her job was with the NJSC.

"I'm a receptionist and tour guide," she said. "I meet visitors who come to the center, and I sometimes take groups through the parts that are open for tourists."

"Do you get a lot of tourists?"

"Of course. It's the biggest scientific instrument ever created." A sly smile at the jury. "Some people think the bigger the better."

I coughed. Haviland looked a little annoyed. "Were you working on December third?"

"Yes," Singer said. "I was stationed at the reception desk in the Feynman Center. That's where I work when I don't have a tour, so I can answer questions, give out maps, that kind of thing."

"So, your desk is the first thing a visitor sees when they enter? The first place they would go to ask a question?"

"Yes."

I could tell Terry was dying to object and ask what the point of this line of questioning was, but he held back. It was probably just what Haviland was waiting for.

"Do you know Jacob Kelley, the accused?" Haviland asked.

"No. I don't think we ever met," Singer said.

"But on December third, you heard his name, didn't you?"

"Yes. There was a woman who asked for him. She seemed quite upset."

"Did the woman say who she was?"

"No. She had three children with her, two girls and a boy, and she said she was looking for her husband and asked if I knew how to contact him," Singer said.

I stood up slowly, staring at her.

"What time was this?" Haviland asked.

"Just before five o'clock."

"How can you be sure of the time, Ms. Singer?"

"Visiting hours end at five o'clock. It was the end of my working day."

Haviland pushed a button on a remote control, and a picture of my beloved Elena appeared on a large screen. "Is this the woman?"

I felt a lump in my throat, just seeing her picture. It had been so long since I'd seen her. It seemed like another life. I felt like I was choking, like I was going to cry right there in the courtroom. They had been there, right there at the NJSC. They *had* split when the varcolac came to the house, and here was the proof.

I realized everyone was looking at me, and Terry was frantically tugging at my sleeve. Judge Roswell glared at me. "Mr. Kelley, sit down."

I sat. "I'm sorry, Your Honor."

Haviland gave me a predatory smile and turned back to the witness. "Ms. Singer, let's be clear. Mr. Kelley claims that he saw his wife and children dead in his house in Pennsylvania more than an hour before you claim to have seen them in New Jersey. Were they dead when you saw them?"

"No, sir."

"Ms. Singer, how long have you been working at the NJSC?"

She blinked at the sudden change of direction. "A little more than a year."

"And in that time, how many visitors have you seen?"

"Oh, hundreds. Gosh, I don't know, maybe thousands."

"And the woman who was looking for Mr. Kelley, had you ever seen her before December third?"

"No, just that once."

"Can you be absolutely sure she was Jacob Kelley's wife?"

Her mouth pouted prettily. "I'm very sure."

"I remind you that you are under oath, Ms. Singer."

"She didn't tell me who she was, but she looked just like the picture," Singer said. "If it wasn't her, then she had a twin sister."

With shaking hands, I snatched one of Terry's legal pads and scribbled a note on it.

Terry read it, looked at me, and wrote, "Why?"

I wrote, "Please, just ask."

He shook his head, but he tucked the legal pad under his arm.

"And what did you tell Mrs. Kelley?" Haviland asked.

"Well, I felt sorry for her, you know?" Singer said. "She said he might be with Mr. Vanderhall, so I looked up the building and told her." She put a hand to her cheek. "I had no idea that her husband had killed the man. The poor woman."

"Objection," Terry said, but the judge was already nodding.

"Ms. Singer," she said. "Whether or not Mr. Kelley killed Mr. Vanderhall has not yet been established. Please limit your answers to the questions being asked."

"Of course. I'm sorry," Singer said.

"Your witness," Haviland said, and sat down.

Terry stood and took the lectern. He flipped through his legal pad for a moment as if marshalling his thoughts. He obviously hadn't planned to interview this woman, which meant he wasn't prepared. The old adage that you shouldn't ask a question to which you don't already know the answer meant that he should just sit down again. He frowned and stared at his pad. I knew he was deciding whether to ask my questions or not.

"Mr. Sheppard?" the judge said.

He seemed to shake himself. "Just a few questions, Your Honor. Ms. Singer, did you happen to notice if the woman you saw was wearing a wedding ring?"

Singer brightened again. "Yes, she was. I always notice that sort of thing. It was a sweet ring, small, you know, but sometimes that means more than some enormous diamond. Maybe the guy doesn't have a lot of money, but then it's really for love, you know what I mean?"

"Did you happen to notice . . ." Terry paused. "Did you happen to notice which hand the ring was on?"

"Well, of course," Singer said. "It was on her left hand. I told you it was a wedding ring; where else would it be?"

I knew the jury wouldn't understand why I was smiling, but I couldn't help it. At least an hour after I had seen them dead, my family had been alive. Singer had seen *my* Elena, not the backward version of her I had found in the house. It meant my theory about them splitting had been correct after all. It meant my family was really alive out there, or had been two months ago. But if that was the case, what had happened to them? Why had no one seen them since?

"Mr. Kelley," Judge Roswell said in her stern voice. Her face was too pleasant to pull it off effectively, and she looked more like a scolding grandmother than a fierce authority figure, but I knew her affable appearance wouldn't stop her from holding me in contempt of court, so I sat down quickly.

"I'm sorry, Your Honor," I said.

"Mr. Sheppard, is there a point to this line of questioning?"

Terry glared at me. "I apologize, Your Honor. I have no further questions."

CHAPTER 17
UP-SPIN

I needed help. Colin had given us a place to stay, at least for the time being, but I needed to figure out what was happening. I needed to find out if it was possible that a different version of my family was still alive, and if so, where they might be. Marek was self-employed, so he had some flexibility, but he still had to fulfill his contracts, not just stay with me all the time. Besides, Ava—his wife and Elena's sister—hadn't been pleased that he had been gone all night without calling, and she didn't like his explanation that he had been with me. She had seen the headlines, too. I only heard one side of the conversation, but she sounded furious and upset.

I left Alessandra in Colin's safe house and borrowed Colin's car. Jean Massey lived in a two-story condominium in Princeton, not far from the college. She understood the physics involved, and she worked at the NJSC. I couldn't just stroll around the facility asking people if they'd seen my wife and kids. The police would still be crawling everywhere, and I was a murder suspect. Jean could ask around though, if she was willing.

She answered the door, and when she saw me, her eyes flew open wide. "Jacob? Is that really you?"

She had a smartpaper in her hand, and I could see the headline on the newsfeed. She knew I had been arrested. "I can explain," I said. "May I come in?"

"Of course." She held the door open, briefly looking out past me to see if anyone else was there. "What's going on, Jacob? The police were all over the facility yesterday, looking for you, and the paper this morning said you had been arrested and your family was missing."

"It's a long story," I said.

She pointed me to a seat in her living room and offered me coffee. The room was sparsely decorated, with a few inexpensive prints and personal knick-knacks. A baby swing sat in a corner, and there was a tiny pacifier on the coffee table next to a stack of diapers and scattered physics journals.

"I left you in Brian's office, and then I never heard from you again," Jean said. "Then the police came and said Brian was dead and asked all sorts of questions about you, and then this . . ." She held up the news article. "Why aren't you in prison? Are you out on bail?"

I explained everything as best I could. I told her about finding Brian in the bunker, about the varcolac, and about seeing the second Brian, and what he had told me. I told her about racing home and finding my family dead, escaping the varcolac again, and evading the police.

She asked a lot of questions, but she didn't once question my sanity or the truth of what I was saying. She seemed to have no trouble at all accepting the idea that there were two of me. I figured she'd spent so much time thinking about quantum physics that it seemed more natural to her than the normal world.

"I'm so sorry about your family," she said. "Really, I can't imagine."

I didn't want to dwell on that. I had a quantum puzzle to figure out and the very real possibility that my family was not dead. I had to keep pushing forward or I would go mad. "The varcolac is a probabilistic entity, like a particle," I said. "I think that contact with him can cause splits, where more than one possible path exists for a time."

Jean thought about it. "So how many splits have there been?" she asked.

I started listing them on my fingers. "Brian was the first," I said. "One version of him I found in the bunker, the other I met up with in the forest. Both versions are now dead, and the second body disappeared, so I assume that means the split has resolved. Then, if my theory is right, my family split, one version leaving the house before the varcolac arrived, and the other version . . ." It was still hard for me to say it aloud. "Their other versions were killed, by the varcolac. We don't know if that split has resolved or not. Finally, me. I'm both here and in prison, so we know my split hasn't resolved yet."

"But that means that Alessandra split twice," Jean pointed out.

I thought about it. "You're right. The first time, she would have split with the rest of the family, one version heading out and the other staying home. Then she split again, one version running away immediately, and the other version not running until after I had seen her."

"And that second split has already resolved," Jean said.

I took a sip of coffee. It was fresh, a quality brand, and it tasted good. "I think the splits resolve when the two paths meet—or become similar enough," I said. "Both versions of her were in the street, running away from the house, so they merged again. The two versions of me are still drastically different, though, so we haven't resolved."

"It still doesn't quite make sense to me," Jean said. "Before it resolves, a particle exists in many places and times, not just two. If this is really possible, why aren't people splitting all the time, and into millions of different versions?"

"I think they might be," I said. I'd been thinking about this on the drive over. "I think that any time anyone comes in contact with the varcolac, there are a million possible paths that split off. Only, most of them resolve again, almost instantaneously, because they're so similar to each other, and you never know it. It's only when those paths are very different—the difference between meeting the varcolac and leaving the house before it arrives, for instance—that the paths persist."

"So half a million possible paths resolved to them getting away, and half a million resolved to them not getting away, leaving two distinct paths," Jean said.

"I think so. When I ran away from the varcolac, I ran out the back door," I said. "If it had come after me a little to the right, however, I might have run out the front door. That could have been the difference between escaping the police and being arrested." I heard crying upstairs. "Is that your daughter?" I asked.

"Yes. Nick will get her. Your reasoning sounds solid," she said. "Crazy, but solid."

"Really? You believe me?"

She shrugged. "I've known you for a lot of years, Jacob. If that's what you say happened, I believe it."

I heard footsteps on the stairs, and then Nick Massey appeared, carrying a baby girl in a pink, cotton dress. I stood and shook his hand. I'd met him a few times before, but didn't know him well.

"And this must be Chance," I said. I looked down at her and frowned. She had a very round face, small chin, almond-shaped eyes, and a large, protruding tongue. She was cute, but I recognized the pattern of her features. I was pretty sure that Chance had Down Syndrome. I looked at Jean. "She's beautiful," I said.

Jean looked away, but not before I saw the pain in her eyes. She picked up my empty coffee mug. "Can I get you another cup?" she asked.

"Sure. Thanks," I said.

When she left the room, Nick shook his head. "Jean didn't tell you, did she?"

"She didn't mention it," I said. I remembered Jean's reluctance to talk about her daughter when she had first let me into Brian's office.

"She didn't show you a picture, either, did she?"

"No," I said.

"She never does. It hit her pretty hard."

"I'm sorry," I said.

"Don't be." Nick picked up the pacifier and slipped it into Chance's mouth. "She's a beautiful girl. She's everything I ever wanted, but not for Jean. She wanted a smart kid. A scientist. Somebody like her. She thought, with a quantum physicist and a Princeton geneticist for parents, it was a lock. As if genetics were that predictable."

Jean returned with a fresh cup of coffee.

"Well, nice seeing you," Nick said, slipping out again with the baby.

"You, too," I said.

"The important thing," Jean said, "is that your family might still be alive. They were heading for the NJSC, so that's where we have to start looking."

I shrugged. "That's why I'm here. I can't really walk around in the open."

"Say no more," Jean said. "I can ask around. If they were there, we'll find them."

"I'm worried," I said. "I have to believe they're still out there, but where? They would have seen the news by now; they would have talked to the police."

"Maybe they have," Jean said. "Maybe they're at the prison right now, talking with the other version of you."

"I'm afraid they may have resolved, back to the dead versions of themselves," I said. "I don't want to think about it, but I'm afraid of it all the same."

Jean shook her head. "No, that's not right. The bodies disappeared."

"What?"

"The article says nothing about your family being dead, just about Brian. They didn't find your family. If they had resolved to their dead versions, their bodies would be there, just like Brian's."

I laughed. "You're right!"

"Now, I can ask around. If they're out there, somebody must have seen them. What are you going to do?"

"I don't know. What else is there to do?"

"I think you should go meet your double. Make sure there actually is a second version of you sitting in jail."

"I can't just walk up to the prison and ask if they have me there behind bars."

"No." Jean held up her smartpaper, which still showed the article. "But it mentions the name of the lawyer who signed on to defend you. You could ask him."

I thought about it. "That could work," I said. "He's not going to turn me in to the cops, anyway."

"And Jacob?"

"Yes?"

"Tell your double that if he needs an expert witness for the trial, he can count on me."

CHAPTER 18
DOWN-SPIN

The prosecution's case was moving toward its climax. Haviland brought his DNA specialist to the stand, who took two hours to give the jury a primer on DNA analysis and make sure every one of them knew that it was irrefutable. The blood on my shoes was Brian's. Scientifically proven. Beyond any reasonable doubt. Terry barely asked any questions on cross; there was nothing to be said.

Haviland's final witness was Officer Emilio Morales, the detective with the New Jersey State Police who had led the investigation. Haviland walked him through the reasons why he had concluded I was the murderer, which meant the jury got to hear a summary of all the evidence against me, laid out by a well-spoken and honest-looking cop.

They covered my apparent motive for the murder—that Brian had taken a shot at my wife—and all of the physical evidence that linked me to the crime.

"Was Mr. Kelley able to provide an alibi for four o'clock AM on December third, the time when Brian Vanderhall was murdered?" Haviland asked.

"No. He claimed to have been home asleep at the time, but no witnesses have been able to confirm that," Morales said.

"Was there any more evidence that Mr. Kelley murdered Mr. Vanderhall?"

"At the murder scene, we have Mr. Kelley's fingerprints and shoeprints," Morales said, ticking them off on his fingers. "He was arrested with the murder weapon in his possession, GSR on his hands, blood on his shoes, and driving the victim's stolen car. What more evidence do you need?"

Haviland said he was done and sat down. Terry cleared his throat and took the lectern for cross-examination.

"Mr. Morales, my client lives with four other people: his wife, Elena; and his children, Claire, Alessandra, and Sean. Why were they not able to confirm his alibi?"

"Mr. Kelley's family has not been seen since his arrest."

Terry pretended astonishment. "Did you look for them?"

"Certainly we looked for them," Morales snapped. "After all that talk about them being dead when Kelley was arrested, we thought maybe he'd murdered them, too."

"So, you asked family members?"

"We asked family members, coworkers, neighbors, friends. We put out an alert for them. Either they changed their identities and went somewhere far away, or they're dead. Personally, I would guess the latter."

"But you never found their bodies."

"No."

"Did it ever occur to you that what my client told you about them might be true?"

"What, that he found the bodies in his house, and then they vanished into thin air before anyone else saw them? I don't know where you're living, sir, but on this planet, bodies don't just up and disappear."

"We'll see about that," Terry said. "No further questions."

"Mr. Haviland?" the judge said.

"Your Honor, I am finished with this witness as well," Haviland said with a self-satisfied smile. "In fact, I have no more witnesses to bring. The prosecution rests."

CHAPTER 19

UP-SPIN

I found Terry Sheppard's office a few blocks from the courtroom in a row of townhouses that had been almost completely renovated as lawyers' offices. You could hardly walk down the street without banging your head on a shingle. I wondered how anyone chose a single lawyer from the crowd. I had no trouble picking because, apparently, I already had. I'd never met Terry Sheppard before, but according to the news stream, he was my lawyer.

Several of the adjoining offices shared a secretary, a heavy woman with curly gray hair and a large flower pin. I told her I didn't have an appointment, but that I was pretty sure Mr. Sheppard would see me right away. Her expression said she'd heard it all before, and she invited me to take a seat, but she made the call. Moments later, a man with a huge mustache opened a back door with a worried expression.

"Jacob?"

I stood. "Mr. Sheppard."

"What on Earth? You're supposed to be in prison. Has there been . . . some change? Were you released?"

"Not released," I said.

With a furtive look around the waiting room, he motioned for me to follow him, which I did. His office was very nice, with leather-upholstered chairs and cherrywood bookshelves stacked with law texts. A childishly painted porcelain mouse, half-hidden on his desk, gave a personal touch to an otherwise professional room. A framed photograph showed a round, smiling woman and a little girl, perhaps six years old, who I guessed was the source of the mouse.

"How did you get out of prison?" he asked.

"I was never there."

He narrowed his eyes. "I met you there for the first time yesterday. You paid a retainer's fee and hired me to defend you. A job that will be made much more difficult if you have somehow slipped away unnoticed."

I chose a leather chair and settled myself into it. "Don't worry. If you call the prison right now, you'll find that they still have custody of Jacob Kelley."

He stared at me, trying to make sense of this. I had pity on him. "Think of me as Jacob's twin brother. That's not quite right, but it will do for now."

Sheppard's eyes flicked right and left, and he blinked several times. I realized he was eyejacked. In a few moments, he said, "It looks like Jacob Kelley has no siblings at all. Mother and father deceased, closest relative an uncle, living in South Philadelphia." His eyes focused on me again. "No twin brothers. So, I think I'll go ahead and make that phone call."

A few more eye blinks and a pause, and he said, "Yes, this is Terry Sheppard. I'd like to inquire about the status of an inmate. Yes. Could you transfer me to the officer in charge of the ward? Thank you." Another wait, during which Sheppard drummed his fingers on the desk. "Yes, thank you, I heard a report that my client, Jacob Kelley, received a black eye in a fight in the yard, and I'm concerned it may affect his scheduled court date. Well, if you can see him, could you just confirm that his face is not injured in any way? No? Glad to hear it. I appreciate it, Officer. Thank you for your time."

Sheppard squinted at me and rubbed at his mustache.

"Clever ruse," I said. "You made sure they could see him without giving the idea that you thought he might have escaped."

"And unless the guard is blind or lying, Jacob Kelley is still in prison. Which means that, despite the evidence of my eyes, you are not Jacob Kelley."

"On the contrary," I said. "I am Jacob Kelley."

"I don't appreciate being jerked around," Sheppard said. "What do you want?"

"I want to meet him. I want to meet the other Jacob."

Sheppard popped the lenses out of an old pair of glasses and lent me a New York Yankees baseball hat as a crude attempt at disguise. I wasn't terribly worried—I didn't think the prison guards probably paid too much attention to visitors' faces—but Sheppard seemed agitated. I told him to relax. They couldn't very well arrest another man as Jacob Kelley when they already had one behind bars.

The truth was, I was more nervous about meeting a duplicate of myself than I was about the guards. The idea had grown on me for several days, but for the other me, it would be an immediate shock. I wasn't sure how I felt about there being another me sharing space in the universe. Would I even like myself?

The version of myself that I was about to meet saw the man with no eyes in the CATHIE bunker, found Elena and Claire and Sean dead just as I did, fought with the man in our living room, but didn't run from the police. He hadn't been to see Colin, and he almost certainly did not know there were two of us.

The guards made no comment about my appearance and ushered us into a glass cage with a silver table and six yellow chairs. After a few minutes of finger drumming and foot tapping, they brought in a man in handcuffs and an orange jumpsuit with a strained, worn look around his eyes. It was me.

The guard unlocked the handcuffs and left the room, closing the transparent door behind him. The other Jacob was staring at me, mouth open.

"Do you know this man?" Sheppard asked.

"Looks like he could be my twin brother," Jacob said.

"You were caught in the varcolac's probability wave," I said.

His mouth opened even wider. "Superposition," he said. "Just like Brian."

I nodded. I held up my left hand. "See the wedding ring?"

"Why is it on your right hand?"

"It's not," I said.

"We're on opposite sides of the Bloch sphere."

"Exactly," I said.

"This is weird."

"You're telling me."

We both laughed in uncanny echo.

"Will someone please tell me what's going on here?" Sheppard asked.

"A Bloch sphere is a concept in quantum mechanics," Jacob said. "It's a geometrical representation of the uncertain state of a particle—say an electron—that's spinning both up and down at the same time."

"How can something spin up?" Sheppard asked.

"It's the right-hand rule," Jacob said. "Take your right hand and curl it in the direction of the spin." He held out his hand in a loose, thumbs-up gesture. "The direction your thumb is pointing is the direction of the spin vector."

"Only his is backward, from my perspective, because to me, that's his left hand," I said. I held out my right hand and curved the fingers the same way, causing my thumb to point down instead. "See? We represent both states at the same time."

"Which of you is the real one?" Terry asked.

"Neither," I said.

"At least not yet," Jacob added.

I eyed him warily and caught him returning the look. It was oddly thrilling for another person to understand me so quickly and so completely. The problem was, it wasn't another person. It was me, and when all this was over, only one version of me could survive. Was this what had happened to Brian? Had he killed himself to make sure his version was the one that lived?

"That doesn't make sense," Jacob said, as if guessing my thoughts. "The two versions are the endpoints of a probability waveform—the real Jacob exists in all possible states between the two of us, with a certain probability. The wave will eventually collapse to be you, or me, or some average value in between. So if Up-Brian killed Down-Brian, that wouldn't make Up-Brian the final version. It would just raise the probability that the final version would be dead."

"Though Brian might not have realized that," I said.

Sheppard held his head in his hands. "What are you two talking about?"

"Okay, look. Every little bit of matter or energy in the universe, whether it's a beam of light or a comet or a bacon cheeseburger, is made of tiny particles," I said.

"They're not really particles," Jacob said. "They can diffract and interfere with each other, so really they're waves. They have a certain wavelength, usually quite small, that governs how they behave."

"Don't interrupt," I said. "It's no good thinking of them as waves, as if they were ripples on a pond. They can be counted. You can have just one. They have some odd wavelike properties, but they're clearly particles."

Jacob was ignoring Sheppard now. "How can you call them particles? They're not Newtonian; they have no classic idea of position or velocity. The 'particle' concept is just a crutch for an inadequate imagination." He turned back to Sheppard. "What we call matter and energy are just simple wave functions. The difficulty some people have in accepting that is purely psychological."

"Waves of what?" I asked.

"What?" Jacob said.

"A wave is the fluctuation of a medium. These waves you're talking about—what is doing the waving?"

"The quantum-mechanical substrate."

I threw up my hands. "And what is that? It's just a word you made up to fill the void in your reasoning."

"They're waves," Jacob said.

"Particles."

"Waves!"

Sheppard stepped between us and waved his hands. "Stop it," he said. "This is insane. What does this all mean? What are you going to do?"

I took a deep breath. Maybe coming here hadn't been such a good idea. "When does the trial start?" I asked.

"Hard to say. The NJSC is a big political sore spot, so the media are running away with this one, poking at the possibility of a politically motivated killing. That will put a rush on the trial procedure, but it will still be months probably."

"That gives us plenty of time to work, then," Jacob said.

"The most important thing is to make sure that the final Jacob Kelley . . ." I said.

". . . whoever he is . . ." Jacob added.

". . . is found innocent of all charges."

CHAPTER 20
DOWN-SPIN

After Officer Morales's testimony, the jury was given an hour and a half to walk the streets and find lunch, or, if they were brave, to eat in the courthouse cafeteria. Lunch for me was a roast beef sandwich and a Coke in a tiny meeting room under the baleful stare of an armed guard. I made it last as long as I could, but a sandwich can only stretch so far. When it was done, I had nothing to do but sit and stare at the walls and miss Elena and the kids.

After lunch, the trial shifted to a new phase. It was the defense's turn to start calling witnesses. Terry stood and regarded the courtroom like a king surveying his new domain, holding on to his lapels. So far, Haviland had been calling the shots, and he had just been doing damage control. Now it was his turn. The physical evidence against me was going to be difficult to overcome, but we had a few tricks up our sleeves. One big surprise in particular, but that wouldn't come out until my testimony at the very end.

Jean was marvelous on the stand. She had dressed up for the occasion, in a classy black pantsuit and high heels. I had never seen her in anything but jeans and a sweatshirt before. She and Terry knocked questions and answers back and forth like professional tennis players, leaving the jury swiveling their heads back and forth in comic time between the two. She was funny, informal, and best of all, comprehensible. Terry was the perfect foil, pretending ignorance while tossing up the perfect leading questions.

"Dr. Massey, we all learned about atoms in school," he said. "We're all made up of them. But tell the jury—just how small are they?"

She smiled. "A piece of tissue paper is about one hundred thousand atoms thick."

Terry pretended astonishment. "Really? But our case is dealing with things even smaller than that—*sub*atomic particles, correct? So how big is, say, a proton, compared to an atom?"

"About a hundred thousand times smaller."

Astonishment again. "So tissue paper is a hundred thousand atoms thick, but a proton is a hundred thousand times smaller than that? What about an electron?"

"An electron has no size at all."

"How can something have no size? Doesn't that mean it's not there at all?"

"It has mass," she said. "And spin, believe it or not, and of course a negative electric charge. But no, it's a point particle, with no actual size to it at all."

"Are there any other particles?"

"Sure. Neutrons, muons, pions, taus, neutrinos, quarks, photons . . ."

"Photons? Aren't those light?"

They went on in that vein, driving the jury through a crash course in basic particle physics. Terry had gotten his nephew to convert some of Jean's illustrations into graphics displays, which he showed the jury on the courtroom's ancient plasma screen.

"So if atoms are made of protons, which are so tiny, and electrons, which have no size at all, an atom is mostly just empty space, isn't it? So if I'm just made up of empty space, why don't I just fall right through this table when I lean against it?" He leaned against the table to prove his point.

"It's because of the electron field surrounding the atom," she said. "They prevent the other atoms from passing through."

She went on to describe the double slit experiment, which shows how subatomic particles aren't really particles, but aren't really not-particles, either. Haviland objected frequently to the relevance of the testimony, but Judge Roswell allowed it, citing the groundbreaking nature of the case and the complexity of the science involved. After several coin and tennis ball illustrations to establish the concepts of superposition and entanglement, they finally got to the crux of the matter.

"So what you're saying is that Mr. Vanderhall could, theoretically, have killed himself, despite the fact that he was shot three times from at least two meters away, and no gun was found in the room," Terry said.

Jean nodded. "He could have set up an entanglement situation with himself. For a brief period of time, he could have been in two places at once, enough time to shoot himself and dispose of the gun before the Brian probability wave collapsed into a single, dead Brian. Interestingly enough, it could have collapsed into the living Brian instead—there was no way to know until it happened."

"Isn't that an awfully convoluted way to commit suicide? I mean, why didn't he just put the gun in his mouth and pull the trigger?"

I thought Haviland might object to the question on the grounds that Jean couldn't know Brian's intentions, but he kept quiet. Maybe he thought the objection itself would lend credence to the whole idea in the first place.

"I can't say what Brian was thinking, or that it even happened this way," Jean said, perfectly following her script. "All I'm saying is, it's possible. Given the technology Brian was researching, it could be done. Suicide is a possible reason for his death."

"That's your professional opinion?" Terry asked.

"It is."

Terry let it go at that, and Haviland took the stand with a show of barely concealed incredulity.

"Ms. Massey . . ."

"Dr. Massey," Jean corrected.

"Ah yes. Doctor. Of course. Do you really expect the jury to believe that the victim made a copy of himself, which shot him and then disappeared into thin air?"

"I'm not saying he did it. I'm saying it is scientifically possible."

"Have you ever made a copy of yourself, doctor?"

"No."

"Have you ever seen anyone else do so?"

"No."

"Have you read in any scientific journal that such an experiment has been made, or even attempted?"

"Not with a human, no." It was a marvelous answer, though deceptive, since it implied such an experiment had been done with an animal. Of course, nothing like it had ever been tried, but Haviland didn't know that. He couldn't press her on it, because once he asked the question, he'd be giving her free rein to defend the concept on scientific grounds.

Haviland dropped a beat, and then said, "Remember that you are under oath, Dr. Massey, and that this is the real world, not science fiction. To your certain knowledge, in any reputable, peer-reviewed, scientific literature, has any copy of a human being through quantum superposition ever been made?"

"No," Jean said.

Haviland threw his hands in the air and let them fall, shaking his head as if this had all been a criminal waste of time. "No further questions, Your Honor."

Jean stepped down from the bench and flashed me an encouraging smile. I nodded back with a look that I hoped conveyed my gratefulness. Not all of my colleagues would have been willing to stand up and be counted with me, to risk the detrimental effect on their careers that media scrutiny of their statements might bring, not to mention the potential of being associated—depending on which way the verdict came out—with a convicted murderer.

CHAPTER 21
UP-SPIN

No one at the NJSC had seen Elena or Claire or Sean. Jean said she had asked everyone she could think of, and no one remembered them being there. The police had been inquiring, too, but of course I couldn't ask them what they'd discovered. As time went by, I found it hard to be optimistic.

Christmas was unbearable. Three weeks had come and gone by then, with no word. My theory that they could still be alive started to sound ridiculous, even to me. Marek said Ava was convinced I had murdered Elena and the kids and hidden the bodies, and her other sisters were inclined to agree. It was putting quite a strain on their marriage, and he rarely came to see me anymore.

I mostly stayed in Colin's safe house, though even there the church held services and events, and I couldn't entirely avoid the sounds of Christmas music and holiday cheer. I didn't know what to say to Alessandra, so I didn't say much of anything. She began to help out around the church: setting up for events, washing dishes, sweeping floors, just for something to do. She could have left me at any time. She could have gone to the police and turned herself in, and then lived with one of Elena's sisters, but she didn't. Not even when I started drinking, more heavily than I ever had before. I hadn't been a drinker in college—there was too much to learn and do. Now I had nothing to do, and the more I could avoid thinking, the better.

It would be months before the trial would start. There had to be all manner of preliminary hearings, and the pretrial, and the discovery process, and myriad motions by both parties, before it could begin. I had missed Jacob's first appearance in court, which occurred only two days after his arrest, and involved his arraignment and the bail argument, although on a murder charge there was no chance of him getting out on bail. The first preliminary hearing was scheduled for early in January. I insisted to Terry on the phone that I wanted to come, but he shut me down.

"You're our ace," he said. "The prosecution has no idea what we have up our sleeve, and if we bring you out now, they'll have two months to work up a way to discredit you, or even get you barred from the trial."

"But how can they do that?"

"I'm your attorney, remember? Trust me, the less the prosecution knows about our case for as long as possible, the more likely we are to win. The preliminary is the prosecution's show—they're on the hook to prove to the judge they have enough evidence to continue. We don't have to reveal anything we've got planned, unless I choose to in order to get evidence struck down. So be patient. Lie low, and let me do my job."

So I lay low. I had promised my double that I would do what I could to prove his innocence, but I was no lawyer; I couldn't help with any of those things. I couldn't think of anything I could do to find my family, either, or even to confirm that they were dead. So I drank and slept and pretended I was fine and told Alessandra that tomorrow we were sure to find them.

"I know what you're going through," Marek said on one of his rare visits. "When I lost my wife, just breathing seemed like more trouble that it was worth."

"Your wife is still alive," I said. "Both of your wives are still alive."

"I expected her to come to the United States, eventually," Marek said, ignoring me. "I was doing it all for her, sending her money, trying to save as much as I could. And she left me."

"What are you telling me?" I asked. "That the pain will go away, in time, and I'll find someone else?"

"I'm just saying, I know what it's like," Marek said. "It's hard. It hurts. It'll keep hurting for a while. But don't let it crush you. Get out of this room. Go do something."

"Where am I supposed to go?"

He shrugged. "You have a daughter. Take her to a movie. Go out for ice cream. Anything."

"I'm drinking too much, is that it?"

"It'll get better," Marek said.

"I don't want it to," I said.

January was even worse than December. I got news that my teaching position at the college had been filled by someone else. I heard that Elena's parents had visited my double in prison a few times, but that most of her family were keeping their distance. Of course, they all thought I was a murderer. The only family I had left was Colin and Alessandra.

"Claire would have been starting to look at colleges about now," I told Alessandra one day. I was sitting on the bed, flipping through pictures on my phone.

"Who cares?" she said.

"What?"

"Who cares? Claire's dead. Everybody knows that but you."

I put the phone down. "Don't say that."

"If they're not dead, then where are they?"

"I don't know where they are. Maybe they are dead. But it doesn't mean we stop caring about them. Claire was your sister. She was pretty and smart and kind, and now she's gone. Maybe she's dead and maybe not, but she was a special person, and I miss her."

"Claire?" Alessandra shouted. Tears were streaming down her face. "All you talk about is Claire and Sean and Mom. What about me? I'm *alive*. I'm *here*."

"I know," I said, bewildered by her outburst. "But I miss them. Don't you understand that?"

She turned away. "Yeah, I understand."

"Alessandra," I said.

She stomped up the stairs. "I know. Just forget it."

I knew I should go after her. That's what a good father would do, but I didn't have the energy, and didn't know what to say. My head was pounding. I picked up the phone again and flipped to the next picture of Claire.

Finally, Colin told me we would have to leave the safe house. "Too many people have seen you here," he said. "The church leaders are getting nervous."

"Where am I supposed to go?" I asked.

"I know people," Colin said. "I can help the two of you get new identities. Go to the West Coast, find a quiet spot, get a job, and try to start over. There's nothing left for you here."

"I can't do that. What about the trial?" I asked.

"What about it?"

"I can't just leave."

"Yes, you can. If they need you, you can come back for a few days. In the meantime, you need to find a new life."

Alessandra came over and touched my arm. I saw that she had already packed a bag with the clothes Marek had brought from our house. "Come on, Dad," she said.

"I'm not ready," I said.

"Yes, you are," Colin said. "It's time. You need to see people. Life goes on."

I stood and turned my back on them. "Why does everyone insist that I move on? Am I supposed to forget my wife and kids? Act as if they never existed?"

"You have a daughter," Colin said. "She needs you."

I shook my head. "I can't."

"So what are you going to do?" Alessandra asked, her voice breaking. "Live in a basement forever? Mom and Claire and Sean didn't make it, but we did. We're alive. You're alive. So live."

I turned back to face her, feeling more exhausted than ever in my life before. "I can't do it, Alessandra."

"Then what?" she asked. "What does that mean, you can't do it? Are you going to kill yourself? If so, then get on with it. I'm tired of you."

"Don't talk to me that way," I said.

"Or what? Are you going to ground me? Take my allowance? You can barely get out of bed. I hate you."

I could feel the heat rising. "Hold your tongue. What would Mom think, if she heard you talking like that?"

"I hate you," she said. "You never loved me. It was always Claire, Claire, Claire."

"That's crazy. Of course I love you."

"Then show it," she said. "Take me away from here."

I opened my mouth to respond, but something was blocking my throat, and before I knew it, I started to cry. It started as a kind of hiccup, then burst out of my throat in strangled sobs. It made me feel ashamed and weak and ridiculous, and I knew it was partly the alcohol, but I couldn't help it. They just stood there and watched me until I got under control.

"I can't," I finally said. "Don't you see? I can't leave. They might still be here somewhere. Maybe it's crazy, but it just might be true. How can I go to the West Coast when it still might be true?"

Alessandra stared at me, and it wasn't disgust in her eyes, as I had feared, but compassion. She nodded slightly, but her eyes were still determined. "So figure it out," she said. "Solve the puzzle. You're supposed to be so smart. Find out what happened to Mom and Claire and Sean. Or track down the varcolac, and we'll kill it. Just let's get out of this basement and *do* something."

I took a deep breath. "Okay," I said.

"Okay?"

"You're right," I said. "We'll do it."

CHAPTER 22
DOWN-SPIN

"The defense calls Marek Svoboda to the stand," Terry said.

Marek took the stand in a suit and tie that I had never seen him wear before. He gave his name, took his oath on the Bible, and sat down.

"What is your relationship to my client?" Terry asked.

Marek explained that he was married to Elena's sister Ava and answered a few more questions about his background.

"What time did you meet Mr. Kelley on the morning of December third?"

"It was about nine o'clock," Marek said.

"And what did you plan to do?"

"His friend Brian had come over to the house the night before. He said and did some strange things and took a shot at Elena. Jacob wanted to go to the NJSC and try to find out what was going on."

"Did he say anything about wanting to kill Mr. Vanderhall?"

"No."

"What about wanting to hurt him or make him pay or anything like that?"

"No."

"So, you met him at nine o'clock in the morning," Terry said. "On December third. Five hours after the prosecution's witness says Mr. Vanderhall was killed. Is that right?"

"That's right," Marek said.

"So, if my client had killed Mr. Vanderhall, he would have to have driven back from New Jersey in time to meet you at nine o'clock, and then drive with you back to New Jersey again. Why would he do that?"

"He wouldn't, if he was the killer," Marek said.

"Objection." Haviland stood. "Speculation."

"Sustained and stricken," Judge Roswell said.

Terry nodded. "When he got in the car with you at nine o'clock, were his shoes bloody?"

"Nope."

"Did he have a gun in his pocket, that you could see?"

"Nope."

"Did you tell the police this, Mr. Svoboda?"

"Yes."

"Did they believe you?"

Haviland stood. "Speculation again, your Honor."

"Sustained," the judge said. "Mr. Sheppard, please stick to the witness's direct experiences."

"I'm sorry, Your Honor. I'll rephrase," Terry said. "When the police interviewed you, did they say whether they believed you or not?"

"They said they didn't believe me," Marek said. "They kept pushing, asking the same questions over and over again, asking me if I was an accomplice."

"And were you?"

"Was I what?"

"Were you an accomplice? Did you help Jacob Kelley kill Mr. Vanderhall or cover it up?"

"No."

"All right, Mr. Svoboda. When you arrived at the NJSC, where was the first place you went?"

"To Mr. Vanderhall's office."

"Why did you go there? Surely you didn't expect to find him in such an obvious place, with the police searching for him."

"Jacob wanted to see if he could find anything that would tell him about Mr. Vanderhall's research," Marek said. "Anything that could explain what Mr. Vanderhall had done in his house."

"And did he find anything?"

"Yes. He found a suicide note."

The courtroom exploded in buzzing. Haviland jumped to his feet, objecting loudly.

"Your Honor, this is the first I have heard of any such document," Haviland said.

"I have no document to submit as evidence," Terry said smoothly. "I am merely asking the witness for his recollection of the events of that day."

"It's hearsay, then," Haviland said, but the judge raised her hand before Terry could respond.

"I'll allow it, Mr. Sheppard," she said. "But you're walking a fine line."

"Thank you, Your Honor," Terry said.

Haviland looked like he'd swallowed a lemon. There was no possible way he and his team could have seen it coming. I hadn't told anyone about Brian's letter, and I didn't have it anymore, since the varcolac had destroyed it.

"A suicide note?" Terry said. "Could you describe it for us?"

"Yes, sir. It was in an envelope with Jacob's name on it, so he felt perfectly within his rights to open and read it."

"Do you remember what the note said?" Terry asked.

"Yes, clearly," Marek said.

"Tell us, to the best of your recollection."

"It said, 'I should have told you about this in person, but I didn't have the nerve. I think it's for the best this way. You're smart; you'll figure it out. Say goodbye to Cathie for me. Brian.'"

I noticed that Marek had left out the "maybe someday you'll join me" line, which we hadn't understood at the time. I was pretty sure I knew what that meant now. At the time he wrote it, Brian still thought that the varcolacs were going to make him a god, immortal and with all their powers. He was expecting to be missing, not dead, and he thought

I could read the notes on his smartpad and figure out where he'd gone, maybe even contact the varcolacs myself and join him. He didn't expect to turn up dead.

"Did you actually read the note yourself, or did Mr. Kelley read it to you?" Haviland asked.

"I read it myself," Marek said. "It was handwritten on password-protected smart paper."

"And Jacob knew the password?"

"He figured it out. It was some number that was important in quantum physics."

"So it was clear that Mr. Vanderhall wanted Mr. Kelley to get this note?"

Haviland shot up. "Objection. The witness can have no knowledge of the victim's intentions, or even that he wrote the note."

"Sustained," Roswell said.

"To whom was the note addressed?" Terry asked.

"To Jacob."

"Thank you. And who is Cathie?"

"CATHIE is a place, not a person," Marek said. "It's the name for the bunker where we found Mr. Vanderhall's body."

"So that's how you knew to go down there?"

"Yes. Jacob interpreted the letter as telling us we should go down to the CATHIE bunker."

"Did Mr. Kelley seem to already know what he would find in the bunker?"

"No, he didn't."

Terry walked Marek through how we had found Brian in the bunker, but how we didn't call the police because we didn't have phone reception. Terry and I had argued about whether Marek should mention the varcolac, but eventually decided not to. It was tough either way. The story didn't hang together very well without the varcolac, but what jury would believe him if he told them we'd been attacked by a demon?

We would be asking a lot of them already. In order to generate a reasonable level of doubt in my guilt, the defense had to present another possible alternative that fit the facts. True or not, if an alternate theory was just as convincing as the defense's theory of my guilt, then there was clearly some doubt as to whether I should be convicted for the crime. The alternative story that Terry was spinning, as had been introduced in Jean's testimony, was that one version of Brian had killed the other one. It was a tough sell already, and Terry didn't want descriptions of alien intelligences confusing the matter.

Marek told the jury that I had been so overcome with grief about my friend's death that I had run away, up the stairs. He described it as a kind of claustrophobia, a need to get some fresh air, and under Terry's gentle questioning, it sounded credible. Marek had followed, both to help me and to see if there was phone reception outside, but there wasn't. That was when we found Brian's car, with the keys still in the ignition, and used it to drive away.

The problem with the story was that it was mostly true, but not quite. All considering, I thought it was the best we could do, but it made me wonder how much of the trial system had to do with truth, and how much of it was a competition between the two opposing sides to see whose fiction was the more believable.

Terry dropped the bomb out of nowhere.

"When you got into the car, you discovered that you were not the only one there, didn't you?"

"Yes," Marek said. "Brian Vanderhall was sleeping in the backseat."

The courtroom erupted in noise, and Judge Roswell had to bang her gavel for order.

Terry feigned confusion. "Let me understand this," he said. "You just told us you found Mr. Vanderhall dead in the bunker, and now you're saying he was sleeping in the backseat. Which is it, Mr. Svoboda?"

"Both. We found him in both places. There were two versions of him.

One was dead, the other was still alive."

Haviland objected again. "Your Honor, this is insane. Mr. Sheppard is turning this courtroom into a circus for the media. I move that Mr. Svoboda be placed under contempt for his mockery of these proceedings and—"

"That's enough, Mr. Haviland," Roswell said. "Mr. Sheppard?"

"This is the alternate theory of the defense, Your Honor," Terry said. "As my expert witness contended earlier, this is a scientifically plausible scenario. Not only is it plausible, but we intend to prove that it actually happened."

"Very well," Roswell said. "Objection overruled."

"Judge, I request a sidebar," Haviland said.

Roswell sighed and motioned the lawyers up to the front. She switched on a noise cancelling system that prevented any of the rest of us from overhearing what was said. I saw Haviland gesticulating and rolling his eyes. Before long, Roswell took her seat again and the lawyers returned, Terry looking serene and Haviland annoyed.

"The objection is still overruled," Roswell said. "Mr. Sheppard, please continue."

Haviland sat, and Terry continued to question Marek. This was the point at which things got a bit sticky, since now that Brian's double had been introduced, his departure had to be explained. Marek said nothing about the Higgs projector, nor Brian's attempt to use it to protect them from the varcolac. He merely claimed that, after explaining some of his quantum research to them, Brian had disappeared.

"Disappeared?" Haviland said. "Into thin air?"

"Yes, sir. Jacob explained it to me as the collapse of a probability wave, but all I know is, he vanished."

"No further questions," Terry said.

Haviland stood, shaking his head in apparent disbelief that such nonsense had been allowed in court. "Mr. Svoboda," he said. "I'd like to ask you about the so-called suicide note that you say Mr. Kelley found.

Did you see the note before Mr. Kelley picked it up?"

I had wondered whether Haviland would ask about the note or just try to ignore it. It wasn't really devastating to his case—his witnesses had already proven that Brian's death couldn't have been a suicide by any normal means. If he didn't ask, however, it would allow the letter to stand without challenge. Haviland had apparently opted to ask.

"No," Marek said. "Jacob found the note and then showed it to me."

"Can you be certain he didn't write the letter at home and then pretend that he found it to remove suspicion?"

"If he wanted to remove suspicion, he would have planted the letter in the office and left it there for others to find, not shown it secretly to me," Marek said. It was a good point, and I saw Haviland wince.

"Let me rephrase. Do you know, beyond Mr. Kelley telling you so, that this note came from Mr. Vanderhall's office?"

"No."

"Where is this note now?"

"I don't know."

This was actually good luck for us. If we had a piece of physical evidence related to the crime in our possession, Terry would have been required to turn it over to the police, or risk considerable legal consequences, both in the trial and personally. Just having knowledge that such evidence had once existed, however, came with no such responsibility.

Haviland laid the scorn on as thick as he could. "So we have no evidence, other than your word, that this so-called suicide note ever existed or—even by your own testimony—where it came from or who really wrote it."

"If you don't believe me," Marek said, stiffening, "then don't ask me any more questions."

"A few more, I think," Haviland said. "You say that when you found Mr. Vanderhall's body, you didn't call the police because you had no phone coverage. Is that right?"

"Yes."

"But the police never received a call from you or Mr. Kelley, not then or later. Are you telling us you didn't have phone coverage that whole day?"

"We didn't call later because we had seen Brian alive," Marek said.

"Ah yes, I see. Just before he magically disappeared, is that right?"

"Yes."

"What about after you stole Mr. Vanderhall's car and drove to Pennsylvania? Did you have phone coverage then?"

"We didn't steal the car," Marek said.

"No? Did you own the car?"

"No," Marek said. I could tell he was getting angry at being disbelieved, but he was keeping it in check.

"Did you have permission from the owner to drive it?"

"The owner was in the car with us."

"Now, I'm confused," Haviland said. "I thought you testified that he disappeared there in the woods. Was he in the car with you all the way to Pennsylvania?"

"No."

"Why did you drive to Pennsylvania?"

"That's where Jacob lives," Marek said.

"But wait a minute. You found Mr. Vanderhall's body dead in the bunker, and you testified that you didn't call police because you didn't have phone coverage. But then, instead of driving back to the NJSC or to a local police station to report what you'd found, you turned and drove in the victim's car back to Pennsylvania. Why did you do that?"

"Jacob was afraid his family might be in danger."

"In danger!" Haviland gave a short, disbelieving laugh and raised his hands to the ceiling. "Now why would Mr. Kelley's family be in danger, if not from him?"

"Brian told him they might be," Marek said. It was a weak explanation, and Haviland knew it. He kept after him like a shark smelling blood.

162

"And as you drove to Pennsylvania, you still had no phone coverage?"

"We did, but as I said, we had seen Brian alive. Besides, Jacob was trying to reach Elena by then, to warn her."

"Isn't it true that you had no intention of calling the police?"

"No, we tried several times," Marek said.

"Weren't you actually running away from the police?"

"No."

"Did you go with Mr. Kelley on the night of December second, when he killed Mr. Vanderhall?"

"No, I did not. And Jacob didn't kill anybody."

"Why did you return to the bunker the next day? Were you hoping to clean up the crime scene? Or did you forget some incriminating piece of evidence? The gun, perhaps?"

"The first time I ever saw the bunker was when we found Brian's body there."

"Mr. Kelley was found with gunshot residue on his hands. How did that happen, if you simply found the body? Did he pick up the gun and fire it a few times just for fun?"

Marek hesitated. There was no good way to answer that question. "We thought we saw something," he said.

"So he did fire the gun?"

"Yes. It was dark, and Mr. Vanderhall was dead, and we were scared."

"Scared? Of what?"

"We thought the murderer might still be there," Marek said, a bit lamely.

"I see," Haviland said. His expression radiated disbelief.

It wasn't good. Marek looked like he was making up answers on the fly, and to some extent, he was. It made me think that maybe we should have come clean with everything and told the jury the whole story, varcolac and all. But I couldn't see how that would have gone any better.

"So, Mr. Kelley fired the weapon in the bunker, but he didn't hit anyone, and then you ran upstairs, but not away from anyone. How many flights of stairs are there up to ground level?"

"Twenty, I think."

"And you ran up all of them?"

"Well, we were mostly walking by the time we got to the top."

"How did you get to the bunker in the first place?" Haviland asked.

"We took a golf cart around the collider tunnel."

"Why didn't you return the same way you came?"

"I told you before, we were scared, and it was claustrophobic down there. We needed some fresh air."

"You're telling this court that you ran up twenty flights of stairs to get some fresh air?"

"Yes, we did." Marek snapped the words, his patience crumbling.

"Isn't it true that you used the stairs because you knew Mr. Vanderhall's car was waiting for you at the top?" Haviland asked.

"No, that's not true."

"Isn't it more reasonable to think that you were fleeing the scene of the crime?"

"No, we weren't doing that."

"I see. No, instead, you want us to believe that you saw Mr. Vanderhall up there, alive and well, and he invited you to steal his car and make your escape?"

"That's what happened! Except we didn't steal—"

"Have you ever sought treatment for alcohol abuse?" Haviland asked.

Marek hesitated, taken aback by the sudden shift in topic. "I've been clean for four years," he said defensively.

"Answer the question please."

"Yes. When my wife left me, I—"

"And have you ever undergone psychiatric treatment?"

"Yes, at around the same time. It was a bad time for me."

"Thank you, Mr. Svoboda. No further questions."

Terry took the lectern again and tried to clean things up, emphasizing the points already made, but it didn't help much. He kept glancing at his watch, and I wondered if he was just trying to draw things out long enough that he could start fresh with my testimony in the morning.

Finally, he said, "Your Honor, I anticipate the next witness to take a significant amount of time. I would like to suggest that court be adjourned and begin with his testimony in the morning."

Roswell agreed, and we all stood. The jurors stretched, trading relieved glances at each other, already anticipating a nice dinner at home or a night watching the stream. To them, this case was an interesting sidelight, an exciting break in their otherwise humdrum lives, or possibly an inconvenience that was costing them sales commissions or badly needed tips. It wasn't their lives hanging in the balance. Was this truly the best system of justice the world had to offer? I searched their faces for any indication of what they were thinking, but I found none. I doubted they were convinced yet.

I shook my head. It didn't matter. We would have a surprise for them tomorrow.

CHAPTER 23
UP-SPIN

Colin let Alessandra and I stay in his house on the condition that I not spend any more than ten hours a day there. In other words, I was welcome to sleep there but not to mope and not to drink. I agreed to his terms. I still didn't have a plan, but at least I was up and moving around. So I did the only thing I could think of. I called Jean Massey and asked if she could meet us for lunch.

We took Colin's car. He was hesitant to let us borrow it at first, but Alessandra reminded him that he was the one insisting that I get out and do things, and how could I do that without a car? I drove carefully, keeping close to the speed limits so as not to draw any attention or get pulled over.

As we crossed the bridge into New Jersey, Alessandra said, "I don't hate you, you know."

I reached over and squeezed her hand. "I know."

"I just didn't think I could stand another night in that basement."

"I'm sorry," I said. "I guess I'm pretty messed up right now. I haven't been much of a help to you." We were silent for a while, then I added, "And I don't love Claire more than I love you."

Alessandra didn't answer.

"She's like your Mom," I said. "She's pretty, she follows the rules, she studies hard. People like her easily. I know what to expect with her, and I'm proud of her. You, on the other hand . . ." She glanced at me, concerned, but I went on. "You're more like me. You're not satisfied doing what other people tell you. You question the rules. You lose your temper sometimes. Claire can get manipulated or run over by other people, but you stand up for yourself. It means we clash more. But it doesn't mean I love you any less."

She considered that for a moment. "Okay," she said.

"Okay? That's it?"

"I don't love Mom more than I love you, either," she said. I glanced at her sidelong, but she was smiling. "I'm good, Dad. Thanks."

We met Jean at Einstein's Brain, a classic American restaurant near the NJSC, which featured cheap food, red vinyl seating, and more pictures and paraphernalia from the great physicist than I had seen anywhere else, even at the Einstein Museum on Nassau Street. They didn't actually have a piece of Einstein's brain at the restaurant, though I knew there was one on display at the Mütter Museum in Philadelphia, about ten blocks from the court building where I was on trial.

Jean had dark circles under her eyes, and her hair looked like it hadn't been brushed, but she put a hand on my shoulder and gave me a compassionate smile.

"How are you holding up?" she asked.

I shrugged. "We're getting through. How are you? You look tired."

"I've been up late working on your trial," she said.

"Thanks," I said. "I hope it's not taking you away from your family too much."

She grimaced. "To tell you the truth, Nick and I aren't doing so well."

"Oh, Jean. I'm sorry to hear that," I said. "I hope it's not because of the trial."

"No, nothing like that. We just don't see eye to eye anymore." She waved a hand dismissively. "It's an old story. But look at you!" Jean hugged Alessandra and exclaimed over how tall she had grown. "I hope my daughter grows up to be as lovely as you," she said.

I remembered Chance and what Nick had said at their house, and I wondered how much of the tension between Jean and Nick was due to their daughter's condition. "I'm sure she will," I said.

We settled down at a table. Jean bought a "Relativity Reuben," and Alessandra and I both chose the "Black Hole Burger."

"What about the trial?" I asked. "What secret strategies have you and my double been planning together?"

Jean seemed a bit relieved at the change in subject. She related the difficulty of explaining quantum physics to a lawyer—"like teaching knitting to a sea turtle"—and her concerns about getting a jury to understand it, much less believe it.

"You can convince them," I said. "What about the footage from Alessandra's viewfeed I sent to Sheppard. Is he going to use it?"

Jean shook her head. "No, he's not planning to."

Alessandra looked up from her burger. "Why not? Then they could actually see the varcolac; they'd know that Dad's story is true."

"He doesn't want to bring up the varcolac in testimony at all. He says the science is hard enough to swallow," Jean said.

"But it's part of what happened," Alessandra said.

"It has nothing to do with Brian's death, that we know of," Jean said. "And Terry's afraid that if we show it, we'd lose the jury entirely. They might just refuse to believe it, and dismiss everything the defense has to say after that. It's like people's home videos of alien abductions. Would you believe it, if you were on the jury?"

"Well, what's the strategy, then?" I asked.

"Terry says the best way to win a murder trial is to have an alternate theory. A way that someone else could have done the crime that fits the evidence just as well as the story the prosecution is telling. If you can do that, then there *must* be a reasonable doubt that the defendant is guilty, because it's equally possible that the alternate person is guilty."

"So who's the other person?" I asked.

"Brian himself."

I made a face. "He didn't commit suicide," I said.

"Actually, I think it's the best explanation," Jean said. "He split, and there were two of him. Brian's always been pretty self-centered. So one of him figured the only way to guarantee his own survival was by killing the other."

I was skeptical. The version of Brian in my car had seemed honestly surprised that his double was dead. In fact, he didn't seem to realize that he even had a double. Brian was an accomplished liar, however—all those years of trying to juggle multiple relationships with women had taught him that—so I supposed I couldn't be sure.

"Listen," Jean said. "I knew Brian, well enough anyway. He was egotistical, self-absorbed, vain. He was in love with himself." I thought that was a bit harsh, but I let it slide. "He would have done anything to save himself," she continued. "Even shoot someone else. Even if that someone else was himself."

"So you think you could stand in front of yourself—the same face you see in the mirror every day—and pull the trigger?"

"It's not unreasonable. Trust me, people will go to any length to secure their own survival, or the survival of someone they love. Things they don't want to do, things they would never normally do. They'll do whatever it takes."

Alessandra stood with a sudden scrape of her chair. Her face was mottled red.

"What's wrong?" I asked.

"I'm just going to the bathroom," Alessandra said.

"Alessandra, she didn't mean . . ."

She walked away without listening. When she was out of earshot, Jean said, "Is she okay? Did I say something wrong?"

I sighed. "When the varcolac attacked, Alessandra saw it kill her mother, and she ran away, straight out of the house, without warning Claire or Sean," I said. "She thinks she's a coward. It probably saved her life, but she thinks it makes her a terrible person."

Jean looked stricken. "I'm sorry. I didn't mean . . ."

"It's okay. You weren't even talking about her."

I ate the last bite of my burger, which was actually pretty good, black hole or no. A poster on the wall advertised the restaurant's coffee while explaining Brownian Motion. I had tried their coffee before, however, and knew better than to try it again.

"There is one more alternate theory Terry has, in case the one with Brian doesn't fly," Jean said.

"Who's the murderer in that one?"

Jean shrugged. "You are."

I almost spilled my soda. "What?"

"Think about it," she said. "It's all about reasonable doubt. If you killed Brian, then the version of you on trial couldn't have done it. How can the prosecution prove that it was him and not you?"

"But we're the same person," I said. "We will be the same person again. Besides, I didn't do it."

"When do you think your split with the other Jacob started?" Jean asked.

"Don't go there. It wasn't until I left the house after my family was killed. The day after Brian died," I said.

Jean was implying that maybe I *had* killed Brian—that the split had occurred much earlier than I thought and my double had killed him while I was home with my family—but I dismissed the thought. What reason would even a different version of me have for doing such a thing?

"The question is, what can I do now?" I asked. "I want to understand what happened, but I don't know where to start. Have you seen any more of Brian's research notes? Anything that would explain more about the varcolac or what Brian discovered before he died?"

Jean shook her head. "I've been all through his things," she said. "Terry insisted on getting all Brian's smartpads back from the police in the discovery process, and I've been going through them all with a fine-toothed comb. There's nothing of significance. What we need is the Higgs projector. Brian's letter that had all the programming circuitry on it."

"They were both destroyed," I said. "The varcolac took one version from Brian and the other from Alessandra and disintegrated them. Though . . ." A thought struck me with a surge of adrenaline.

"Though what?" Alessandra asked, coming back to the table. Her eyes were red, and I guessed she had been crying in the bathroom.

"The letter," I said gently. "There was a letter from Brian that came to the house the day the varcolac came. When I was at the house, I saw the varcolac take it from you and destroy it. But that wasn't in your viewfeed."

"I don't understand," Jean said.

"Alessandra split briefly," I said. "One of her left the house; the other stayed. I saw the version of her that stayed, and I saw the varcolac take the letter from her. But this Alessandra was never there." I turned back to Alessandra, trying to keep my voice calm. "So what happened to the letter? Did you have it when you left the house?"

"You mean, after it killed Mom, and I ran away?" Alessandra's voice caught, and I thought she might start crying again.

"I don't blame you for that," I said. "But I need to know. What happened to the letter?"

Alessandra was very still, remembering. "I saw it on the coffee table, and I opened it. Nobody was explaining anything to me, and I thought maybe I could find out for myself. When Mom came in to tell me we needed to go, I shoved the letter into my pocket and pretended to be reading a fashion magazine."

"So then, when the varcolac arrived . . ."

"The letter was still in my pocket," she said. "I didn't know it was important."

My heart was racing. "So it split with you," I said. "That means there was a third version."

"Wait a minute," Jean said. "If the varcolac could sense the existence of this letter from miles away and go teleporting to your house just to destroy it, how could it not know that there was another version of it out there?"

"I don't think it did sense it," I said. "When it killed Brian, it assimilated him. It drew him into itself, and then its face looked a little bit like Brian's, as if it had incorporated Brian into itself. I think after that, it knew everything Brian knew. Brian knew a copy of the letter had gone to my house and where my house was, so the varcolac knew, too. But it didn't know everything."

"Well, what happened to the third version?" Jean asked. She leaned forward. "Where is it now?"

Alessandra shrugged. "I don't know. When I remembered about it later, I looked, and it was gone."

I let out a breath, disappointed. "It resolved," I said. "It split, and then it resolved again."

Jean shook her head. "It shouldn't have. Alessandra resolved with her other version because their paths became close again. But the letters followed different paths. One was burned; the other got away. It's still out there somewhere."

"You mean, it just fell out of her pocket? That's just as bad. We'll never find a letter that fell out of her pocket somewhere in the neighborhood a month and a half ago."

"We'll never find it if we don't look," Jean said.

I hadn't been back to our house since the day I found Elena and Claire and Sean dead, and it felt surreal to pull into the driveway now, just as I had done a thousand times before. It was a bit of a risk to be here. We didn't know our neighbors well, but there could be trouble if anyone saw and recognized me. I could have let Jean come by herself, but I was up and doing things now; I didn't want to go back to waiting for someone else to do something for me.

I stepped over the threshold, feeling a strange sense of displacement. Elena's body had lain right there, empty and broken, but there was no sign of her now. I walked through the house in a daze, seeing familiar objects as if they were unfamiliar, remembering laughter and life along with the still agony of death. Which was true? When all this was over, what would remain?

While we were here, there were some personal effects I wanted to collect from upstairs. I prowled through the rooms, which looked as cluttered and normal as if we had never left. Alessandra went into her bedroom and emerged with a battered stuffed rabbit, given her the day she was born. In Sean's room, I saw the Legos and the army men and remembered the half-finished spaceship and how his shortened arm had been on the wrong side.

In my room, I saw the bed where Elena and I had slept and made love, and I remembered Claire lying there with her mirrored T-shirt. Were my children truly dead? Or were they prisoners of the varcolac? Was there a difference? I sifted through the accumulation of things on our dressers, but I found nothing but painful reminders of our old life.

Back downstairs, we all met up again. "So where should we look?" I asked.

"Why don't we just take it in order?" Jean suggested.

We walked through the events of that day from Alessandra's perspective, choreographing her movements from the moment she picked up the letter from Brian. We moved from the living room into the kitchen. I remembered sitting there with Elena, watching Brian's gyroscope spin. Anything left in that room would already have been found by the police, but we looked anyway. The trashcan was empty. I traced my hand along the countertops and browsed halfheartedly through the cabinets. It was odd to see a variety of canned goods and boxed cereals and snacks there, as if the tenants were out for the day and would soon return.

"Where to now?" Jean asked.

"Outside," Alessandra said. Something in her voice made me look back. Her teeth were clenched.

"You did the right thing," I said. "You couldn't have done anything if you'd stayed."

She relaxed slightly. "You can't know that," she said.

"Actually, I can know it. Because the other version of you did stay and didn't do anything except give up the letter to the varcolac. Because you ran, we have a chance here." I opened the back door and held it open for her. "Lead the way."

Alessandra stepped out ahead of me, and Jean and I followed. We spread out across the backyard, searching the ground for signs of paper. There had still been snow on the ground that day, but the yard was dry and brown now. If the letter had been dropped out here, it would have blown away long ago.

We reached the fence. "You climbed over here?" I asked.

Alessandra nodded. I ran my eyes along the base of the fence. A stunted bush grew right against the chain link, and some vines twisted their way up. Under the bush, I saw a scrap of white. A piece of paper, dirt-encrusted and half-buried. I bent over and picked it up, shaking it to knock loose the dirt. My name was written on the front.

"This is it," I said. It had been lying out here for weeks, however, soaked with rain and snow, and then drying out in the sun. "I'm not sure what's left of it."

Back inside, at the kitchen table, the three of us crowded around it. In most cases, a piece of smartpaper could withstand a little water, but this had been exposed to the elements for months. I smoothed it out against the table, and then entered the password. The letter came up on the screen, still legible, although dark lines crisscrossed the paper along the fold lines, where the paper had been the most damaged. I entered the second password, and the programming circuits sprang into view.

I took some time familiarizing myself with them, with suggestions and questions from Jean. Alessandra, unfamiliar with coding principles, lost interest in the conversation and started raiding the cabinets for something to eat. I discovered that there were core, indecipherable modules that must represent the equations provided to Brian by the varcolacs. Built around those modules, however, was a great deal of code I could understand, presumably added by Brian to interact with and control the core modules.

Before long, I was starting to make sense of it. "Look, he's got a set of subroutines here to create particular effects," I said. The subroutines had names like GroundStateSpin, MacroDiffraction, StrongNuclearForce, and Tunneling. There were different versions of each, and optional circuitry that was cut off from the system that provided still more variation. "He was experimenting," I said. "Interacting with the modules in different ways, seeing what they could do."

There was even a subroutine called TeleportExperimental, with an intriguing comment that read, "Do not use before solving destination bug!!!"

"There's a lot here," I said. "It must have taken him months to write all this."

I spotted some graphics modules, and realized that the code was designed to work with a pair of eyejack lenses. I went upstairs, rummaged in a drawer until I found the pair that had come with my phone, and brought them back down.

"Let me try it. I don't want you killing yourself," Jean said.

"You're our star witness," I said. "Besides, there's an extra one of me. I'll do it."

"You have a daughter."

I gave her a look. "So do you."

Jean held up her hands, relenting, and I put the lenses in my eyes. They quickly recognized Brian's smartpaper as being in range and synched to it. I initiated the main program, and the now-familiar tugging sensation began in my chest, like a bass thrumming so deep I couldn't hear it. A basic menu appeared over my vision with the subroutine names. I scrolled through and selected GroundStateSpin, since I thought I could guess what that might accomplish.

Overlaid on my vision, a curved, double-headed arrow appeared. When I looked at an object in the room, the arrow would move over it and the object would highlight. I chose a tea kettle on the counter and blinked at it. It started spinning, just like the gyroscope, its spout whipping around and around like a boy on a merry-go-round.

It was incredible. I could move things with my *mind*. Jean and Alessandra stared at it, transfixed. I made the tea kettle stop, and started twirling the flour canister. Best of all, the energy for the spin was coming from the ground spin state of the particles. We could turn generators with this technology, maybe solve the world's energy problems.

What could the other subroutines do? I went back to the list and chose Tunneling. I still had the flour canister selected, and now, in my vision, a cone projected out from the center of the canister and into the room. I found I could rotate the cone around the canister and change its length. On the other side of the kitchen wall from where the flour canister stood was the living room, and I knew there was a small, decorative table standing against that wall. I aimed the cone directly through the wall and blinked.

The flour canister disappeared. At the same moment, there was a tremendous cracking sound like a gunshot. It was too loud just to be the canister shattering. I raced around into the living room, followed closely by Jean and Alessandra. The decorative table was smashed into splinters and covered in flour. Shards of table and porcelain were embedded in the wall.

Hastily, I quit the program and shoved the Higgs projector into my pocket. The thrumming sensation stopped.

"What were you trying to do?" Alessandra asked.

"I was trying to tunnel the canister through the wall and have it land on the table," I said. "I think it appeared *in* the table instead, and the stress of all that matter suddenly appearing in the middle of already-existing matter tore the table apart."

"It looks like we'll have to be more careful," Jean said. She held out a hand. "May I give it a try?"

"Let's not try it again just yet," I said. "I want to study the programming a little more, get a better understanding of what a module does before running it. I don't know how well Brian tested his software, either—I don't want to blow up a city block because he accidentally used English units in one place instead of metric." I looked around the room where Elena had died. I felt tired. "I want to get out of here," I said.

Driving back, Alessandra asked, "Why did the varcolac want to take that letter anyway? It can do all this magic stuff without it."

I shrugged. "How could we know? This was an alien encounter, from both sides, neither of our species comprehending the other. The varcolacs originally provided the equations for the core modules to Brian, probably in good faith, but we don't know what that information meant to them. Maybe it was simply a kind of textbook, an explanation of who they are and how they're made. Regardless, when Brian put this together"—I gestured at the smartpaper—"it had some effect that they didn't like, and they wanted it back. Who knows what changes this has made in their world? It could be killing them, or causing some other disruption—we just don't know."

"This is the creature that murdered Mom and Claire and Sean," Alessandra said. "It's not just misunderstood. It's a killer."

"I'm not sure if it means to be," I said. "You could be right—it could be acting out of rage or simply enjoy killing; I don't know. But look how it took Marek apart and put him back together. Look how its body is so awkwardly assembled out of different parts. It's trying to understand us, and not getting very close. I doubt life and death even mean the same thing to it as they do to us. The idea that a being's total existence is enclosed by a piece of matter is probably incomprehensible to them."

"So it was all, what, some kind of cosmic accident?" Alessandra asked, anger simmering in her tone.

"If anyone's to blame for this, it's Brian," I said. "He thought he could trade with a radically different intelligence and come out ahead. He was greedy and stupid. The varcolac . . . we have no idea what motivates it. All we know is that it wanted to reclaim Brian's copies of this programming."

"And it killed people to get it."

"Yes," I admitted. "It did."

"Is that programming a threat to them? Could you use it to hurt the varcolac?" Alessandra asked.

I remembered Brian making the varcolac disintegrate, at least momentarily. "Maybe," I said. "Brian said the varcolac gets its power from exotic particle leakage from the collider, such that when he used his circuitry to eliminate those particles, the varcolac lost its coherency. So I guess, if we learn enough about how to use the projector, perhaps it would be a threat."

"Well then," Jean said. "I guess we'd better learn."

CHAPTER 24
DOWN-SPIN

"That was a train wreck," I said. Terry had come again to visit me in the prison meeting room. He sat in one of the yellow chairs, looking tired. I paced the room. "Marek looked like he was lying, because half the time, he was."

"It wasn't that bad," Terry said.

"I was embarrassed to put him in that situation," I said. "He's one of my only loyal friends, and I hate that he had to perjure himself on my account."

"He told the truth where it counted," Terry said. "He told the court that he saw Vanderhall alive. That's crucial for our case, and it was important for the jury to hear him say it."

I let out a sigh and threw myself down in a chair. "It's only important because we're trying to prove that Brian killed himself. Which I don't believe for a minute. The Brian I saw in the woods didn't know that another version of him was lying dead in the bunker."

"He wouldn't necessarily tell you . . ."

"No. He didn't know. I'm sure of it."

"It's not that important," Terry said.

I raised an eyebrow. "The truth isn't important?"

"Look," Terry said, running a hand through his hair. "I've been a defense attorney most of my career. People hate me. They think I don't care about truth, that I just try to set criminals free because the money is good. They don't understand when I say that the truth is irrelevant to my work, just like it's irrelevant to the prosecutor's work. My job is to present all the evidence and arguments that may demonstrate your innocence. The prosecutor's job is to present all the evidence and arguments that may demonstrate your guilt. The judge makes sure we play fair, according to the rules. But ultimately, it's the *jury* who decides what really happened.

"It doesn't matter to me, as far as my job is concerned, whether you killed Vanderhall or not. It also doesn't matter to me if he killed himself. But the fact that there's another explanation that fits the facts; that *is* important. Maybe you killed him. Maybe somebody else did it. The point is, there's more than one workable explanation, and that means the case against you isn't proven. It doesn't mean you're innocent, but it does mean that, under our law, you can't be convicted."

I thought about it. "I see your point. It still seems wrong to try to convince the jury of something we know isn't true."

"I'm trying to get you out of jail," Terry said, exasperated. "I'll use every trick I can."

"Why don't you use my double as the scapegoat?" I asked. "Show him to the jury, take his fingerprints, show that the physical evidence that matches me could match him just as well."

"It won't work," Terry said.

"Why not?"

"For one thing, you're the same person. If I understand all this, you're just momentarily following different paths. You're not twins. He's you."

"But what if he killed someone, and I didn't? Should I be held responsible?"

"For another thing," Terry said, "you're going to resolve again, right? Eventually? What then?"

"We should at least bring him out," I said. "Let everyone see that there really are two of me. It would make Jean and Marek's testimony much more believable."

"We'll bring him out. Trust me on this," Terry said. "Testimony is like a fireworks display. You can't use up all your explosions at the beginning. You have to orchestrate it, slowly gain momentum until all your points come together at the end, in a huge finish. You have to save your biggest surprises for the end. It gives the other side the least opportunity to knock your argument down or distract the jury. We'll put your double on the stand, but not until the last minute. You'll go first, to tell your story, and we'll give Haviland all the rope in the world to hang himself. Then, we bring out your double. The proof that it's all really possible."

"As long as my probability wave doesn't resolve before then."

Terry yawned hugely. "True enough," he said. "If that happens, there's nothing I can do."

CHAPTER 25
UP-SPIN

"Court is now in session for the People versus Jacob Kelley, the honorable Ann Roswell presiding," the court officer bellowed.

Alessandra and I sat in Colin's house, watching on the stream as my trial finally began. I had begged Sheppard to let me come and sit in the courthouse, but he had flatly refused. I told him I could disguise myself, that no one would ever know, but he wouldn't hear of it. All it took was one person to recognize me, and the game would be up. I argued that we should let the world know right away—hold a press conference and tell the truth—but Sheppard said that was a sure way to lose. Roswell hated to have the course of her trials manipulated by the media, and she was likely to sequester the jury and ban me from the courtroom.

So I sat and watched and tried not to let the talking heads drive me into a rage. They all seemed to assume my guilt, and they reveled in the bloody drama of a man murdering his friend. They speculated endlessly about my missing family as well, mostly to wonder where I had buried the bodies. The cameras zoomed in close on my double as he sat at the defendant's table in stony silence.

We heard the opening statements, and then Officer Peyton described coming to our house after Brian fired at Elena. When I heard my wife's voice on the 911 call, I clutched the arms of my chair nearly hard enough to snap them. It brought an unwelcome memory of Elena holding on to me while we waited for the police to arrive, how she felt in my arms, how she smelled. I wasn't sure I could keep watching, but I remembered that the other Jacob didn't have a choice. If he could do it, I could do it. I stayed in my seat.

To distract myself, I studied Brian's code. It really was incredible that he could have written so much of it by himself, but I figured that once he realized what it could do he probably worked on the software day and night. The varcolac had destroyed the other versions I knew about, and since nothing like this had been found in Brian's office, I was probably holding the only existing copy. To be safe, I replicated the whole thing onto a fresh sheet of smartpaper.

After the trial finished for the day, Alessandra and I went to the movies and watched two films in a row, drowning our stress in giant Cokes and buckets of buttered popcorn. I slept fitfully, dreaming of Haviland's pointing finger and of a pitiless jury announcing a guilty sentence. The next morning I was exhausted, but we turned the trial on again anyway and heard Officer McBride testify about matching the gun with the bullets in the bunker. Despite the importance of the outcome, the pace of the trial itself was tedious, and I caught myself drifting off a few times. That is, until the testimony of Sheila Singer.

The camera caught my double's obvious shock, and I felt the same way. Singer had seen Elena and the kids—three kids, even Alessandra—alive! After all the searching and wondering, here was actual proof that they had split. At least an hour after I had seen them dead, they had still been alive.

Alessandra gripped my hand.

"It might not mean anything," I said, though my heart was pounding against my chest. "They've been missing for months. They might just have resolved shortly after this woman saw them." In fact, as I said it, my excitement started to fade. Of course, they must have resolved. They couldn't possibly have been driving around New Jersey for these past several months, looking for me. Their probability wave had collapsed, Alessandra's to the version of her sitting next to me, and the others into their dead bodies.

"That doesn't make sense," Alessandra said, when I voiced my doubts. "Their bodies disappeared. They couldn't have resolved to those versions."

"Then where are they now?" I asked.

Her eyes searched mine, looking for hope. "I don't know. But there's a chance, isn't there?"

I stood. "Come on."

"Where are we going?"

"To the NJSC. To find out for sure."

As I drove across the bridge to New Jersey, Alessandra said, "Even if they are alive, they're not *my* family, are they? They're *hers*. My double's."

"It doesn't work that way," I said. "Your double is you. You are your double. If she's really out there, then when the probability wave collapses, you'll resolve into a single entity again."

"Meaning either her or me."

"No, mathematically speaking, the probability wave includes all possibilities between you and her. The two of you represent the opposite vectors of the Bloch sphere, the edges of the spectrum. So you could resolve into a mixture of both of you. Are likely to, in fact."

"And what will that version of me remember?"

"Not a version of you. You. I don't know what you'll remember, but it will still be you. It's as if you had to make a decision, whether to buy the red dress or the black dress, and you imagined what it would be like if you went down either path. When you finally made the decision, you wouldn't lose any part of yourself, just because you didn't go down the path of choosing and then wearing the black dress. This is the same. The path that turns out to be reality doesn't change who you are."

"It does if I don't remember being on this path. If I won't remember being me, the me who I am right now, then it very much changes who I am."

I couldn't argue with her—I had the same fears for myself. Time in prison had changed the other Jacob, had made him a different person than I was. How much of *me* would be left when we joined back up again? Was I defined by my memories, or by something else?

In a sense, none of us was ever the same person we'd been a year ago, or even an hour ago. We were more like a long chain of different people, each connected to the others by a memory of what had gone before and an expectation of what was to come. What defined Jacob Kelley, if it wasn't my connection to previous versions of myself made possible by my memories? What if someone swapped my memories wholesale for another person's—would I still be myself? Or would I be him?

Disturbing thoughts, but thoughts that were hard to dismiss, given the forking of my personality and memories in two directions. If I split again at this very moment, and one of me turned left and the other right, which path would *I* follow? The *real* me who was thinking these thoughts right now? Both of us would remember thinking these thoughts, but we couldn't both be Jacob Kelley, could we? It was a tangle, and one with no way out that I could see. I wanted to encourage my daughter, but I had no true encouragement to give.

"I'm sorry," I said. "I'm scared of what will happen myself. I don't have all the answers." I shrugged. "In fact, I probably don't have any of them."

Her face softened, and she leaned over and kissed me lightly on the cheek. "Now you're being honest," she said. "What's your plan?"

"To find out what happened to them. After that, who knows?"

The days were warmer now. Leaves had returned to the trees, and flowers were in bloom, but the long trek through the Jersey Pine Barrens looked more or less the same as it had the morning I drove out with Marek to find Brian dead on the bunker floor. My thoughts kept going round and round about waveform collapse and what it meant, hoping Elena and the kids might still be alive somewhere, but trying not to hope too much.

We arrived, and I parked in the visitors' lot. Sheila Singer was still back in Philadelphia at that moment, giving testimony, so we wouldn't be able to question her. That was for the best, since she would also recognize me as the accused and probably call the police rather than talk. Now we just had to hope that no one else recognized me, though I thought our chances were pretty good in the visitors' center. The real scientists rarely came here.

The atrium of the visitors' center was cathedral-large, with high glass windows and a hanging model of the super collider hanging above our heads. Displays with names like *The Quest For Unification* and *Baby Black Holes* stood against the walls, with interactive models of atoms and informational touch screens. The young Asian woman behind the central desk was attractive in a studious way, with a pageboy haircut, large glasses, and a man's button-down shirt. I approached her while Alessandra drifted off to look around the room.

"Hello," the receptionist said with a bright smile, "How can I help you?"

"Do you know Sheila Singer, by any chance?"

"Sure, I do." The smile faltered. "But she's not here today. I'm sorry . . ."

"No, I know that. Do you work with her often?"

"Most days. We flip coins for the tours, because, to tell you the truth"—she lowered her voice—"it's a bit boring sitting at the desk all day."

I tried to sound conversational. "I'm sure it is. How long have you been working here?"

"Since nine o'clock."

"No, I mean—"

"Oh! Sorry. A little more than a year." Her forehead wrinkled. "Why do you want to know?"

"See, I work with the district attorney's office," I said. "Ms. Singer is testifying today about something she saw here several months ago, and we like to double-check our facts." This claim seemed unlikely to me for several reasons, but I hoped she wouldn't question it.

"Oh, this is about the case!" she said. "I was jealous that Sheila got to testify and I didn't. It's so exciting, you know?"

"Then you were here that day? When the woman came asking about Jacob Kelley?"

"I certainly was. It was right at the end of the day, and the woman looked frantic, and the oldest girl looked like she might have been crying." She crossed her arms. "But Sheila was the one who actually talked to them, so she gets the court appearance and interviews with all the reporters."

"And did Sheila tell the woman where she could find her husband?"

"Well, she didn't know, did she? I think she just offered to call our manager. Then the woman asked about Dr. Vanderhall, and sure, Sheila knew him all right."

"She did?"

"Oh, sure. They had a bit of a fling a ways back. Dr. Vanderhall has a bit of a reputation—I mean *had* a reputation. I probably shouldn't say that about him when he's dead, but you know, I told her it wouldn't turn out well, and of course it didn't."

"What did Sheila say then?"

"She told the woman where to find Dr. Vanderhall's office, and she said thank you and left."

"Do you know where she went after that?"

The receptionist gave an odd shrug and looked out the window. "Well, I assume she went to Dr. Vanderhall's office. Where else would she have gone?"

"That was the day they found Dr. Vanderhall dead," I said.

"Well, yes, it was, wasn't it? And her husband was the murderer," she said, still not making eye contact.

"Suspected murderer," I said.

"What?"

"He hasn't been convicted. He might not have done it."

"Yeah." She waved a dismissive hand. "But they wouldn't have arrested him if they weren't pretty sure."

"I see what you mean. Thanks for your time."

I found Alessandra sitting on a bench near a display called *Supersymmetry: The Thrilling Story of How the Universe's Most Elusive Particles Were Found*. Her unfocused expression told me she was eyejacked again. "What are you looking at?" I asked.

"Sheila Singer's eyejack viewfeed history."

"Really? You can do that?" I asked.

"It wasn't that hard. I jumped down a chain of friends until I found a circle that included her. Most people aren't that careful when it comes to security, or they just don't care who sees their stuff. They just leave the default privacy settings, which supposedly limits access to your circle of friends, but really leaves it open to your friends' circles, etc. Somebody who works at the same place my father used to work isn't that many jumps away from me."

"Well, what did you find? Can you see what she saw last December third?"

"There are thousands of hours of viewfeeds here. Looks like she's a Lifer."

"A what?"

Alessandra rolled her eyes. "A Life Logger. She keeps her eyejacks recording twenty-four/seven, so it's a full record of her life. The viewfeeds aren't very well organized or titled, though." She paused a moment, and her eyes flicked from side to side. "Wow. I wonder if she knows *that* viewfeed can be publicly accessed." Alessandra cocked her head and squinted. "I didn't know anybody could be that flexible."

I cleared my throat loudly.

"It's an aerobics class, Dad."

"Right," I said. "Moving on."

"It might take me awhile to go through all this," Alessandra said.

"You should be able to narrow down the time pretty well," I said. "She said she saw Elena just before five o'clock on December third."

"The problem is, she didn't index by time."

"Okay, I get it. I'll leave you alone."

I wandered the displays for a while to let her search in peace. Most of them exaggerated the NJSC's accomplishments in overblown and misleading language, sometimes claiming what seemed like outright falsehoods to me, but which might simply have been attempts to express the truth in simple enough language for the average tourist to understand. I kept glancing over my shoulder, nervous that someone would come in who would recognize me, and I finally suggested to Alessandra that we go out for lunch, and she could continue the search there. I found a soup and sandwich shop I used to frequent, but fortunately I realized my mistake before actually going inside. I was bound to be recognized, if not by the staff, then by former coworkers on their lunch break. I chose a diner instead, and ordered chicken sandwiches for both of us.

The food had arrived by the time Alessandra found the right view-feeds in Sheila's library. I still had my lenses, so I synched to Alessandra's phone, and we watched together.

We saw the Feynman Center's atrium from a view behind the desk, and there, as Sheila had described, were Elena, Claire, Alessandra, and Sean, looking lost and upset. I heard Alessandra—the Alessandra next to me in the seat—gasp as she saw herself. It was one thing to know you had a double; it was another to see it with your own eyes. I just watched

Elena. At the same time that I had been finding her dead on the living room floor, she'd been out there, alive, and looking for me.

Elena met my eyes—Sheila's eyes, really—and said, "I'm looking for my husband, Jacob Kelley. Do you know where he is?"

Sheila checked her screen. "I'm sorry, I don't know who that is," she said. "Kelley? Does he work here, or is he a guest?"

"He used to work here, a few years ago," Elena said.

"I'm sorry," Sheila said. "I don't know where he would be. Do you want me to get my manager?"

"No," Elena said. "He was here to see Brian Vanderhall. Can you tell me where his office is?"

"Oh, yes. We know who he is." The view shifted, and Sheila traded looks with the other receptionist—the young Asian woman I had just spoken to at the NJSC. I realized I hadn't thought to get her name. "His office is in the Dirac building. Go out these doors and take a right . . ."

"I'll take her there," the Asian receptionist said.

"Are you sure? I thought you never wanted to see him again," Sheila said.

"I'll just show them where the building is. It'll give me an excuse to cut out of here a few minutes early."

"Oh, so you'll leave me to close up," Sheila said.

"That's the basic idea," the other one said. She winked. "Come on," she said to Elena, "I'll take you."

As they walked out, Elena dialed a number on her phone and listened. Now it was my turn to gasp. She was calling *me*. That call, the one that had come just in time to distract the policeman before I hit him—it hadn't been Alessandra calling with Elena's phone. It had been *Elena*, calling to see where I was. If she had called five minutes earlier or five minutes later, I would have answered the phone. I would have *talked* to her. I would have known she was alive right from the beginning.

Sheila watched long enough that we saw them head out the door in a little train, Claire following the Asian woman in the front, and Elena taking the rear. When it was clear there was nothing more to see, I blinked furiously to shut off the viewfeed.

The chicken sandwich was growing cold on my plate. It took me a moment to remember where I was.

"She lied," I said. "They both lied. Sheila didn't mention the Asian woman at all in her testimony, and they both said it was Sheila who told them where to find Brian. Neither of them said anything about actually leading them to Brian's office." I pounded the steering wheel. "I didn't even get her name."

"That's not much of a lie," Alessandra said. "What does it matter?"

"Sheila referred to the other woman never wanting to see Brian again. That implies a past relationship, and given Brian's reputation, probably a romantic one."

"So? From what you've said, there are probably a lot of young women there with a former romantic relationship with him."

"The question is, why are they lying at all? What are they hiding?"

On the drive back to the NJSC facility, Alessandra eyejacked again to track down the name of the woman who had lied to us. It didn't take her long.

"Lily Lin," she said. "Right off of Sheila's friend list."

"Lin?"

"That's what it says. She works at the Center, lives nearby. Looks like a lot of her family's in law enforcement."

"Wasn't there a Lin who was a police investigator, who testified at the trial?"

"Brittany Lin. Looks like it's her sister."

"You're kidding me. So Brittany could have doctored the evidence to protect her sister. An actual police cover-up?"

"I guess."

"Great job, Alessandra."

She smiled, a genuine smile of pleasure. "Alex," she said.

"What?"

"I know you and Mom like to use my full name, but call me Alex. That's what my friends call me."

My first thought was to say that I didn't realize she had any friends, but I managed to swallow that thought before it came out. I knew she was talking about friends online. "Alex," I said. I rolled it around in my mouth. I didn't like it. It completely lost the old Italian beauty of her given name. But it meant she was including me in her list of friends. I decided not to complain. "Alex it is. Do you think you can find Lily's viewfeed of that day?"

"Looking. We got pretty lucky with Sheila. Not everybody's a Lifer, you know. "

"I can't imagine why anyone would be," I said. "What's the point of recording your whole life? Most of it's pretty dull. Special occasions, okay, I get it, but—"

"Some Lifers are extremely popular," Alessandra said. "They have thousands of people watching them, all the time."

"So people with no life of their own spend their time immersed in someone else's? That's a pretty sad—"

"I've had mine recording for over a year." Her tone was belligerent, challenging me to object.

I closed my mouth. A year? Everything that she saw in our home, available online? I almost made a sharp comment, something to the effect of airing our family's dirty laundry in public, but I stopped myself in time. She was talking to me. She had just volunteered information about herself. I would be a fool to shut her down.

Instead, I just said, "Why?"

She rolled her eyes. "Welcome to the twenty-first century, Dad."

"I mean it," I said. "I don't get it. Why share video feed of every second of your life with complete strangers?"

My sincerity must have come through, because she answered seriously. "It makes me feel connected. People comment on my life, people across the world sometimes. They understand what I feel, cheer me on, give me advice sometimes. Not a lot. I don't have a big following."

"But . . . what about privacy?"

She shrugged, a barely discernible twitch of one shoulder. "Not a big deal, Dad. To your generation, maybe. Not to me."

"Do you watch other people's?"

"Sure. My friends, a little. Mostly strangers. I find people I like and follow them for a while."

"But . . . why? Isn't it boring just watching somebody else's life? I mean, it's not like a movie. Nothing much happens to people most of the time."

She sighed, as if forced to explain something obvious to an idiot. "There are apps that cut through the chatter. They key off of statistically uncommon visual patterns, raised voices, rapid eye movement—stuff like that. If you just want to see the highlights, you can. Sometimes it's pretty interesting just to watch the raw feed, though."

"Really? People tune in and just watch you do your homework or eat dinner?"

Alessandra—Alex—threw up her hands. "Haven't you ever read a blog?"

"Sure, I just—" A little pop of understanding stopped me. I actually got it, a little bit. "You're saying the appeal is similar to a personal blog. Someone talks about the ups and downs of his or her life; others tune in to the drama."

"Exactly like. Viewers leave comments, get worked up, have little flame wars sometimes. The most popular personalities become super-celebrities. They live their whole lives in front of millions of people."

I was silent for a bit, digesting this. The pine trees kept coming. When I was young, my mother had been suspicious of my Facebook account and had no clue how widespread or popular a phenomenon it was. I was starting to realize that the tide had turned and what I dismissed as a teenage game was, in fact, a serious cultural force.

I stole a sideways glance at her. "Is that what you want to be? A super-celebrity?"

Another minimalist shrug. She looked out her side window and didn't answer. I took this to mean that yes, at least at some level, she did want that, but she didn't want to open herself up to mockery or admit to longing for unlikely stardom. I could think of a dozen reasons why living your whole life in front of millions of people was a terrible idea, destructive to relationships, certain to cause an identity crisis, but I knew a turning point in our relationship when I heard one. Either I could tell Alex my mind, and she would never tell me hers again, or I could show myself willing to listen without judgment—something I wasn't sure I'd actually done with Alex, ever.

"That would be pretty cool," I said. "To have a celebrity in the family."

She shot me a look, afraid that I was making fun of her. Then she smirked. "Pretty cool?"

"What, people don't say 'cool' anymore?"

"Not in this decade."

Alex was able to discover that Lily Lin did indeed have a viewfeed covering the time when she had walked Elena and the kids to Brian's office, but the file was locked and not open to the public. With a little stretching of the speed limit, Alex and I arrived back at the Feynman Center before closing time. Lily Lin was no longer behind the desk. Instead, a thick-set man with an even thicker mustache stood in her place and scowled.

"Excuse me," I said. "We're looking for Lily Lin."

"I am looking for her, too," the man said, his irritation plain in his accented voice. He sounded a bit like Marek, so I guessed an Eastern European country. "She has been gone forty-five minutes and no notice."

"Oh no," Alex said. "She ran. You told her you were part of an investigation. She must have panicked."

"Has she ever gone home early without telling you?" I asked the man.

The man shook his head and bared his teeth, like a dog with a scrap of meat. "No, she is never running away like this before." The word *running* came out like *runnink*. Russian?

"She's the killer!" Alex said.

"Killer? What killer?" the possibly Russian manager asked.

I sighed. "I'm investigating the murder that happened here last December."

"And you think . . . Lily?"

"I just want to find her."

"She took purse," the manager said. "Left computer logged on."

"She left in a hurry, then. Do you have security cameras?" I asked.

"Certainly. We can . . . Lily!"

I followed the manager's gaze to see Lily Lin walking toward us, clutching her purse. Her eyes and nose were red, and her makeup was smeared.

"I'm sorry, Mr. Egorov," she said.

"You have been gone forty-five minutes!"

"I know. I'm sorry."

"Where have you been?"

"In the bathroom."

"For forty-five minutes?"

"She's been crying," Alex said.

"You know something, don't you," I said. "Either you didn't tell the police everything, or else your sister is covering for you."

Lily wiped at her eyes. "I don't know what you're talking about."

"Yes, you do," I said. "The day that woman and her children came, it wasn't Sheila who brought them to Brian Vanderhall's office. It was you."

"Who are you?" she asked.

"I'm investigating Vanderhall's death. We know you took a viewfeed of the incident. We'd like to see it."

She took a step backward. "No," she said, shaking her head. "No, I can't do that."

"You won't have to testify," I said. "We just need to know the truth."

"Go away. I don't know anything."

"You shot him, didn't you?" I said. "Your sister is law enforcement; she must be protecting you. We know you were dating Brian. When he left you, well . . ."

"He wanted me to shoot him," she said, her expression panicked now. "He made me do it. He said it wouldn't hurt him."

"So it was an accident," I said.

"No! I mean, yes, I shot him, but it didn't hurt him," Lily said. "It worked, just like he said it would. The bullet went right through."

"So how did he die?"

"Isn't it obvious? He must have been playing around with it and shot himself, or maybe he got his new girlfriend to do it, only this time it didn't work, and he blew his brains out. Serves her right. I hope she saw it happen. I hope his brains splattered all over her."

"New girlfriend? Who was this, specifically?"

"I don't know her name. There was always a new girl, and never the same one for long." She wiped her eyes and sniffed. "Can you believe I actually thought he was going to marry me?"

"Why didn't the police discover all this?" Alex asked.

"Let me guess," I said. "Your sister overlooked the fact that you were a recent lover of the victim, and thus a natural suspect."

"No, she interviewed me," she said. "She knew I was a suspect. But

I had an alibi. I was with my brother and his wife that night. She *knew* it wasn't me."

"So what are you hiding?"

"I'm not hiding anything," she said, but she glanced at the doors as if contemplating her escape.

"The viewfeed," I said. "Can we see it?"

"No. Who are you, anyway? I don't have to show you anything."

"Please. It might help us find them," I said.

Lily gasped. She pointed at my face. "Oh my gosh!" she said. "You're the guy! You're the one who killed Brian!"

"I didn't kill him," I said. "You just said yourself that you thought it was an accident."

"You're supposed to be in jail!"

"Time to go," I said. We headed for the door.

"Mr. Egorov, quick! Call the police!"

We pushed out through the double doors. "Ridiculous woman," I said.

"She's upset," Alex said.

"She might know where they are, but she won't show us," I said. "I'm not inclined to be generous."

We jumped into the car. I tried to reach Terry on the phone, but all I got was a voice mail message saying that he was in trial proceedings and would return my call as soon as he was able.

"Hopefully, the police will think she's crazy when she calls," I said. "Since I'm obviously on trial right now, not driving around New Jersey."

The phone rang. "Terry?" I said.

"No, this is Nick Massey," said an angry voice on the other end. "I'm looking for my wife."

It took me a moment to switch gears. "Wait, what? Who is this?"

"Nick Massey." He stressed each syllable as if I were an imbecile.

"You're looking for Jean?"

"That's what I said."

"I haven't seen her."

"Listen up, asshole," Nick said. "I don't have to catch you in bed together to know what's going on. She's barely been home for weeks, and now she's not even answering my phone calls. If she's leaving me, fine, but I need to know the score, and we need to settle up in court. If she doesn't want me or Chance, she could at least have the decency to tell us to our faces."

I opened my mouth, then shut it again, not sure how to respond. This was completely out of the blue, and I didn't need any more problems. "You've got this wrong," I said. "I'm not sleeping with Jean. She's helping me with my court case. She's an expert witness."

"Put her on the phone."

"She's not here. I've seen her, but not today. I don't know where she is, but my guess would be the Philadelphia courthouse."

"A husband knows, Mr. Kelley. She's not just busy with some court case. She's been emotionally checked out for months, and now I know why. She's sleeping with you, and she's left me and Chance behind."

"Look, I'm sorry for that, really, but I had no idea," I said. "If I see her, I'll tell her you called."

"Do that. And think about whether a woman who abandons her child is really somebody you want to be involved with."

"I'm not sleeping with her, Nick."

"Well, if that's the truth, I apologize. But I'm pretty sure somebody is."

The second I hung up, the phone rang again in my hand. This time it was Terry. "Jacob, where are you? We're putting you on the stand this afternoon."

"What? Today?"

"Of course! Listen, if you're not here in less than an hour, you're going to miss your chance. This whole thing hangs on you being here."

"We have new evidence," I said, and explained to him what we'd discovered. "We have a witness, one of Brian's old girlfriends, who says that Brian was using the gun to perform dangerous experiments on himself. He convinced her to fire it at him, and maybe other people as well."

"It's not very much," Terry said.

"What do you mean? It's an alternate theory if I ever heard one."

"We already have an alternate theory. It's too late to switch gears. Besides, the judge is going to be very suspicious of any new information materializing this late in the trial. Will your witness testify?"

"Uh, no, probably not. Not willingly, anyway."

"It won't work. Too many desperate lawyers try to throw up smokescreens at the end of a trial. Opposing counsel would scream foul, and the judge would agree."

"And they're not going to scream foul about me?"

"Of course, they are. But that's our ace in the hole, and I don't think there's going to be anything they can do about it. It's worth the risk."

"This woman's a more credible suspect than I am. She should at least provide some reasonable doubt."

"If we had her a month ago, maybe. Today, we have to stick with what we have. Get back here in an hour, or we won't have anything."

CHAPTER 26
DOWN-SPIN

T erry stood and announced the next and final witness. Me. I felt the eyes of everyone in the courtroom on me as I walked to the stand. The room looked different from this perspective. I felt the jurors watching me, and I met their eyes with as honest an expression as I could muster, just like Terry had coached me. He said jurors always liked when a defendant testified. It gave them a chance to hear the defendant's side of the story, something that seemed strangely missing in most trials. Despite the appeal to the jury, defendants almost never testified, and for a very good reason. It gave the prosecution the chance to ask tough questions and bring things into the court record that might otherwise be kept out, like a criminal past or incriminating statements previously made. It also meant a guilty client would have to lie, straight-faced, to the court and make the lie stick. Not many lawyers were willing to take the risk.

Terry thought this was one of the rare times that the benefits outweighed the risks. My story was so bizarre that presenting it in any other way but through my voice would be laughable. Jean had laid the scientific groundwork, and Marek had given his first-hand account; now I just had to tell them the story from my perspective. We expected Haviland to make my claims sound ridiculous, but we had set a trap for him which might just turn the trial around, if it worked.

Terry had coached me on how to behave. Don't smile. Don't fold your arms across your chest. Keep your hands away from your mouth. Never say, "To the best of my knowledge." Don't mumble. Speak confidently. Sit up straight. I was so busy trying to remember all these tips, I barely had time to worry about what I was going to say. Maybe that was part of the idea.

At the lectern, Terry shuffled his papers and took his time. I guessed he was trying to raise the suspense, to heighten the sense that whatever had gone before, this was the part of the trial that really mattered. I hoped he was right.

"Mr. Kelley," he said. "Did you kill Brian Vanderhall?"

I waited a beat, just like he taught me, then leaned forward into the microphone. "I did not."

"Did you cause his death in any way?"

"No, I did not."

"When was the last time you saw Brian Vanderhall alive?"

"On the afternoon of December third."

Terry paused to let that sink in. "Other witnesses have testified that Brian's dead body was found, by you, on the morning of December third."

"Yes, that's true," I said, enunciating clearly. "I found Brian's dead body in the bunker in the morning. I also saw him alive that afternoon."

Even though Marek had said essentially the same thing, the courtroom erupted in a buzz of noise. The camera flies whizzed around my face. Haviland actually laughed and clapped his hands together, apparently thinking his case was as good as won. I kept my face solemn, neither smiling nor acknowledging the reaction.

Judge Roswell pounded her gavel—I wondered how often she actually got a chance to do that—and the room quieted.

Terry pretended to be astonished by my claim. "Are you suggesting Brian Vanderhall rose from the dead? Or is it time travel, perhaps? Or does he have an identical twin who was hidden away by his parents at birth?"

"None of those," I said. "This admittedly unusual event was a direct result of Brian's research into quantum fields."

Terry stepped me through it, point by point. We could have taken a different tack, tried to frame my story in completely normal terms, leaving Brian out of it, or else not told my story at all. But I had told the police the truth when they interrogated me, which meant the whole story was on record. If I left out the unbelievable parts, Haviland could just trot them out and use them to make me look ridiculous anyway.

It was better to come out with it and treat it seriously, in hopes that the jury would do the same. Jean had already laid the scientific groundwork for Brian temporarily being in two places at once. I reiterated Marek's testimony about how the note Brian had left led me to the CATHIE bunker. I described the pair of resonators I found there, and what they meant in terms of the macroscopic realization of quantum effects. I said nothing about the spinning objects in the room, or the man with no eyes, or of Marek being pulled into pieces. Instead, I skipped ahead to when we found Brian in the back of his car.

Here, Terry stopped the narrative. "Are you certain it was Brian Vanderhall?"

"Completely."

"How could you tell?"

"I've known Brian for more than a decade. It was his face, his hair, his voice, his mannerisms and style of speech. He talked to me about the resonators, which practically no one knows about, much less understands. There's no question it was him."

"What happened to him? Where is he now?"

"The quantum waveform resolved."

"What does that mean?"

"It means the two Brians—the one who was dead on the bunker floor and the one who was sleeping in the back of his car—combined to become one again. There was just as much chance that the resolved version would be the living Brian, but unfortunately for him, it turned out to be the dead one."

"So ultimately, it's still true that Brian was killed by the gun in the underground bunker?"

"Yes. It's just that a shadow version of himself—another possible Brian, if you will—persisted for a short time afterward."

"Could the shadow version of Brian have killed the first version in a bizarre form of suicide?"

"As Dr. Massey testified, it's scientifically possible. My professional opinion agrees with her analysis."

"Do you know who killed Mr. Vanderhall?" Terry asked.

"No."

"Were you there when he died?" Terry asked.

"No, I was still at home in bed."

"How well did you know Mr. Vanderhall?"

"Quite well, for more than ten years, as I said. We attended college together and worked together. Before last December, I hadn't spoken to him in two years, however. Not since I left the NJSC."

"Were you good friends before that?"

"Yes. Best friends, I would say. He was the best man at my wedding."

"And now you've been accused of killing him. Had you ever been convicted of a crime before this?"

"Nothing more than a speeding ticket."

"No felonies? No driving under the influence?"

"Nothing."

"Tell us, how has this accusation of murder impacted your life?"

Terry persisted on that topic at some length, trying to paint a picture of me as an upstanding citizen and gain the jurors' sympathy for my wrongful imprisonment. It would have been easier if Elena and the kids were here, and he could show a tearful family. It all felt fake to me, though it was in fact true, and I understood it was necessary to gain a rapport with the jury. Finally, he covered the physical evidence and had me explain how I ended up in possession of the Glock and with Brian's blood on my shoes. As his last question, Terry asked me again, point-blank, whether I had killed Brian Vanderhall or in any way caused his death.

"No, I did not," I said.

"Thank you, no more questions." Terry sat down.

It was the best I could do. I had told my story, hopefully seeding some doubt in the minds of the jurors, and now I just had to survive cross-examination. Haviland stood to take the lectern. He was practically cackling with glee as he took the stand, rubbing his hands together and barely keeping back a smile. He obviously thought he was going to roast me alive.

"So let me get this straight," he said. "You're claiming to have seen the victim, Brian Vanderhall, alive and walking around after he died."

"Yes."

"And you expect the court to believe that this is"—he made a show of holding a document out in front of him, as if reading from the official record—"'scientifically possible.'"

"Yes."

Terry had warned me not to rise to Haviland's jibes. He would try to bait me into an angry or defensive response, but I was supposed to remain calm. The trick was to answer the questions, not the tone.

"Mr. Kelley, is your wife in the courtroom right now?"

"No."

"Why not? Doesn't she support you during this difficult time?"

"My wife is dead," I said.

"Oh yes? Did you kill her, too?"

Terry shot to his feet like a rocket. "Objection. Harassing the witness."

"Overruled," Judge Roswell said. "Mr. Kelley, you may answer the question."

"I did not kill my wife," I said. "I have never killed anyone."

"You said your wife was dead. How did she die?"

"I don't know," I said. This wasn't quite true, but the truth would completely derail my testimony, and no one would believe it.

"You don't know?" Haviland said. "Didn't you tell the police that 'a strange man came into the house and killed them'? Are those your words, Mr. Kelley?"

"Yes, they were my words to the police interrogator."

"Do you retract them now?"

"No. There was a man there, and I believe he killed them, but I don't know for certain."

"Was the man Brian Vanderhall?"

"No. This was after Brian's probability wave had already resolved."

Haviland gave me his incredulous look. "So let me get this straight. Your story has two disappearing magicians in it, one who came back from the dead, and one who killed the rest of your family?"

"Objection," Terry said.

"Sustained," Roswell said. "Mr. Haviland, please rephrase."

"Did you recognize the man who killed your family?" Haviland asked.

I was getting irritated. "No. I said I don't know who he was. I wasn't there when it happened. When I arrived at the house, there was a man there, and I believe it was him who killed them."

"Did the police apprehend this man?"

"No."

"Didn't you tell police upon your arrest that the bodies of your wife and two of your children were in the house?"

"Yes, I did."

"Did the police find those bodies when they went inside?"

"No, they did not."

"Wouldn't it be more accurate to say that your family is missing, Mr. Kelley? After all, it's been months, and neither your family nor their bodies have been found, isn't that right?"

"Missing may be an appropriate description," I said.

"Did you and your wife have a fight the night before she went missing?" Haviland asked.

"No!"

"Did you hit her?"

"I didn't hit her. I have never hit her."

Haviland turned a page of his notes. He stacked the pages and rapped them against the lectern to even the edges. I thought he was probably giving the jury a chance to consider why a wife might take her children and leave home without a trace.

"I see," he said finally. "Mr. Kelley, have you ever struck someone in anger?"

I paused. I knew exactly what incident Haviland was referring to, and I really didn't want to talk about it.

"Answer the question, please," Haviland said. "Have you ever struck someone in anger?"

"I was protecting my wife."

"I'll ask again. Have you ever struck—"

"Yes. We were at the health club, and this guy was harassing my—"

"Yes or no will do." Haviland gave me a patronizing smile. "Who was the man you struck?"

"His name was Martin Slosser."

"Where did this incident take place?"

"At the Granite Run Health and Fitness Club."

"How many times did you hit him?"

"I'm not sure."

"Four or five times?"

"Something like that. I'm not sure."

"You weren't counting?"

"Of course not."

"Is it safe to say you were out of control, Mr. Kelley?"

"He attacked my wife!"

"Did he attack her physically?"

"Not exactly. He was saying crude things to her, sexually suggestive things, with an implied threat."

"So you made sure he knew what would happen if he harmed your wife."

"I was angry. I hit him."

"Just a little? Did you bloody his lip and send him off?"

"I don't understand the question."

"What were the man's injuries, Mr. Kelley?"

"He lost consciousness for a short while."

"Was he not taken to Riddle Hospital by ambulance and treated for a concussion and contusion of the brain?"

"He was taken to the hospital, yes. I don't know what he was treated for."

"You told the jury a moment ago that you had never committed a crime. Wouldn't this be considered assault?"

"No charges were pressed," I said. "I don't know what it would be considered."

"So you knocked a man unconscious for speaking rudely. What would you have done if he actually touched your wife?"

"I can't say what would have happened."

"Is it safe to assume you would have reacted even more strongly?"

"I don't know. It didn't—"

"What if he threatened her with a loaded gun? What if he fired that gun at her head?"

I nearly lashed out with an angry response, but I caught myself just in time. I saw Terry at the defense table, making frantic, tiny shakes of his head. He had told me a dozen times not to fall prey to the rhythm of the prosecutor's questions. Take your time. Breathe. Answer at your own pace.

I took a deep breath. I counted to five. "Your questions are hypothetical," I said calmly. "I can't possibly tell you what I would have done in a situation that never occurred."

"I have another one for you. Think back to your time as a competitive boxer in Philadelphia. Do you remember a man named Vinny Russo?"

My muscles clenched. I knew he was baiting me, trying to goad me into a violent reaction. "I remember him," I said through clenched teeth. "It was a long time ago."

"He was in a sexual relationship with your mother?"

"Yes."

"According to the police report, you found him and your mother engaged in intimate relations in your South Philadelphia home."

"Yes."

"You walked in on them while they were copulating on the couch?"

"Yes."

"Did you hurt Mr. Russo?"

He had the police report. There was no point trying to color the truth. "I hit him as hard as I could."

"Which, as a competitive boxer, was pretty hard."

"Yes."

"Did you hit him just once?"

"He got up, so I hit him again."

"According to the police report, you broke his nose and knocked out three teeth?"

"If they say so."

"They also say Mr. Russo was so frightened for his safety that he ran outside without his clothes."

I stifled the sudden smile that came with the memory. "That's right, he did."

"But, according to you, you've never committed a violent crime."

"I've never been convicted of a crime, no."

"That's not quite the same thing, is it, Mr. Kelley?"

"When I need to, I can protect those I love. That's not the same thing as being violent."

"Was your mother an unwilling participant? Did she want you to rescue her from this man?" Haviland asked.

"We all knew Vinny," I said. "He was a jerk. He was taking advantage of her. If either of her brothers had found him instead of me, it would have been worse."

"It's safe to say, though, that you take a violent, protective stance about the sexuality of the women in your life."

"What does that mean?"

"That if you feel the sexuality of your mother or wife or daughters is threatened, you react violently."

"It's not a crime to protect the people you love," I said. "It doesn't mean I killed anyone."

"How would you describe Mr. Vanderhall's romantic relationships?"

The sudden change of topic threw me off. "I'm sorry?"

"His relationships with women. His sex life, if you will. How would you describe them?"

"Varied and short-lived. He always had a woman he was with, sometimes more than one. He liked the excitement of the chase, but didn't have the patience for an actual relationship. Somehow, women were attracted to him despite this."

"Did he ever have relationships with married women?"

"Pretty commonly, yes."

"Were their husbands aware of these relationships?"

"Not usually, no. At least at first. He got into some trouble that way."

"Did you always know which woman he was with?"

"No. Not even when I was working with him, and certainly not for the past few years."

"So you wouldn't necessarily know it if Mr. Vanderhall was conducting an affair with someone you knew. Such as, for instance, Elena, your wife."

I probably should have seen it coming, but I didn't. He caught me blindsided, and I stood up in the witness box, seething.

"Mr. Kelley, you must sit down," Judge Roswell said sternly.

It took me a moment to respond. I was drowning in a sea of rage, not just at Haviland, but at the whole impossible situation: at Brian Vander-hall, at the justice system, at the other Jacob, at the unreasonable absurdity of quantum physics, even at myself. It poured through me, half-blinding me, a torrent in my ears. Finally, I got control and took my seat.

Terry had been objecting loudly, and now that I was seated, the judge listened to his objection that the prosecution was harassing the witness. Roswell agreed. "Unless you are prepared to bring actual evidence that Mrs. Kelley was sleeping with the victim, then you will abandon this line of questioning. I will not tolerate fishing or baiting in my courtroom."

Haviland apologized, but he didn't seem sorry. I realized he had gotten just what he wanted out of me: an angry reaction in front of the jury. "Have you ever sought professional help to control violent tenden-cies, Mr. Kelley?"

"I don't have violent tendencies."

"Answer the question, please. Do you need me to repeat it?"

"No," I said.

"No, you don't need me to repeat the question, or no, you—"

"No, I've never seen a shrink about violence," I growled. He was intentionally irritating me, and I knew it, but I still couldn't help being annoyed. He was playing games with my life. I didn't like his games.

"So just to review," Haviland said. "You claim that, despite the fact that you were the only person able to enter and leave Mr. Vanderhall's office, and despite the fact that you were found in possession of the gun that killed him and with his blood on your shoes, you had no involve-ment whatsoever in his death."

I put as much honest certainty as I could into my voice. "Yes. I did not kill him."

"Instead, you expect the jury to believe this fantastic tale of photo-copied physicists?"

"It's the truth."

"That Mr. Vanderhall was both dead and alive at the same time?"

"Yes."

"Well, perhaps you know what you're talking about—you're a scientist, after all." This drew a few chuckles. "Tell me, from your experience, have you ever been dead and then walked around the next day?"

"No."

"Have you ever read a peer-reviewed scientific paper that suggests that it is possible to do so?"

"No."

"Have you ever been in two places at once?"

"Yes."

"Do you have even one scrap of evidence that . . . what did you say?"

I smiled. "Yes, I have been two places at once."

Haviland glanced at the judge and then back at me, unsure how to proceed. "Mr. Kelley," Judge Roswell began in a stern tone, but I spoke up quickly.

"Your Honor," I said, making sure everyone in the courtroom could hear me. "This is what I've been testifying to all along. Not only is it possible for a person to be in two places at once, I am doing so at this moment." I glanced at Terry, who nodded. It was time. I pointed to the courtroom doors, which were just now opening to reveal a man dressed exactly as I was, in a simple black suit and tie. It was the other Jacob, my double. "In fact," I said, "here I am now."

There was a noise of shifting seats as everyone in the courtroom turned to look. Heads swiveled back and forth as they compared the other Jacob's appearance to mine. I sat up straight, offering everyone a clear view of my face. My double walked confidently toward the front.

The showmanship was a risk, but it certainly captured everyone's attention, and I knew the moment would be played on every feed in the country. Haviland was floored. He stared at Jacob and then back at me, for once at a loss for words. The jury looked back and forth as if they were viewing a tennis match.

Judge Roswell stood, her kindly face now rigid with fury. "Mr. Sheppard!" she barked. Terry stood, almost snapping to attention. "Is it your intention to turn my courtroom into a circus?"

"No, Your Honor. I apologize."

"Bailiff, will you please remove this man from the building."

"But Your Honor, this is one of my witnesses," Terry said.

Her eyes narrowed. "You told the court that Mr. Jacob Kelley would be your last witness."

"Yes. This is Jacob Kelley."

"Which one, Mr. Sheppard?"

"Both of them, Your Honor. This is the defense's case, and the whole point of Mr. Kelley's testimony. This is no circus trick or identical twin—Mr. Kelley has no siblings. He is actually in two places at once, just as Brian Vanderhall was on the night of his death."

"Your Honor, this is ludicrous," Haviland said. He was red in the face and puffing. "I demand a mistrial."

Judge Roswell used her gavel for the second time that day. "The jury will return to the deliberation room and await instructions," she said, her voice cutting through the buzz in the courtroom. "Mr. Sheppard, Mr. Haviland, Mr. Kelley, and . . . the other Mr. Kelley. Come back to my chambers without saying another word."

She left her dais with a swirl of black robes. The four of us followed her meekly through the doors and into a paneled office filled with the requisite shelves of law journals and mahogany furniture. There were only two chairs besides the judge's. The lawyers took these, leaving Jacob and I to stand.

Roswell gave an exasperated sigh. "Terry, what's come over you?" she asked, dropping the formality of address she used in the courtroom. "It was a tough case, but I didn't think you were this desperate. I'm strongly considering a mistrial and slapping you with a heavy fine for wasting the court's time and money."

Terry laid a document on her desk, a few pages folded back to show a highlighted section. "It's all true, Ann. I have the DNA results right here. These two are the same man."

Roswell didn't even look at the document. "Rubbish. Identical twins have the same DNA; you know that."

"Look at them. Really look at them."

Jacob and I moved so we were shoulder to shoulder and stood up straight. She looked. I knew the most remarkable thing wasn't how identical we appeared, but the fact that, standing like this, you could see that we were mirror images. Our faces, side by side, were symmetrical in a way that neither twins nor any clever makeup could duplicate. She studied us carefully, but showed no sign of what she thought.

"David?" she said finally.

"It's all nonsense, of course," Haviland said.

"Don't talk," Judge Roswell said. "Look."

He turned in his chair and studied us for a long moment. "You've got to be kidding me," he said. "Really?"

We nodded in unison. "Really."

CHAPTER 27
UP-SPIN

I thought if Judge Roswell could be convinced, we would be home free, but it wasn't so easy. She believed we were who we said, but she still wasn't pleased. The worst of her glare was focused on Terry Sheppard.

"This is a miscarriage of justice," she said.

"Why?" I asked. "We're innocent."

Her eyes swiveled toward me like Gatling guns looking for a target. "I don't know that. Seems to me you had twice as much opportunity to kill him if there were two of you. What I do know is that this is going to play havoc with the court system. Your little stunt went out on the national feeds. That means that by tomorrow every convict in the pen is going to have his lawyer filing appeals that it wasn't him who did the crime, it was the other guy who looked just like him. How will any charge stick if there could be a doppelganger out there doing things in your name? It's a disaster."

"But we are the same person," Jacob said. "One passport, one driver's license, one social security number. If we did something wrong, we're equally culpable. Eventually the waveform will collapse, and we'll be in one place again, too."

The judge's eyes pinned Jacob for a moment, then turned back toward Sheppard. "A disaster," she repeated. "Terry, I thought you had better sense."

"I can't help the legal precedent," he tried. "It's the truth. These two are the same man. And if they can be the same man, then their story that Brian Vanderhall was split in two is equally plausible."

"Don't give me your rationalizations. I don't want to hear it." Judge Roswell actually pointed a scolding finger at Sheppard like a mother might a naughty child. "You hid the truth from me and the prosecution to get an edge. You put up a gigantic smokescreen that will turn everyone's attention away from the matter at hand: whether your client actually killed Brian Vanderhall. I've never been as disappointed in a former clerk than at this moment. When I hired you, you had principle. Promise. I never thought to see you resorting to cheap theatrics to win a case."

"It's not a smokescreen," Terry said doggedly. "It demonstrates that Vanderhall shooting himself is a plausible story."

"It was a vaudeville show, and it has drastic implications for the trial system, as you would know if you thought beyond this one case. It violated the spirit of the discovery process, if not the letter of it. It was cheating, Terry."

"But, Ann . . ."

"Call me, 'Your Honor,'" she snapped. "Or better yet, don't talk at all. You could have brought this to me weeks ago. Both parties could have made arguments in private, and we could have decided how to proceed to ensure fairness. How can we have a fair hearing now? I'm tempted to declare a mistrial, but thanks to you, I don't see how we can select another jury that will be any less biased than the one we have." She considered for a moment. "I will instruct the jury that they are to consider the evidence as presented without reference to whom they may or may not have thought they saw coming through the doors. The other Mr. Kelley will not testify. Mr. Haviland, you will complete your cross-examination, and then we will move to closing arguments. Neither of you are to refer to this incident in the courtroom again."

"Your Honor, Mr. Sheppard has made a mockery of you and this court with this charade. He should be removed from the case," Haviland said.

Judge Roswell narrowed her eyes at him. I thought he had gone too far by implying Terry had made a fool of her. "That won't be necessary," she said. "However, Mr. Kelley"—and now she looked at me—"if I see you within a hundred yards of my courtroom again, or appearing on the news before this trial is over, I will have you arrested for murder as well. Don't think I can't. Is everyone clear?"

We all nodded glumly, except for David Haviland, who positively smirked.

Disaster. It had seemed like such a good plan, but it was all falling apart. The jury had seen me, briefly, so maybe it would influence their verdict despite Roswell's instructions, but as she had pointed out, the existence of two of me wasn't evidence that I hadn't committed the murder. With the judge instructing them to dismiss what they saw, the jurors would assume it had been a trick of some kind—much easier than actually believing my story. And there were still the fingerprints, and the gun, and the bloody shoes. My double would have to endure the rest of cross-examination, and the judge was likely to give Haviland wide latitude in his questions. This wasn't going to fall my way.

Roswell called the bailiff in to escort me off the premises, and I was left on the sidewalk while the trial continued on without me. I stood outside the courthouse, not sure what to do next. Alex was inside, but I couldn't go in and tell her where I was. She would only have seen me go back toward the judge's chambers and then not come out again.

I looked around and saw someone jogging toward me. "Jean!" I said.

"What happened back there?" she asked.

"The judge was mad at our little stunt. I'm banned from the courtroom. Could you do me a favor?"

"Anything."

"Go in and tell Alex that I'm out here?"

"Sure thing."

Jean ran back up the courtroom steps. Two minutes later, she came out again with Alex and Marek, who had been inside watching the court proceedings as well. We found Colin's car in the parking garage and climbed in, Alex in the passenger seat and Jean and Marek in the back. I sat in the driver's seat and shut the door. I didn't turn the engine on, because I didn't know where to go.

"Here's the thing," I said, twisting to look at them. "I don't know how much longer I have left. I don't know if the jury is going to exonerate or condemn me, and I don't know when or how my waveform is going to collapse. I think it's too late for any of us to affect the outcome of the case. So with the time I have left, I want to figure out what happened to the rest of my family."

"Count me in," Jean said. I thought about the phone call from Nick and decided that I wouldn't mention it. It wasn't really any of my business, and Jean, whatever her problems, had been a good friend to me. She had to work out her family problems on her own, and if she didn't see fit to confide in me, I wasn't going to interfere.

Alex slipped a hand over and squeezed mine. "Count me in, too," she said. I gave her a warm smile. Neither of us mentioned that she, too, didn't know how long she had left, or just who she would be when her waveform collapsed.

Marek didn't say anything, but I knew he was in. Over the preceding months, he had shown himself to be as good a friend as I had ever known. Certainly a better friend than Brian Vanderhall. He didn't say much, and he didn't get sentimental, but he wasn't going to leave me until this was all resolved, one way or another.

I checked my phone and saw that there was a message from Lily Lin. "Hang on," I said. "This might be important."

The message was brief, but there was a link to a viewfeed. She had decided to let us see it after all.

Quickly, I explained to the others what we had learned from Lily. "She was the last person to see them," I said. "This might tell us what happened."

My heart was pounding as I waited for the others to sync their lenses to my phone. When everyone was ready, I played the feed.

The beginning was familiar—we had seen it before from Sheila's point of view. Elena asked about me, and Lily offered to take her to Brian's office. This time, however, we kept watching. They left the Feynman Center and headed along the gravel path toward the Dirac building. It was December, so the sky was already dark. A sliver of moon hung over the horizon. Lily wore a sweater, but no coat, and she hugged herself as she led the way.

Suddenly there was a man on the path in front of them. He didn't step out of a building or out from behind a tree; he just appeared. Even from this distance, the bones of his face looked wrong, and his elbows and knees bent awkwardly. He had no eyes.

Lily took a step back, and I could see the look of confused fear in Elena's eyes. The varcolac advanced, its forward motion not hindered by its awkward gait. Lily shrieked and backed out of its way. The varcolac ignored her.

Elena stepped in front of it, blocking it from the children. "Who are you?" she asked. "What do you want?"

It reached out to her, and I cringed, expecting a repeat of the death scene from my house. Instead, a portion of space seemed to rotate on invisible hinges, and a dozen more varcolacs appeared, identical copies of the first, surrounding the party on the grass. The children screamed and huddled close as the varcolacs advanced. When they had formed a tight circle, the space around them rotated again, like a three-dimensional trapdoor, and when it returned to its original position, Elena, the children, and the varcolacs were gone. Only Lily was left, her view blurred by her tears.

The viewfeed ended. This was why Lily hadn't told anyone what she had seen. It was horrible and impossible, and who would believe her? She had been only too glad to avoid testifying in court.

But now I was one step closer to learning what had happened to my family. It was possible, maybe even probable, that the varcolacs had killed them, but not certain. Despite the fact that they hadn't been seen for months, it was conceivable that their waveforms might *not* have collapsed. There was no way to tell where the varcolacs had taken them, or even if it was a *where* in the traditional sense, but it was possible—just possible—that they might still be alive.

I twisted in my seat to face the others. "They must have had a copy of the Higgs projector letter," I said. "The varcolac realized they had split, and after it destroyed the copy that Alessandra was holding, it went back to the NJSC to destroy the other version."

"Wait," Alex said. "I'm confused. Just how many copies of this letter were there?"

"By my count, there were four," I said. "Brian had the original letter, and he split, making two. One was destroyed in the pine forest; the other he mailed to me. That version split twice, both times with Alex. One version went to the NJSC, one stayed at home and was destroyed by the varcolac, and the other she dropped by the fence, where we retrieved it. As far as we know, I have the only copy left."

"What should we do?" Jean asked. "Go find Lily again? Maybe she knows more."

"No," Alex said. "We need to find the new girlfriend."

"That's right!" I snapped my fingers. "Brian had already dumped Lily when he died, but she mentioned a new girlfriend, someone Brian had left her for. Someone else who was helping him with his experiments."

"Who was it?" Jean asked.

"She didn't know."

"Doesn't sound like much of a lead."

"If we could find her, though, she might know more about how Brian died. She might even be the murderer. She might have pulled the trigger at Brian's request, like Lily said, only the experiment went wrong. Or she was angry at him, and there was the gun, loaded and in easy reach, and she grabbed it and shot him," I said.

"But he was found in a fingerprint-locked room. Only you or Brian could have locked it," Jean said.

"Or else someone who knew how to reprogram the lock."

"The police looked for that. They said it hadn't been reprogrammed in years," Jean said.

"Okay, then someone who both knew how to reprogram the lock and hack its internal logs so nobody could tell."

"Doesn't sound like the type of woman Brian usually slept around with," Jean said.

"Look, someone killed him. It wasn't me. The varcolac isn't likely to use a gun. That leaves other people. So someone must have gotten past that lock," I said.

Jean made an exasperated noise. "We've had this conversation a dozen times. Logically, the only person who could have locked the door and left the room was Brian himself. The other version of himself."

I sagged against my seat. I still didn't think Brian had killed himself, but she was right, we weren't getting anywhere. Besides, my goal wasn't to solve Brian's murder anymore. It was too late for that. Now I just wanted to find my family.

"We need to go back to the NJSC," Jean said.

"We've been there three times this week," Alex said. "What else are we going to find?"

Jean leaned forward. "We have to find whatever it is the varcolac wants. In order to know where it took your family, we have to know where it is. We have to find the varcolac. The only way to do that is to go back down to the CATHIE bunker."

I started to shake my head. "That's not a good idea. You haven't seen it, Jeannie, not in real life. It nearly killed us."

Jean crossed her arms. "If you want to find them, that's where we have to go. That's where the answers are."

A sudden rap on the car window made me jump. I looked out to see a journalist peering in at me. "Mr. Kelley? Can I ask you a few questions?"

"Time to go," I said. I turned the car on and pulled it into gear.

The journalist rapped on the window again. "Mr. Kelley?"

I rolled the window down an inch. "I'm innocent," I said. "I have nothing more to say." I backed the car out of the parking lot. He followed me and stood in front of the car, blocking my exit. I drove toward him anyway.

"Wait," he said, but he didn't have the courage to stand his ground with me bearing down on him. I didn't stop, and he jumped aside at the last minute. "Hey!"

As soon as we reached the street, another journalist spotted me and ran in our direction, camera drones whizzing ahead of her. "Court must have let out," I said. "We should have gotten farther away." More of them appeared, like seagulls after bread, materializing out of nowhere. I blasted the horn and pulled away, leaving them calling after me from the curb.

"Where are we going?" Jean asked.

"Where do you think?" I asked. I didn't like it, but I had to admit that she was right. There was no way around it. The super collider ring was the varcolac's lair, if anything was, and if we wanted answers, we had to go back down into it.

CHAPTER 28
DOWN-SPIN

W aiting for a jury to come back with a verdict is the worst sort of
torture. The seconds drag by, and there are too many of them
in each minute. Sometimes, when I looked at the clock, I could
have sworn it went backward. Not that the time really mattered. There
was no deadline. The jury was free to take all week to make a decision if
it needed it.

Haviland's final interrogation of me had been bloody and merciless.
He dragged me through my story detail by detail, making me repeat it
again and again, until it sounded as hollow and ludicrous as a fairy tale.
Along the way, he asked me if I believed in gnomes, Bigfoot, or the Loch
Ness Monster, or if I'd ever been abducted by aliens, each time shrugging
as if, given my tale, these were reasonable points to establish. Terry stared
stonily ahead, giving no indication that he noticed the beating we were
taking.

When the bloodbath was finally over, the lawyers delivered their
closing arguments. Terry made a valiant effort, reminding the jury that
the only physical evidence the prosecution had against me showed that I
had been at the scene, which I had freely admitted. It didn't prove that
I had pulled the trigger. There were no witnesses that placed me at the
scene at the actual time Brian had been killed. The prosecution had provided no motive for me to commit such a crime, beyond their contention
that I was a violent man. He didn't push the science, except to claim that
significant evidence had been brought to bear to demonstrate the plau-
sibility of an alternate theory. Roswell frowned a bit at that and seemed
about to interrupt, but she let it slide. He ended by reminding the jury
that they didn't need to believe the alternate theory entirely, only be able

to see that things could have happened in more than one way, and thus that my guilt had not been proven.

Haviland, on the other hand, was triumphant in his closing argument, almost gloating. He ridiculed my "pseudoscience," even provoking a laugh from one juror. Then he grew solemn and sermonized on the ills of causing the death of another human being, the need for society to protect its own, and the responsibility of each juror to their fellow citizens. He summarized the evidence in rapid style, and he dismissed the attempts of the defense to spin a plausible alternative story as "fanciful" and "desperate." He glossed over the idea of motive, and harped instead on the "reasonable doubt" theme of his opening, claiming that any reasonable person would have no doubt who had killed Brian Vanderhall.

When both lawyers had finished, Judge Roswell gave the jury their instructions. She ordered them severely to consider only the evidence, not the lawyer's questions or statements "or anything else you might have seen." Only what was officially entered in court record was to be considered.

"One final thing," Judge Roswell said. "I'm afraid that I'm going to have to call for this jury to be sequestered until a verdict can be reached. If you reach a verdict this evening, you will not be further inconvenienced. If not, however, you will not be able to return to your homes until the case is decided. Meals and lodging will be provided to you."

The announcement was met with groans and traded looks by the jurors, and I was struck again by how insignificant this case was in the lives of these men and women. Even if they were conscientious people—and I had no reason to doubt it—this would all be over for them in a day or two. They would return home to their families and their lives and, after regaling their friends with tales of their murder trial for a week or so, forget all about it. They probably cared more about whether their court-provided hotel room would have HBO than they did about the ultimate outcome of the case. Perhaps I was being too cynical, but from where I sat, I wasn't feeling too optimistic about the legal system.

Roswell fixed them with her evil eye, no doubt picking up on the same reactions. "Ladies and gentlemen of the jury, do not allow your desire to go home prevent you from giving this case your full efforts. A man's life hangs in the balance. Should you keep a dissenting opinion to yourself, and not speak up against the ideas of your fellow jurors, you may be punishing an innocent man, or allowing a guilty one to go free. Our system of justice entrusts you with this responsibility, believing that you will treat the determination of this man's guilt or innocence with the same gravity as you would if it were your own."

With that, the jury stood, faces unreadable, and filed out of the room. I sat in the same chair I had warmed for most of this interminable week, waiting. There was a lot of dead time in a trial, so I had already spent a great deal of time waiting in this room—waiting for the jurors to arrive, waiting for the lawyers to finish a sidebar with the judge, waiting for any of a hundred secret rituals the judge performed in hushed voices with her aides, the court recorder, the court officers, the bailiff, and any of the other unidentified people who went in and out, disrupting the flow of the trial. I had studied at length the room's elegant crown molding, its bland oil paintings, its massive chandeliers. There was nothing left to distract me from a bitter reflection on my situation.

Someone else was living my life. That the someone else was technically me didn't help very much. *He* was running around free, going where he pleased, hanging out with my friends, eating at restaurants, and spending time with my daughter, while *I* returned to my jail cell each night and would probably be convicted of murder. The prospect of our waveform collapsing didn't provide much encouragement: the more like *him* the final Jacob turned out to be, the more *I* would cease to exist. The more like *me* the final Jacob turned out to be, the more likely it was that I would spend the rest of my life in jail. I was helpless, while the man who was living my life investigated things without me. What if he discovered a way to force the waveform collapse and choose which way it resolved? I could hardly fault him for making the obvious choice.

It was strange how I had begun to use the third person to describe my other self. Jacob was me in principle, but it felt less and less like that was true the more our experiences diverged. We had both been the same person the day Brian died, but were we anymore? It was hard to say.

And still the jury didn't return. Every time someone coughed or a door opened or closed, my stomach muscles clenched in a jolt of panic, thinking that the jury was back. The waiting was agony. I asked to use the restroom, though I really didn't need to, simply to get up and move around.

The bailiff took me to a special restroom separate from the ones open to the public. Sitting alone in the stall, looking up at the narrow, barred window, I thought about suicide. I wasn't even sure how I would do it—a shoelace around the light fixture? A piece of broken glass to the wrists? I wouldn't technically be dead, if I did it—Jacob Kelley would still be alive. Eventually, only one of us could live anyway, and it seemed better that it be him. I didn't think I could really do it, though, at least not using the brutal and chancy means available. These were just the idle reflections of a man feeling cheated by life.

Fifteen minutes after I shuffled back into the courtroom, the jury finally reappeared. They were welcomed by the scrape of shifting chairs and the rustle of papers as the courtroom came alive again. The jurors' faces were somber, giving no hint of the verdict. They filed in awkwardly and a few glanced down at their chairs, as if uncertain whether they were supposed to sit. Finally, after a few false starts, they all sat down.

"Ladies and gentlemen of the jury, do you have a verdict?" Judge Roswell asked.

The chairwoman stood. "No, Your Honor." She looked embarrassed. "We didn't have enough time to talk through everything, but the officer said we had to come back in now."

I glanced at the time. It was five after eight.

Roswell didn't look surprised at the lack of verdict. I guessed she had ousted them because it was past closing time, and her question had been mere formality. "Do you feel that with more time you will be able to reach a verdict?"

"Yes, Your Honor." There was no hesitation, so I figured the group must have been asked the question already, and were just now repeating it for the record.

"Very well," Roswell said. "Court will reconvene tomorrow at eight o'clock, and your deliberations can continue at that time. The court officers will direct you to your hotel and answer any questions you might have."

"How can we get our clothes for tomorrow?" one juror blurted out.

"You will be able to call for a family member or friend to bring you what you need. If that is not possible, considerations will be made. Please direct any further questions to the court officers. Court is now adjourned."

The packed gallery erupted in noise. Terry slid a thick sheaf of papers over to me. "In case you want to review the relevant case citations," he said.

I gave him a strange look.

"Your double asked me to give this to you," he said. "He said you should read it carefully."

I nodded and tucked the papers under my arm. I stood quietly, looked at no one, and allowed the bailiff to lead me out.

I had only been in my cell for five minutes when a guard told me I had a visitor. I had just seen Terry, so it could only be the other Jacob, come to apologize or commiserate. I really didn't feel up to seeing another reminder of the life I wasn't living.

"Tell him I don't want to see him," I said.

This was enough to prompt a raised eyebrow from the bored guard. "You're refusing your visitor?" He didn't care one way or another, but most inmates would go see anyone at all, even a cop, just to get out of their cells and relieve the boredom. I considered the alternative: another round of interminable waiting and bitter contemplation. "I ain't waiting all day," the guard said.

"Fine, I'll see him," I said.

"Move it, then."

We walked back to the space-age meeting rooms, with their transparent walls and molded yellow chairs, where someone was waiting for me. It wasn't Jacob. It was a uniformed cop, a big guy with a blond crew cut and red blotches on his pale skin. I recognized him as Officer Peyton, the man who had responded to Elena's 911 call.

I dropped into a chair across from him. "You here to post my bail?" I asked sarcastically.

"No."

"It's only ten million dollars. A nice round number."

"Mr. Kelley, I was at your trial."

"Yes, I know. For the prosecution. You told the jury all about my motive for murder."

The blotches on Peyton's face grew more pronounced. "I'm sorry about that."

"Yeah, I bet."

"I saw what happened in court today." He said it quietly, almost whispering, as if he were having trouble getting the words out. "There were two of you, just like you said. I saw you both as clearly as I can see you now. Unless you have a secret twin brother that there was no record of, you must be telling the truth."

"Imagine that."

"If you're telling the truth about that, then maybe you're telling the truth about the rest, too. That there were two of your friend Vanderhall and you really did see him at your home at the same time that he was dead in the bunker."

"So you believe me now," I said.

"Some of it, anyway," Peyton said.

"Fat lot of good that does me. Tomorrow is when they decide to put me away for life."

Peyton shrugged. "Maybe they'll find you innocent."

"I can't say how encouraged I am by your legal expertise," I said.

"It could happen. They were talking a long time in there, and they didn't decide yet. Maybe this whole thing will just blow away."

I jumped to my feet, shaking. It had been weeks since I punched anything, and I was only barely restraining myself from knocking that soft, pale face of his inside out. "I found the dead bodies of my wife and daughter and son. Everyone I know thinks I'm a murderer." I leaned over and shouted into his face. "This thing will not just *blow away*!"

The guard outside yanked open the soundproof door. "Everything all right in here?"

"We're fine," Peyton said. "We're not done yet."

The guard gave his stick a menacing wave in my direction. "Sit down," he said. I threw myself back into the chair. The guard left.

"That day when I came to your house, I saw something," Peyton said. "Something I never told anyone else about." He hesitated. "I saw a ghost in your back yard." He looked at me expectantly, but I just stared back at him. "Esposito and Ashford walked around the house first, and they didn't see anything, but I took a look afterward. There was a ghost standing in the middle of your yard, no footprints anywhere around, just standing there surrounded by smooth, unbroken snow. And then it was gone."

He waited again for a reaction, but I didn't give him the satisfaction.

"The ghost just disappeared," Peyton went on. "But it was like turning more than disappearing, you know? Like going around a corner, but there was no corner there. Have you ever seen anything like that?" He sounded desperate for me to validate his experience, to confirm he wasn't crazy.

"You didn't think this was important to mention in your report?"

"No, of course not. What would I say, that I saw a ghost in your back yard? I wasn't even certain I saw it."

"Don't give me that. You were certain. But in your testimony in court, you told the jury that your search turned up nothing, no evidence of any other person besides Elena and me who could have fired that gun. You lied to save yourself from ridicule. At my expense."

"How would it have helped you if I admitted to seeing a ghost? They wouldn't even have let me testify."

"What you saw was what we have been calling a *varcolac*," I said. "And maybe the prosecution wouldn't have called you as a witness, but the defense might have. You want me to tell you that you aren't crazy. Why weren't you willing to return the favor?"

"Look, I was just doing my job. I came; I took your statements; I filled out my report. When it comes down to it, I don't know that you didn't shoot your friend. Or that your twin didn't."

"Neither of us did. I hadn't been near the NJSC in years when Brian died. If he'd bothered to take my name off his lock when I stopped working there, the police never would have come looking for me. They would never have connected me to this crime at all."

"That's not true. They had a tip that put them on your trail before forensics ever deciphered the lock."

"A tip? You mean somebody actually called the New Jersey State Police and gave them my name in connection with Brian's murder?"

Peyton nodded. "McBride made it seem in the trial like it was his smart police work that made the connection between you and the weapon and the murder, but that wasn't really the case. An anonymous caller made the connection, and then Media and New Jersey started talking and matched the gun with the bullets. It was only afterward that they connected your name with the lock, and it seemed pretty cut and dried from there. The evidence was fitting together."

"Except that I didn't do it."

"The jury's supposed to decide that. That's how the system works. We just try to collect enough evidence to be confident enough to make an arrest."

"And then you only testify in court to the parts that make me look bad."

Peyton stood up. "I'm done here. I'm sorry I came. If you really didn't kill him, I hope the jury finds you innocent."

He stood and motioned at the guard to unlock the door. The guard came in, but just as Peyton was about to leave, I cleared my throat.

"Listen," I said, "the man you saw: it wasn't really a man. It was a different kind of being, a creature made up of quantum entanglement. If you ever see it again, just run."

"Man? What man?"

"The ghost you saw in my back yard."

"It wasn't a man."

"What? I thought you said—"

"The ghost I saw was a woman."

CHAPTER 29

UP-SPIN

Jean, Alex, Marek, and I found a dirt path leading from the highway into the pine forest that must have been used by construction vehicles when the accelerator tunnel had first been dug. I moved the chain while Jean drove the car through, then I reattached the chain on the other side. This allowed us to park in a less conspicuous place, off the main road, where passing troopers were less likely to spot an abandoned car. I draped a few fallen pine branches over it, just to make sure.

This was the emergency exit that Marek and I had come through before, but I still needed GPS to find it. The ground was covered with needles, and the pine trees all looked the same. I had hoped to take the freight elevator down, but it needed a key to start, so we were stuck with the stairs, all twenty stories of them. Marek and I were fine, but Jean was panting when we reached the bottom, and Alex was breathing hard, though she hid it well. It wasn't going to be easy to get everyone back up top again.

I led the way toward the CATHIE bunker itself, listening for any unexpected sounds. The door to the bunker was taped off with yellow crime scene banners, which I tore away. Inside, the trash and broken instruments and glass shards had been cleared away, tagged and stored as evidence. Most of the surfaces had been dusted with aluminum powder in the search for fingerprints. I took a step inside. Nothing happened.

The others followed me in. There was nothing left to find here. There was still some equipment and most of the tables and wires, but the resonator experiment had been destroyed, and the police had certainly already found anything of interest. Against a table leaned two push brooms that the police must have left behind. Certainly Brian had never swept the floor, but it was clean now. Marek picked up one of the brooms and started sweeping it through the dust on the floor, but I doubted he'd find anything.

The mirror was still on the wall. I peered into it. It showed me my reflection. I studied the eyes, but they were just my eyes.

"This is where Brian first made contact with them, using the resonators as a kind of quantum radio," I said. "At first, they were helpful, providing him with the information for the Higgs projector, but at some point he must have harmed or betrayed them."

"Why do you say that?" Jean asked.

"Well, the varcolac has been pretty hostile. The first thing it did when it came out of the mirror was to destroy the resonator equipment. Maybe that was random destruction—even exploratory destruction, like a toddler dropping a glass to see what will happen—but maybe not. Maybe Brian had previously trapped it and forced it to do what he wanted."

"What, by drawing a pentagram on the ground and burning candles?" Jean asked.

"I'm just theorizing." A sudden surge of frustration made me pound both my fists on the tabletop and yell.

Both Jean and Alex jumped. "What?" Jean asked.

"I have no idea what to do here. We're just spinning our wheels. We can't recreate Brian's work, because it's destroyed. We can't summon a varcolac, and even if we could, we wouldn't know how to learn anything from it. We don't know anything at all."

"Let me see the Higgs projector," Jean said.

"What are you going to do?"

She pulled a folded sheet of smartpaper out of her pocket. "I've been dabbling with some code," she said. "Diagnostic only—it might help us understand how Brian used the projector to summon the varcolac and keep it at bay."

I hesitated. The potential dangers of fooling around with the projector were serious, but it wasn't reasonable for me to keep it solely to myself. Jean had been a faithful friend through all this, and there was no questioning her quick intelligence. If she thought she knew a way to use it to find out more than we knew now, I trusted her. I handed her the projector.

She synched the data on her smartpaper to the projector, and I could tell by the way her eyes flicked back and forth that she was interacting with it through her lenses. I was amazed that, given the brief look she had gotten at the programming before, she could have remembered enough of the interface to write subroutines of her own.

I felt the now-familiar tugging sensation in my chest, and I knew the projector had been turned on. "What are you doing, Jeannie?" I asked. I hoped she had more of a clue than I did. The device held incredible power, perhaps even the ability to summon and control a varcolac. But what was it doing, right now, to the integrity of my DNA, or my cellular structure, or my identity? To the basic laws of our universe? We just didn't know.

I got a partial answer pretty quickly when Alex suddenly clutched my arm and gasped. I looked up to see that the room contained, not one, but dozens of varcolacs. Surrounding us.

"Turn it off, Jean," I said. "Whatever you're doing, turn it off."

The varcolacs all had the same not-quite-human look about them, as if taken apart and put together too hastily, but they weren't all identical. There were male and female faces in the crowd, but they didn't always correspond to the male and female bodies. There were some different skin colors, but racial characteristics were as mixed up as everything else. Disturbingly, several of the faces bore some resemblance to Elena, Claire, Alex, and Sean. They were preternaturally still.

"What do we do?" Alex whispered, turning her head toward me slightly, but unwilling to take her eyes from the varcolacs. "Tell them we come in peace?"

The creatures glided forward, joints bending awkwardly, giving the impression of a nest of spiders. There was no way around them.

I cast around for some kind of weapon. The iron bar I'd used down here before had made no impression whatsoever, and in my house the man with no eyes had effortlessly snapped a poker in two. Standard weapons weren't going to accomplish anything.

The varcolacs closed around us. I'd seen what could happen if they got too close, seen them kill Elena and Brian, seen a steel microscope crumpled like paper, seen Marek torn limb from limb. I pushed Alex behind me, shielding her with my body, for all the good that would do. They didn't speak or make any expression of hostility or hatred. They just kept coming.

Marek wielded his broom like a quarterstaff and stepped forward, cursing loudly in Romanian. He swept the handle in an arc through three varcolac bodies, but they shimmered and diffracted around it just like before. There was no way to touch them.

Jean was hastily doing something with the projector. She stepped forward, holding it out like a charm, and incredibly the varcolacs drew back. The projector seemed to be causing them some kind of pain; when she pointed it in their direction, they shied away, back against the walls, and they shimmered, seeming to become more insubstantial. They had no eyes to track her movements, but their attention was clearly on her and on the projector in her hand.

"How did you do that?" I asked.

It didn't hold them back for long. As she was pushing them back in one direction, they circled around and approached her from the rear.

"Watch out!" Alex said, and Jean spun in time to push them back the other way.

"I'm going to clear the door," Jean said. "You won't have much time." She held the projector out in front of her and stepped toward the door, clearing an escape path. "Run!"

We all ran, Jean right behind us. Alex headed back toward the stairs, but I knew there was no way we were going to make it back up twenty stories with any speed. Perhaps the varcolacs would find the stairs just as difficult, but I wasn't counting on it, and once we were stuck in the stairwell with them coming up behind us, there wouldn't be any other options. We'd be trapped.

"This way," I said. I ran the other direction, into the accelerator tunnel. I hoped that the golf cart Marek and I had driven might still be there, or else that the police or a maintenance guy had left one behind, but no such luck.

Alex tried to use her phone to call for help, but of course she got no reception. "There are call stations every mile," I shouted. "If we can make it there, we can ask them to send a vehicle to come and pick us up."

The varcolacs followed us silently. They ran awkwardly, lurching as they came, but it didn't seem to slow them down. I thought Alex might be the one to fall behind, but she was fast and ran with a natural stride, and Jean quickly caught up with us. Ultimately it was Marek who started to drop back—as strong as he was, he was heavy, and he didn't run as much as I did. There was no point in me slowing down to help him. I couldn't carry him. The best I could do was encourage him to run harder.

"Come on!" I shouted. "It's all those bacon cheeseburgers! Move!"

He growled at me and put on another burst of speed, nearly catching back up with us, but his breath was coming in big gasps.

"And don't you get any crazy ideas about stopping to delay the monsters while we escape," I said between my own panting breaths. "We're almost there."

I didn't actually have any idea how far we were from a call station, nor how quickly they would be able to send someone out to get us. I realized that I had to be far enough ahead, however, that I would have time to make the call before the varcolacs overtook me. I started putting on more speed, trying to widen the distance between me and them. The muscles in my thighs ached, and my side was starting to burn. I generally ran a few miles four or five days a week, but I obviously hadn't been keeping up with that recently, and it was more of a light jog anyway, not a sprint.

Finally, I saw the call station up ahead against the collider ring wall: a green-painted booth with a phone inside. Not only that, but someone was already there. It must be a maintenance worker, calling in. Maybe he had heard some part of our confrontation, or had seen some evidence of damage, and was calling in for instructions. He must have a golf cart or other vehicle. I shouted to get his attention.

As I ran closer, however, I could see that he wasn't on the phone. He was just leaning against the station, arms crossed as if waiting for something. A chill passed through me as I recognized his bearing and the general wrongness of the shape of his body. A few more steps, and I could see his face clearly enough to be certain. It was the man with no eyes, the first varcolac we had seen, the one who had killed Brian and Elena and Claire and Sean.

He stepped out in front of us, legs spread wide. Alex screamed, but I kept running. If we stopped, we had no chance. We had to get past him.

The man with no eyes straightened his arms out in front of his body and clapped, as if smashing two cymbals together. A shock wave of some kind knocked me off my feet. I saw Marek, Jean, and Alex go down as well. I sat up, dizzy, struggling to get to my feet again. Jean was on the ground next to me.

I pushed myself up to my knees just as the man with no eyes clapped again. I felt the side of my head strike the concrete. The last thing I saw before everything went black was the circle of varcolacs advancing all around me.

CHAPTER 30
DOWN-SPIN

I called Terry Sheppard from prison and told him what I had learned from Peyton, particularly how the police had been given my name by an anonymous caller. Terry doubted it would do any good with the verdict this late in the game, but if new information came to light, he said, it could certainly help with the appeals process. That wasn't very encouraging, but I left him to it. He said he would track the information down, but I was left with the distinct impression that he wasn't in a great hurry. It was evening, and I knew there wasn't much hope of getting any New Jersey state cops assigned to the case on the phone, and not much hope, even then, of getting them to help. They wanted me put away; they weren't going to admit to anything.

So I was surprised when only two hours later I was pulled out of my cell and brought to meet two visitors. The visitors were Terry and an investigator he had put on the case—introduced only as Bill, someone he said he hired often. Bill apparently knew his business, because he'd already somehow gotten a hold of a recording of the anonymous tipster's call. They both looked exhausted.

"Looks like you were right," Terry said. "They did originally act on the basis of a tip. Unfortunately, that fact is not obviously significant to the case, which hangs more on forensic evidence than on eyewitness testimony. If the police had found the tipster, that might just mean they would have one more person to speak against you."

"But who was it?"

"We don't know," said Bill, who looked a little like Terry, but without the mustache. I wondered if they were related. "She didn't leave a name, and the call was traced back to a pay phone at the Lakehurst Diner Restaurant."

"She?" I asked, remembering Peyton's ghost.

"Yes, it was a female caller," Terry said.

"When did this call come in?"

"2:07 PM. After you found Vanderhall's body, but before the New Jersey cops connected with the Media cops. Probably about the time you were down in that bunker."

"Well, can I hear it?" I asked.

"Hear what?"

"The recording of the call."

"Not much to it," Bill said. He pulled his phone out of his pocket and pressed a few buttons. A female voice spoke out of it.

"Yes, I'm calling with information about a murder."

"Can I have your name, please?" asked another female voice.

"It's about Dr. Vanderhall. He was killed last night, and I saw who did it."

"Let's start with your name, please," the voice said calmly.

"Don't you want to know who the murderer is?" the caller asked.

"I'd like to know who you are. If you're afraid, we can protect you, but we can't protect you if we don't know who you are."

"It was Jacob Kelley. He was the murderer."

"We will certainly look into that. Now, can you tell me your name?"

Bill shut off the recording. "The caller hung up after that. Not much to go on, except that she fingered you for the crime. So it's probably someone who knows you."

"I know who she is," I said dully.

"You recognized the voice?"

"As soon as she spoke," I said. "Didn't you recognize it?"

Terry bit his lip and slowly shook his head. "No . . . though it sounds a bit familiar."

"It's Jean Massey," I said. "Jean Massey is the murderer."

CHAPTER 31
UP-SPIN

The blackness swirled, lighter blacks competing with the darker ones. I couldn't feel any part of my body, but I was still conscious. As my vision cleared, I could see sparks in the darkness, not like stars, which were always far away, but more like fireflies. They were white, tiny, and moved quickly, blinking off and back on again. I tried to track the movement of one, but found that I couldn't. What were they?

The more I watched, the more I could sense there was a pattern to the movement, and I thought I could discern some meaning in it. Colors. Texture. Temperature.

The constant motion was making me feel sick. I tried to close my eyes, but I found that closing them didn't make any difference to what I could see. The motion seemed to intensify. The more I watched, the deeper I could see into the cloud of lights, and now I was watching millions or even billions of them. Not only that, but I could see forward and backward in time, as well. I saw that each light was not eternal, but had a lifetime, interacting with other lights, altering their shape and their purpose. In fact—and this came like a jolt of new sight, a pattern coming into focus—the whole constellation of lights was connected. It was a single system.

As soon as I realized that, I saw that this system of lights was just one of many, and that each system had its own span of existence through time. The systems interacted with each other, trading millions of lights among them, composed of different sets of lights from one moment to the next, but still tracing out a continuous path as a single system.

Was this how the varcolac saw the world? What were these systems I was seeing? Humans? The varcolacs themselves? Or were these only the beginnings of more complex ideas? Perhaps the systems I was now perceiving were only cells or bacteria. As this thought occurred to me, my sight leapt to the next level of complexity, and I saw systems of systems, each composed of trillions upon trillions of lights, and I knew that I had not even come close to the end. The concept now in place, my vision jumped back, and back, and back again, perceiving each departure as a new combination of particles, all intertwined, all shared and traded, yet somehow distinct.

Finally, I opened my eyes. At first, I thought I was simply viewing the next level of complexity, the systems upon systems, and I suppose I was. But there was something hard and cold against my face. I had hands again, and legs. I was back in the real world, at least as I understood it. My face was pressed against a concrete floor, and I could see the pebbly, sand-colored surface, feel the rough texture on my cheek and forehead. There was light coming from somewhere above me, and a persistent buzzing sound, like a high-voltage electric fence.

I lifted my head and looked around. I was still underground, somewhere in the accelerator ring structure. It was an enormous, dimly lit, concrete room, and I recognized it. It was a sub-basement below the collider ring, an access room for the electric power coming into the collider from the grid. Thick bundles of cable stretched across the floor, running in different directions and across each other. The bundle that ran right in front of me was thicker than my leg and a riot of different colors, all twisted together. Near the walls, the bundles converged, forming super-bundles that passed into conduit pipes. Banks of switches covered one of the walls, out of reach.

All of the crisscrossing bundles of wire divided the floor into spaces of different shapes and sizes, like a skewed chess board. In many of these spaces were people, one person to a space, lying asleep or unconscious. To my right, I saw Marek and Alex, each in their own spaces. To my left were four more people, the sight of whom made my breathing quicken and my heart rate spike. It was my family—Sean, Claire, Alessandra, and Elena, lying there as if they'd just gone to sleep for the night. None of them was moving, but I could see their chests rise and fall with each breath. They were alive.

CHAPTER 32
DOWN-SPIN

I paced my prison cell, drawing irritated looks from my cellmate. I had to get out. The next day, a jury of my peers would pronounce their verdict, and the more I sat around in prison, the more convinced I was that the verdict was going to be guilty. I was pretty certain I knew who the real murderer was, but it was too late to prove it to anyone—at least, not until a lengthy appeal process—and in the meantime, Jacob was out there somewhere, trusting her.

Why had she done it? I had no idea. Money? Power? Fame? All of those were possible, if she could have controlled the technology Brian had discovered. It promised a solution to one of the first dreams of science: unlimited energy. And that was only the least of it. What might one do with a device that could alter the Higgs field? Control the random probabilities of the universe? There was evidence that quantum fields stretched through time as well as space . . . could one undo a bad decision? Unexplode a terrorist bomb? It would change the world.

It seemed likely that Jean had been Brian's newest girlfriend, and I suspected she had been involved in the science all along. She had probably written a lot of the subroutines that interacted with the Higgs projector's core module. I didn't know how she had killed him, exactly, but given what I did know, I could imagine how she might have done it. I knew the varcolac could appear and disappear at will. He wasn't human, of course, but it demonstrated a basic truth about matter: it wasn't as solid and real as it appeared to be to us. Mass itself was a quantum property, delivered to a particle via the Higgs field the same way a magnetic field could deliver an electric charge. If you could manipulate the local Higgs field with enough precision you could walk through walls, change your weight, possibly even reverse gravity. If Jean could do those things, it would have been easy for her to shoot Brian and then escape the locked room. Though she also might have had the skill to hack the logs and frame me.

But it didn't matter how she had done it. What mattered was that I was stuck in here while a murderer ran free and my family was in danger. Tomorrow the jury would deliver a verdict. I was pretty sure that verdict was not going to be in my favor, which meant that this was my last night in this temporary holding cell. Tomorrow I would be moved to whatever maximum security prison they reserved for murderers, which I might never leave again.

It was only then that I remembered the sheaf of papers Terry had given me. I started paging through them lethargically, not sure what I was supposed to learn. He had said my double told me to read it carefully, but I wasn't sure what I could find that would matter at this point. Why didn't he just tell me what he wanted me to find instead of hiding it in a mountain of thick legal documents? I was feeling abandoned and sorry for myself. If there had to be two of me, why couldn't I have been the one on the outside instead of the one stuck in jail?

My mind wandered as I flipped pages. Peyton had described the ghost woman he saw as ethereal and thin, but he admitted that the street lights had been mostly behind her, putting her in silhouette. Peyton's description of the ghost's disappearance—and the fact that she hadn't left any footprints—certainly suggested a varcolac. Was it a female varcolac? Or the same varcolac manifesting a different parody of a human body? If so, why had no one else seen it? Why was it there? Peyton's story provided more information, but instead of shedding any light on the overall mystery, it just made it more opaque.

Finally, I reached a page that was a little bit thicker than the others. The text was just another unintelligible legal case document, but I could tell from the thickness and texture that it didn't belong. I ran a finger across it, and the legal text disappeared. Smartpaper.

It wasn't illegal for prisoners to have smartpaper, so at first I wondered why my double had gone to the trouble of concealing it. Then I realized what it must be. A copy of the Higgs projector. My double must have come to the same conclusion I had—that the jury was unlikely to find me innocent of the charges. If I wanted to get out of prison, I would have to accomplish it another way.

When the lights dimmed on the cell block at nine o'clock, I climbed into my bunk, but I didn't sleep. Using my body to block what I was doing from casual view of any guards that might walk by, I experimented with the Higgs projector, figuring out what it could do. I didn't have much time. I had to act that night, while I still could.

It wouldn't be easy. The walls of my cell were metal, and beyond them were other cells. There were armed guards and locked gates and video cameras and fences with razor wire. I waited until the midnight shift change, wanting to act during that confusion, however slight an advantage that might give. I stood right next to the door of my cell, watching. Prison is a predictable place, with strict schedules and discipline. The advantage to the guards is that it reduces stress and complaints and fights among the inmates. The advantage to me was that I could know exactly what would be happening at any given time.

I held the Higgs projector against the door. It had an electromagnetic lock, not a mechanical one, controlled from a central switchboard in the guards' room. In general, this type of lock was more secure, because it was immune to picking. But magnetism, however strong, was driven by the exchange of subatomic particles. I ran a small subroutine I had discovered during my experimentation and heard a satisfying click. The door drifted subtly ajar.

I couldn't turn invisible or walk through metal bars or teleport outside the prison. What I could do wasn't much, considering, but I hoped it would be enough.

"Hey!" I shouted. "Hey!" I banged on the bars. "Guard!"

The guard was a big white man gone to fat, and not the most conscientious of the staff. His name was Leary, or Leavy, or something like that. He came lumbering over with a sour expression on his face. "What's the problem, Kelley?"

I pushed the door open, showing him. "Some idiot forgot to lock my door," I said. "I'm getting out of here tomorrow; I don't want any trouble on my last day."

Leavy's face went from annoyed to astonished in a moment. He slammed the door in my face and rattled it to make sure it was secure. "Musta left it a little open," he muttered.

"What, no thanks?" I shouted at his receding back. "I'm going to tell the shift manager how ungrateful you were!"

I hoped that would be enough incentive to make him report the incident, or better yet, to go find a maintenance guy to check the door, so he could pass off the problem to someone else and still be able to say he'd done everything he could. Regardless, though, I had to act now. I popped the lock again.

This time, however, I walked straight out and over to the next cell. I popped that lock, too, and opened the door. "Time to party," I said. I didn't wait for a response. I ran from cell to cell, unlocking them all and swinging open the doors. These weren't hardened criminals; most were either awaiting trial or in for less than five years. Being caught trying to escape would add a lot of time to their sentences. For many of them, it wasn't worth the risk, and they stayed in their cells, or shouted at me to get back in mine before I got somebody shot. There were enough mischief-makers, however, glad for a chance at freedom, or even just to relieve some boredom and cause some trouble, that the block was soon full of prisoners. My ruse had already gone unnoticed much longer than I'd been expecting, so when a siren started wailing, I wasn't surprised.

"Let's go!" I shouted. The door to the cell block was also electromagnetic, so I popped it and held it open while the others rushed through, yelling and whooping war cries. Once they were all out, I quietly walked back to my cell and shut the door.

It took the prison guards almost an hour to round up all the escaped inmates. A few of them had been pepper sprayed, a few were bruised or bloody, but nobody had been shot, and nobody had actually escaped. Before they could figure out who to blame, however, they needed to find another place for the prisoners on my cell block. They couldn't very well leave us where we were, since there was clearly something defective with the locking system. I only hoped they did so before anyone studied the security cameras too closely and saw what I had done. The place was in chaos, with Leavy pompously telling anyone who would listen how he had followed the proper procedures.

The problem was, the prison was already overcrowded. They couldn't just move us to another wing, because the other wings were all crowded, too. In fact, prisoners were sleeping in the gymnasium and on the floor in classrooms, since the dormitories weren't large enough to house the population. It was a statewide problem, and the prisons didn't have the budget to build new wings. I thought I knew where they would put us. In fact, I was counting on it.

After another half-hour of deliberation and several arguments between angry officials, they made the decision I'd been waiting for. They decided to house us in the temporary modular jails they had just had shipped in. The new jails were like trailers—mobile plug-and-play units that were apparently a lot cheaper than permanent structures. They were completed and supposedly secure, but had not yet been officially approved by the security committee. Best of all, they stood at the very edge of the prison compound.

The decision was made. We were shackled, shouted at, and told to leave our personal belongings behind, since we'd be returning to our usual cells the next day, once they sorted out the lock problems. Some of the prisoners, still riled from the near-escape, gave some trouble, but I went along meekly.

They took us five at a time, three guards pushing us in the right direction, while a fourth checked our names off a clipboard. One by one, we were unshackled, led into a tiny, one-person cell barely larger than a bathroom stall, and locked in. The guard with the clipboard yanked on each to make sure it was secure.

Once I was locked into my cell, I waited until several more groups of five had come and gone, to make sure I had the rhythm down.

Elena.

I blinked, suddenly distracted, certain I had seen her. Was I going mad? There was no one here, just me and, outside my cell, the guards and the other prisoners. The sensation had been strong, not so much a visual cue, as if I had actually seen her in the flesh, but a mental one, as if I *knew* I had seen her. I shook it off. I couldn't be distracted by such things right now. When the guards left the next time to get another group of prisoners, I popped the lock on my cell, slipped through, walked out the back of the modular prison . . . and nearly collided with a guard.

They had placed one of the guards on the back door. I liked the man, too; his name was Jerry, and he had a steady, calming manner with the prisoners instead of keeping control with curses and insults. I didn't have time to do anything with the Higgs projector, so I took care of the problem the old-fashioned way. In the half-second of surprise before he could reach for his gun, I punched Jerry in the face as hard as I could. He dropped without a sound. I took his gun from his holster and kept running.

I wondered how long it would take them to notice. If not for Jerry, they probably wouldn't have detected my absence until they had all the other prisoners secured, and possibly not even then. Hopefully, no one would try to call Jerry soon. I still had a lot of other problems—my orange prison jumpsuit, for one—but for the moment, I was free.

I broke into a run, since no one seeing me walking would mistake me for anything but a prisoner anyway. I was nearly off the prison grounds when the electric shock knocked me off my feet.

It came straight out of nowhere. As my head cleared, I saw my daughter Alessandra crying out in pain, and then just as quickly the vision was gone. I thought I had run afoul of some new prison security measure, but no prison guards came running. They were still focused on the prisoner transfer, and seemed unaware—so far—of my escape.

I got up again, wary now, but no new shock came. I was outside the prison walls, but not off the grounds. A razor-wire fence circled the prison and the visitor parking lots, with a vehicle check center. There was a maintenance pickup truck in sight that I could conceivably steal, but I didn't know how to hotwire a vehicle, and even assuming I could find some clothes to replace my jumpsuit, I didn't know the protocol at the gate. That meant I had to go over the fence.

It wasn't electrified, and I reached the top easily. It was a barrier meant more for keeping the public out than keeping prisoners in. I was in the shadow of a large maple tree, mostly blocked from sight from the prison itself, but I still had to hurry. I didn't know how much time I had before my absence was discovered.

I had often looked at the tops of such fences and wondered how hard it really was to avoid the sharp parts. Now I found out. This was the kind with large loops of steel, cut to create many sharp points, rather than twisted wire. I found it was a lot more difficult than it looked, and by the time I made my way down the other side, my arms were bleeding from a dozen places, I had several cuts on my legs, and there was one deep gash along my ribs.

The cuts burned, and I was starting to wonder if this had been a good idea. I didn't think I was bleeding enough to worry about, but I had certainly left some blood on the fence, which meant they would know exactly which way I'd gone once they realized I was missing. I had to get a vehicle, and I had to get some clothes, and I had to do it fast.

As I ran down the hill leading away from the prison, I heard the sirens begin to blare.

CHAPTER 33
UP-SPIN

I didn't know if she was real; I didn't know if she was my Elena or some other version; I didn't know if this were some quantum heaven or hell where we were already dead, but it didn't matter. I had spent so long missing her, wishing for this moment, and fearing it would never come. I had imagined it a hundred times, how we would run together and collide in an embrace. I jumped to my feet and ran toward her.

I made it about two steps before I remembered how the wires in the bunker had become electrified when the power was on and we saw the varcolac for the first time. I stopped, windmilling my arms, as the hairs stood up on the back of my neck.

"You can't cross the wires," a voice said from behind me. "They're electrified."

I turned to see Jean, in her own space, only she was awake and interacting with the Higgs projector in her lap.

"Are they all asleep?" I asked.

"Sort of," Jean said, not looking up from what she was doing. "I just brought you out of it, and I'm working on the others. He has each of you in a kind of bubble where time stops, or at least slows way, way down."

"I was like that, too?"

"Yes. As I said, I brought you out of it. I'll have the others out soon."

I looked around in astonishment. "It's as if the varcolac is putting us on ice for later experimentation." I remembered how the varcolac had assimilated Brian after killing him, incorporating his knowledge into its own. "Or for something worse," I added.

Marek stirred and opened his eyes. I warned him about the wires and filled him in on where we were. The others woke one by one, and I told them the same thing. I greeted Elena, Claire, and Sean with tears in my eyes.

"You're alive!" I said. "I can hardly believe it. I've been so worried for you."

"Where are we?" Elena asked. "Do you know what this place is?" I could see she was rattled, but she kept her voice steady.

"I think we're in some part of the accelerator's electrical backbone, where the electrical system connects with the grid," I said. "It's way out along the circle, miles away from the Feynman center."

"How long have we been here?"

"It's March," I said. "You've been down here for four months."

Elena got to her feet, angry, astonished. "What are you talking about?"

"What's the last thing you remember?" I asked.

"I remember walking toward Brian's office to find you. We asked a girl from the front desk, and she was leading us to the right spot. Halfway there, this man arrived. He just appeared out of nowhere."

"He's not a man, really. It's hard to explain," I said.

"And you're saying it's been months? We've just been asleep down here all that time?"

"Not exactly." Jean spoke up for the first time. "You were in a kind of slow time bubble. You weren't asleep; you've barely aged at all."

"I was falsely accused of murdering Brian," I said. "There was a trial. We've been looking for you all this time."

Silence. It was already too much information, and I'd only begun to scratch the surface. Claire and Alessandra and Sean were still sitting on the floor, looking stunned. Elena's eyes darted from place to place.

"Are we trapped?" she asked.

"We're prisoners of that man who kidnapped you," I said. I looked from one frightened face to another, seeing their panic rise. I wasn't doing this right. I was scaring them instead of reassuring them. I took a deep breath and stood up.

For the moment, convincing them that several months had passed wasn't important. In fact, considering the alternative—spending several months awake in a varcolac prison—the fact that they had somehow lost the time seemed like a blessing.

I looked at Sean, noting that this living version of my son had his short arm on the left side, just like I remembered. This was *my* Sean. I tried to put a confident tone in my voice. "How are you doing, Sean?" I asked. "Are you holding up?"

He gave me a brave smile. "I'm okay, Dad."

"Claire? How are you? Did those creatures hurt you?"

Claire started to cry. "I'm fine, Daddy," she said. "Just scared."

"I'm here, too," Alex said. I turned my attention to her, surprised by the bitterness in her tone.

"Of course, you are," I said, and then I realized that this was Alessandra, not the Alex I'd spent the last few months with. This was the Alessandra I'd always dismissed as a lost cause, preferring her more stable, smarter, and prettier older sister. I realized now that the alienation in that relationship had been mostly my doing. I looked at Alex, who Jean was just now bringing out of unconsciousness.

Alex pulled herself to her feet and saw the rest of us. "The wires are electrified," I said quickly, before she could find out the hard way. "Don't try to step over them."

Alessandra looked Alex up and down. "Who on Earth is that?" she asked.

It was tough to explain, but Alessandra took it better than I expected. Of course she did—she was Alex, too, only I hadn't taken the time to really know her. Once introductions were made, the two girls couldn't stop talking, both with a kind of awe that they were talking to someone who was, in essence, themselves.

They seemed to be able to forget, for the moment, that we were trapped underground as the prisoners of a monster. It wasn't so easy for Elena. She looked at me, horrified. "Which one is the real her?"

"Both of them are real. Both of them are Alessandra."

"How is that possible?"

"It's what Alessandra would have been if she'd been kidnapped, and what Alessandra would have been if she hadn't been kidnapped. Either one could have happened, only in this case, they both did." I prayed she wouldn't ask why there was no second Claire or Sean. We would have to cover that eventually, but I didn't want to have to tell her now.

"But . . . they can't both just keep on being Alessandra, can they?"

I shook my head. "No, they can't. Eventually they'll converge back into one person again."

The fear in Elena's eyes sparked into anger. "Did Brian do this?"

"Indirectly."

"The man who kidnapped us, then?"

I sighed. "It's actually not a man. It's a quantum intelligence, a member of another intelligent race that we've been calling varcolacs."

"An alien?"

"Of sorts."

"What does it want?"

"I don't know. It has a vastly different experience of life than we have. I don't know what it understands or thinks of us, and I have no idea what it wants."

There was a disturbance in the air. We all felt it. Claire cringed and covered her face. A moment later, the varcolac stood over Alex, regarding her with its sightless face. Alex froze, staring up at it, her body rigid. It smiled. It was the first time it had made a facial expression of any kind, and it was hideous, stretching back its lips and showing far too much of its teeth.

"We don't have anything you want," I said. "Please let us go."

The varcolac didn't reply. It reached down, lifted Alex by her upper arm, and twisted. The move was casual, but Alex screamed, and we heard bone snapping.

"Leave her alone!" I shouted. I hurled myself toward her, thinking that with enough momentum I might break through the electrical fence and reach them, but it exploded in sparks and threw me back again. I tried to get up again, but my muscles twitched with the pain, and I slipped back down. I cast about for something to throw, anything that could get past the wires, but there was nothing.

"Please let her go," Elena said. She stood at the edge of the wires, pleading with the varcolac. "What do you want from us?" she asked. "This is my daughter. Please."

"Jean!" I said. "Do something."

"I'm sorry," Jean said. "I was just trying to help you. I didn't mean for it to end this way."

"It doesn't have to end," I said. "You can fight it, can't you? Hurry!"

Jean shook her head sadly. "I'm sorry," she said. "I never meant to hurt you. But I have to think of my own family, too."

This wasn't making sense. "What are you talking about?"

"I have to think of my daughter," she said. She gripped the smart-paper, *turned* just like the varcolacs had done, and disappeared.

I stared after Jean in open-mouthed astonishment, but I didn't have time to think about it. The varcolac dropped Alex on the floor and walked across the wires toward Elena.

"No!" I shouted at it. "Come on, fight me! I'm right here!"

Elena cowered away, but the varcolac advanced on her with inhuman speed and grabbed her by the throat. It lifted her as if she weighed nothing and thrust her in range of the bundle of wires separating my square from hers. An arc of lightning shot up from the wires into her body. She screamed and arched her back, her arms and legs jerking uncontrollably while the lightning danced and crackled. She kept screaming and screaming, the sound wrenched out of her body with barely a chance for her to take a breath.

I shouted, too, a bellow of helpless rage, as I tried to reach her, casting about for some weapon, desperate to find a way through, although I knew that even if I could get through, there was nothing I could do against such an enemy. Finally, I dropped to my knees, crying, begging the varcolac to let her go. Why was it doing this? What did it want?

The varcolac opened its hand. Elena's scream died and she fell motionless to the floor. I shouted her name, but I could see her chest rise and fall. She wasn't dead.

The varcolac was intelligent; I knew that. It must have a motive, though it was possible we would all die without ever knowing what it was. Was it experimenting with matter-based life forms just to see what would happen? Was it punishing us for destroying its time bubbles? Was it looking for the Higgs projector? Maybe such a surge of power would be beneficial for one of its kind and it was trying to help Elena by giving her more energy instead of trying to kill her.

I couldn't think straight. I felt dizzy, perhaps from the electric shock, and I thought I might fall over. For a brief moment, I had a vision of driving through a pine forest in a tiny car that was not my own. Where did that come from? Was I succumbing to fear and exhaustion? I shook my head. I couldn't check out now; my family needed me. I didn't know what to do, but I couldn't just do nothing.

Elena still didn't move. Alex rocked back and forth slightly, her eyes unfocused. The others huddled in their squares, frozen or crying softly.

As suddenly as it had come, the varcolac disappeared.

CHAPTER 34
DOWN-SPIN

My house was more than twelve miles away from the prison, and Swarthmore College, where I worked, a few miles beyond that. It was too far. I needed somewhere I could go quickly to change my clothes, somewhere that wouldn't be the first place the police would look for me.

The Granite Run Health and Fitness Club was located on Pennell Road in Lima, about five miles from the prison in Thornton. It was close enough. Before my arrest, I had run two and a half miles every morning—the distance from my home to the college—and I frequently ran in the five kilometer races that local municipalities held. I wasn't built for speed, but I could cover five miles in a little more than half an hour. I decided that I was better off racing the police than sneaking around trying to avoid them, so I took off running as fast as I could.

While I ran, I unzipped my jumpsuit halfway down, pulled my arms out, and then tied the sleeves around my waist. I hoped that a guy running in orange pants and a white T-shirt would be less conspicuous than a guy in an orange jumpsuit. I steered clear of Baltimore Pike, figuring it would be swarming with cops, but there was an old line of train tracks that hugged Chester Creek, and I aimed for that instead. It was mostly in the woods, where I was less likely to encounter any people, and it was easy to run along it without twisting an ankle. Best of all, it would lead me nearly to the fitness club's back door.

I repeatedly heard sirens, and once I saw the flashing lights of a police car, but if they were creating a perimeter, they either missed the train tracks or underestimated my speed. I reached the club without incident and slipped inside. There were only three cars in the parking lot, and I avoided being seen as I made my way through the halls.

I had a locker here with a change of clothes. I was breathing pretty hard—prison life had not been good for staying in shape—but I shoved the jumpsuit into the trashcan and put on the sweats and T-shirt from my locker. Now all I needed was transportation.

I checked the showers. One of them was running, and based on the little Nissan Flash in the parking lot, I was pretty sure I knew who was inside. It was Frank Reed, a guy I knew slightly from working out together, whose locker wasn't far from mine. The lockers had combinations, of course, but a lot of people didn't bother spinning them. I found Frank's, checked inside, and found some business clothes, a wallet, and a ring of keys.

I hated to steal, but I was beyond such considerations. I needed a car, and I didn't have time to quibble. I scribbled a quick note that said, "Frank, I'm sorry. I'll return it unharmed and with interest, if I can." I left it in the locker and took the keys.

The Flash was a tiny car—electric and made of lightweight materials. I thought I might even be able to pick it up if I had to. Frank was a small guy and fit easily. I wasn't and didn't. But it was a car, and once I wedged myself inside, I was on my way down the road, heading for New Jersey.

As I crossed the bridge, I had a sudden vision of the varcolac standing over me. Every muscle in my body tensed—I could see the varcolac almost as clearly as I could see the road in front of me. It wasn't like a dream or a vision; it was more like I had a second pair of eyes in a completely different place, feeding images to my brain.

I knew what was happening. Jacob and I were becoming one person again. The electric shock must have been from him; maybe it was even the reason the probability waveform had started to collapse. I could tell that he was underground right now, probably in the accelerator tunnels, and that the varcolac was there. I couldn't see everything that was happening; only the occasional glimpse.

I stepped on the gas. I didn't know how much time I had left.

With the help of the car's GPS system, I found Jean Massey's neighborhood and pulled up to her front door. I stepped out of my car, eyeing the place warily. The tiny yard was neatly mowed, with a small flowerbed under the eaves. I couldn't imagine Jean doing any gardening, so I guessed this to be Nick's work. Suddenly, I remembered the phone call—Nick, accusing me of sleeping with his wife. But that had been the other Jacob, not me. I had been in prison at the time, but the memory flashed into my mind as if I had actually experienced it.

I knocked on the door. Nick answered, wearing a white polo shirt and slacks and bare feet.

"Hi, Nick," I said. "Is Jean—"

"She's given you too much as it is," Nick said. "I'm sorry, but this is our family time. She's not available."

I shoved my foot in the door before he could close it. "Is she with your daughter right now?" Some of my urgency must have come across in my voice, because he stepped back. I pushed inside. "Your daughter's in danger," I said. "Where is she?"

He believed me. I didn't know how Jean had been acting since she arrived, but clearly it hadn't put his mind at ease. I followed him up the stairs and down the hall.

"Honey?" Nick called.

I walked slowly after him and peered into Chance's bedroom. It was empty.

"Jean?" Nick said, and then louder, "Jean!"

"She took her," I said. "They're gone."

Nick stood in the center of the room, surrounded by Chance's things—her changing table, her crib with blankets still tangled and warm, a scattering of baby toys—and bellowed his wife's name.

CHAPTER 35
UP-SPIN

E lena sat up with a groan. I was by her side in an instant, as close as I could get with the bundle of wires between us.

"Are you all right?" I asked.

"My head hurts."

"I'm so sorry."

She pressed fingers into her temples. "Not your fault."

I wanted to hold her in my arms, to stroke her hair and press her close. My space was roughly square, with three edges made of bundled wire and one edge against the wall. I examined the spot where the wires passed into the wall, but there was no way to cross it. I started to kick the wall. The wall was made of cinder blocks and didn't budge, but I kept kicking anyway, thinking that if I could knock loose even a small amount, then over time I could widen it, tear some of the wall away, and then get around the wire barrier to Elena.

"Use your keys," Marek called. He was in a center square, out of reach of a wall, but I understood what he meant. I pulled my keys out of my pocket, chose the largest one, and started scraping the wall close to the floor. A little dust drifted down, and a shallow scratch appeared. I kept scraping. It was going to take a long time to make any progress this way, but it was better than just waiting for the varcolac to come back and start hurting my family again. I scraped until my muscles ached, but I accomplished little more than a small pile of dust on the floor. It wasn't going to work.

I noticed Alex scrabbling at a round metal grating that covered a drain on the floor. I wasn't sure what she would accomplish if she got it loose—the drain was far too small for her to fit inside, and probably didn't lead anywhere very helpful anyway—but at the least she would have a piece of metal, a possible weapon if it came for her again. It was difficult for her to make any headway, since moving her broken arm made her gasp with pain.

"Here," I said. I tossed my keys across the gap. They flew across the wires with no ill effect, landing on the floor at her feet and sliding a few inches. She used a key as a lever, trying to pry up the grating, but it wouldn't budge and there were no visible screws. I wondered if it was welded to the pipe underneath, or if the concrete floor had just been poured around it, holding it fast. Whatever the reason, it wasn't moving.

I had found my family, but now I was going to lose them again. The varcolac was going to come back and torture them all while I watched, and eventually they would all die, and still the varcolac wouldn't kill me: it would just smile hideously and watch my reactions, and maybe kill Marek, too, just for fun.

I paced my cell. I had to *do* something. I couldn't just sit here, help-lessly waiting.

I started looking at the wires. Where did the energy for the electric shock come from? The varcolac must be manipulating the electromagnetic field somehow, allowing a free flow of electrons out of the wires and into anyone who got too close.

What if I could get higher? If I crossed the wires close to the ceiling, would that be far enough away not to cue the electric shock? The ceiling was wooden planking and beams, with no drop ceiling to hide the pipes and wires. There weren't many secure places to hold on, and I realized it would be very difficult to climb around up there. Besides, I couldn't reach it, and I had nothing to stand on to lift me higher. That wasn't going to work either.

"What's going to happen to us?" Alessandra asked. She was sitting calmly in her square, not doing anything. Claire had been crying more or less constantly since we'd been here, erupting into tears again just as she seemed to get under control. Alessandra hadn't cried at all. My heart went out to Claire and her anguish, which was perfectly understandable under the circumstances, but once again, I was impressed by Alessandra. Why had I never seen it before?

"We're going to escape," I answered her. "I don't know how, but we're going to find a way."

"I didn't mean that," Alessandra said. "I meant, what's going to happen to the two of us." She nodded at Alex. "Her and me."

I stopped my manic pacing. "You're the same person," I said. "She is you. At some point, you'll come together again." In fact, I was a little surprised their wave hadn't collapsed already. Their paths had converged again; their situations were practically the same. I supposed we didn't know all the rules yet. Maybe the longer the separation, the harder it was to come together.

"That's not quite right," Alex said. "You keep saying that we're the same person, but I don't think it's really true. We *started* the same, but we're different people now. We might react the same to a lot of things, but not everything. We know different things, and we have different memories."

"Then . . . one of us has to die?" Alessandra asked.

"No," I said quickly.

"Sort of," Alex said. "Don't sugarcoat it, Dad. We have to become one person again. That might mean just you, or just me, or some combination of us where we remember a little of both. We don't know for certain."

"You don't look scared," Alessandra said. "How can you not be scared?"

Alex laughed. "*You* don't look scared either."

They shared a look and a subtle smile.

"I still say you're the same person," I said. "Who *you* are is constantly changing. Who you were in third grade is different from who you are now, but it was still you. Right now you're just experiencing two different states at once. Like going back in time and seeing an earlier version of yourself."

Alex looked sad. "I know you're trying to encourage us, Dad. But if we converge, and I don't remember all the time you and I spent together, then it doesn't feel to me like *I* will exist anymore. Not this me, anyway."

"Your memory isn't everything," I said. "You forget things all the time; it doesn't make it not you. All of the cells in your body will be completely replaced in a few years, but you will still be here. Memories come and go. You don't remember being born, or even being two years old, but those experiences are still important to who you are. If, when you converge, you don't remember some things, those things will still be part of your identity, your personality, your growth as a person."

Alex didn't respond. Instead, she looked at Alessandra. "If I'm the one who doesn't make it," she said, "then get my viewfeed and post it. Let people know about me."

"Me, too," Alessandra said. "Promise?"

"I promise."

"First things first," I said. "We have to find a way to get out of here."

CHAPTER 36
DOWN-SPIN

"My best guess is that she went to the NJSC," I told Nick. "That's where her equipment and research is. That's where I'm going now."

"I'm coming with you," Nick said.

"I'm an escaped murder suspect. You'll be aiding and abetting," I said.

"I don't care about that. In fact, I'll drive. Hide that little toy car in my garage, so they don't find it here."

"Sounds good," I said. "One more thing—do you have a pair of eyejack lenses I could use?"

We switched cars as quickly as we could, and then Nick floored the accelerator. "We won't get there faster if we get pulled over," I said. "If the police recognize me, we won't get there at all."

He nodded in agreement, but he didn't slow down. On the way, I explained what I thought Jean was trying to do. "She can manipulate the Higgs field," I said. "She can change the wavelengths and basic constants of normal matter, which means she can control how it behaves to an almost magical degree. The real issue, though, is that the Higgs field extends across multiple universes. Which means that the probability waves she can influence extend there as well."

"You're losing me," Nick said. "What does that mean in English?"

"It means she can access alternate versions of your daughter. She can dip into other universes to change how probability waves resolved in the past. It means she can retrieve versions of your daughter that might have been if different choices had been made . . ."

". . . or different genes had expressed," Nick finished. "She wants to 'cure' her Down Syndrome, doesn't she?"

"That's my guess," I said.

His knuckles turned white against the steering wheel. "She's been talking like that for months. I told her it would just be killing our daughter and replacing her with someone else. I thought it was just crazy talk, though, not that she could actually do it."

"I'm not sure how well she can control it, either," I said. "She can't have studied it very thoroughly before Brian's death, and she certainly hasn't tried something like this before. No one has. She could end up killing Chance and not replacing her with anything."

Nick gunned the engine and zipped through an intersection just as the traffic light turned red. He was silent for a moment, then said, "Jean killed Brian, didn't she."

I sighed. "I'm pretty certain she did."

Nick slammed a palm against the steering wheel. "How could this have happened? We were so perfect for each other, so in love. I thought we were happy. Then Chance was born, and it was the best thing that ever happened to me, but Jean was so upset. So angry. She felt ripped off, somehow, as if life had cheated her. Her dream of how things were going to be had been swept away.

"But it was our daughter, you know? Jean couldn't see that. She had been planning to breastfeed; she'd been reading all these books about brain development, bought all the right toys and music, and suddenly, none of it mattered anymore. She left me to feed her, talk to her, put her to bed. She would just sit there and let Chance cry. Then after a while, she just stopped coming home."

I didn't know what to say. I rested my hand on the stolen gun in the pocket of my sweats. I didn't want to shoot Jean. I was no marksman; I wasn't sure I could hit her even if I tried. If she was holding the baby, I wasn't even going to point the gun in her direction.

"Can I use your phone?" I asked. I cringed as soon as I said it, realizing that it was an insensitive response to Nick's story, but Nick didn't seem to mind. He pulled it out of his shirt pocket and handed it over.

It was the new, slim type, about the size and thickness of a credit card. I tapped the screen, searched public records for the listing for Officer Richard Peyton of the Media police force, and called him. He picked up after the first ring.

"Peyton."

"Officer Peyton, this is Jacob Kelley."

A beat of silence. "Where are you, Mr. Kelley?"

"I want to turn myself in. But I will only do it, personally, to you."

"All right. We can do that. Where are you?"

"At the NJSC."

"I have no jurisdiction in New Jersey."

"Only to you," I said, and hung up.

Two minutes later, we careened into the NJSC parking lot and jumped out of the car. We headed straight for the Dirac building and Jean's office. Nick made a phone call and when we arrived, Carolyn Spiers, the building's administrative assistant, was holding open the door.

She did a double take when she saw me. "Aren't you supposed to be in jail?"

"They let me out on good behavior," I said. "We just need to see Jean."

"I don't think she's here," Carolyn said. Her desk was right in front of the entranceway. "I would have seen her come through."

"We'll check anyway," I said.

We didn't knock. I held the door handle down, quietly counted to three, and we rushed in. I had the gun out, but I kept it pointed at the floor. Jean was standing behind her desk, looking down at Chance, who was lying on her desk on top of papers and writing implements. Jean had the Higgs projector and she was manipulating circuitry symbols on its surface. Chance watched the smartpaper, transfixed, occasionally batting at it with a chubby hand.

Nick started walking toward them, but I held up a hand. I didn't know for sure what Jean could or couldn't do, but the situation required careful handling.

"You can't stop me," Jean said. "Just leave me alone."

"What are you doing?" Nick asked. "If you don't want Chance, just leave her with me. I'll take care of her. You don't have to have any part of her."

"I do want her," Jean said. "That's what you never understood. You love her defect, her extra chromosome. I love *her*. I want her to be whole."

"She is whole, Jeannie. She's her. She's Chance."

"Would you want to have the problems she will have?" Jean asked. "Do you want to trade places with her? You're being emotional, Nick, not practical."

Nick took a step forward, pleading. "She needs our emotions. She needs our love."

Jean's eyes blazed. "Don't you *dare* tell me I don't love our child. You have no idea the things I've done for her."

"Like Brian?" I asked.

Spots of color bloomed in her cheeks. "Brian betrayed me. He deserved everything he got."

"You were his new girlfriend, weren't you? The one he dumped Lily Lin to be with," I said.

Nick's head jerked at me, then back to Jean. "Brian Vanderhall? That's who you were sleeping with?"

"For all the good it did me," Jean said bitterly. "Yes, I slept with him, Nick. I did it for us, for Chance. I was everything he wanted: sexy, compliant, the female assistant to the brilliant scientist. Only I was different, because I understood the research, understood its implications—sometimes faster than he did. I swallowed my pride, accepted that he would overlook my contributions when he published, because I knew what this discovery could do.

"I knew it could change the past. Just a quirk of luck, that extra chromosome, like the random collisions and emissions of particles that happen a trillion trillion times a second. It didn't have to happen. It shouldn't have happened. We could undo it, choose a different path, a different random possibility. And we did it, Brian and I. We found the quantum intelligences, spoke to them, learned from them. Out of their knowledge and our own experimentation, a technology was born, more powerful even than I had been expecting."

"But then Brian wanted to destroy it," I said. "He took it away from you, without telling you what he was doing."

"He was afraid." Jean's voice oozed contempt. "He thought it was too powerful, that the intelligences would demand it back. I told him that power was the only way to keep them under control."

"He came to my house to show me and ask my advice," I said. "You followed him to my house. You're the ghost Officer Peyton saw in the snow outside. Then you followed him back to the bunker and killed him there, not realizing there was another version of him still alive."

"He betrayed me," Jean repeated. "I gave him my body, and I gave him my mind, and he didn't give me anything in return."

Nick was looking back and forth between us in growing consternation. "But you defended him," he said. "You spoke out in his favor at his trial."

"She had to get close enough to me to find the projector," I said. "She didn't know where it was."

"I didn't want to hurt you or your family," Jean said. "I didn't know Brian would mail the projector to you, or that you would end up accused of the crime. I was honestly trying to help." She pressed a button on the pager several times. On the table, Chance blurred and became a montage of babies, some happy, some crying, some kicking, some reaching, some clapping hands.

I slowly lifted my gun and pointed it at Jean's head. I wasn't going to shoot with Chance so close, but I hoped Jean wouldn't know that. "Step away from her," I said.

Jean made a guttural sound, like an animal's growl. "I told you, I'm not going to kill her. I love her." She looked back down at Chance, whose image started shifting through the medley of different possible Chances. Some of them became a little more solid, a little more real, while others faded into smoke.

"Last chance," I said. "Step back."

"Leave me alone," Jean said. "You can't win this." She flicked her eyes, and the gun was yanked out of my hands and clattered uselessly into the corner. She had the Higgs projector synched to her eyejack lenses, and she was much more adept at using it than I was.

But she wasn't the only one with a Higgs projector. The one I had used to escape from prison was in my pocket, synched to the lenses I had borrowed from Nick. I didn't know how to do much with it, and I had a feeling Jean had some custom subroutines in her version that she had written herself, but I had to try.

My mind raced. I remembered how I had tunneled the flour canister into the decorative table in my house when we found the projector . . . and a wave of dizziness hit me. That had been my double, not me. Once again, I was remembering something that I, the Jacob in prison, had never done.

I remembered how the table had exploded. I could tunnel a bullet or even a paper clip into Jean's brain, and she could do the same to me. I didn't want to kill her, though. I wanted to get the projector away from her. The problem was, she might have no such reservations about killing me.

One of the possible Chances became clear, a new version with a beautiful face, slimmer, with clear, round eyes and a closed mouth. "There she is!" Jean cried, exultant, her eyes wet with tears. "There's my child!"

CHAPTER 37
UP-SPIN

"W hy doesn't the varcolac have any eyes?" Elena asked.

"I have no idea." It didn't seem like a very pressing question. I was pacing again, angry, intent on finding a way to escape. "We barely understand who or what it is. It's utterly alien—just not the kind from outer space. Though, for all I know, maybe it travels in space, too."

"Is its body real? Can it be hurt or destroyed?" Elena asked.

I considered it. So far, we had seen no evidence of weakness, though the body seemed physical enough. I wasn't sure that, even if we could destroy the body, it would have any effect on the creature itself. "It must have fabricated its body in imitation of humans. Maybe it just doesn't realize that eyes are an important feature."

"Or they were too difficult," Alex said. Alex and Alessandra's voices were so identical that I had to look to see which of them was speaking. Alex still cradled her broken arm. It filled me with fury to see her hurt and not be able to help her, so much so that it was a moment before I realized what she had said.

"Too difficult to make eyes?" I said. "A creature who can jump between universes and who plays with reality like clay?"

"Could be. He hasn't mastered facial expressions, that's clear. Eyes are expressive," Alex said. She shrugged, which jostled her broken arm and she gave a little moan.

"You're doing great," I said. "Hang in there. We'll get you out."

The idea that there were things that were beyond the power of the varcolac to accomplish was encouraging. Of course, Alex might be wrong.

The varcolac might wear no eyes because it found them redundant or repellent. But it was something to think about.

I began pacing again, tracing the limits of my cage, trying to find some chink in the armor. I had no tools, no weapons. I had a solid cinderblock wall on one side and an invisible electric fence on the others. It was a simple and effective prison.

"Please stop," Elena said. "Sit down."

I kept pacing. "There must be a way out," I said.

"And you'll find it if you sit and explain it to me," she said.

She had always known me better than I knew myself. I sat.

"Now why is all this happening?" she asked.

I skipped over most of the details and jumped to the main point. "Brian Vanderhall and Jean Massey found a way to alter the Higgs field in our universe."

"What's the Higgs field?"

"It's a background field that gives particles their properties," I said. "It affects how much mass things have, what kinds of elements are possible, what their properties are—really, just about anything. Assuming you can control it, you can play God. Break the laws of time and space."

"And what does the varcolac have to do with it?"

"What do you mean?"

"You said these creatures have always been here, in our universe, unseen but present. Why can we see them now? What changed?"

I opened my mouth, then closed it again. I realized that I didn't really know. It was possible that they could do it all along, but something tickled at my memory, something Brian had said . . . "That's it!"

"What's it?" Elena asked.

"Brian said the varcolac was tied to the collider. That it feeds off of the exotic particles the collider produces, and draws from its power. And here it is, operating out of the collider's central power hub. It's not roaming the world, going wherever it wants to. It has to stay close to the collider, or at least it has to keep coming back again. The collider is what keeps it going, giving it the power to make these physical manifestations. There are hundreds of electromagnets here drawing thousands of volts every second." I drove my fist into my other hand. "That's got to be it."

"What does it mean?" Marek asked. "What do we have to do?"

"We have to shut off the power to the collider," I said.

"Can we do that from here?"

I shook my head. "We can't even touch the wires, never mind reach the breaker boxes. Besides, they're computer-controlled; I doubt it's a matter of simply flipping some switches. There are probably passwords, or even physical keys. What we need to do is call the control floor, and get them to shut the power down."

"How do we do that?" Elena asked. "Our phones don't work down here."

"No, we're too deep. We need someone outside to do it for us," I said.

"Which is impossible," Marek said.

I closed my eyes. I saw a flash of Jean Massey, of her office at the NJSC, of Chance lying on her desk. The other Jacob might have his own troubles to deal with, but at least he was free to move around and use his phone. "Maybe not impossible," I said.

CHAPTER 38
DOWN-SPIN

Jean's hand hovered over the Higgs projector, just moments from erasing the life of her child. The original Chance was still there, in the flesh, but the physically perfect version was superimposed over her, like a second movie projected onto the same screen.

I flicked my eyes through the projector subroutines and chose Strong-NuclearForce. A selector icon appeared in my vision, and I used it to select first Jean, and then the office wall. Jean and the wall were suddenly attracted to each other by a force far stronger than magnetism. She was hurled sideways and crashed hard into the paneling.

It wasn't enough. I ran toward her, hoping to grab her projector, but before I could reach her, I was thrown backward against the wall. I got up, ready to retaliate, just in time to see a swivel chair come crashing down on top of me. The metal base struck the side of my head, and I saw sparks. She was too fast for me, too accustomed to the interface and familiar with the subroutines.

Chance started to cry. Her face turned red, and she clenched her tiny fists while her wails filled the room. Jean rushed back to her, put a hand on her chest, and made soothing noises.

I tried to get up again, but my vision swam. I saw Elena in an underground room, and in that moment, I heard a voice saying, *Turn off the power*. I didn't have time to think about what it meant. I scrambled to my feet and fumbled with the StrongNuclearForce pointers again.

"This is none of your business!" Jean screamed at me. "Just leave me alone."

My pocket burst into flame. I threw myself back onto the floor and rolled to put out the fire on my pants. It worked, but the projector was burned beyond recognition. The message "Signal lost" flashed briefly in my vision. Just that quickly, Jean had won.

Nick tried to run for the desk and grab Chance while Jean was distracted, but she threw him aside like a rag doll.

"I was a friend to you," Jean said to me. "I didn't have to help you with the trial. I could have just left you to take the fall, but I didn't."

"You helped me because you thought I might lead you to the projector," I said.

"It doesn't matter. I'm finished with you. I'm going to do what I think is right, and nothing you do will stop me."

"It's another murder," I said. "You're planning to kill your own daughter."

Jean stroked Chance's hair and ran her finger along one cheek. "To cure her," she said. "I don't expect you to understand."

An explosion echoed through the room, unexpected and deafening. Jean cried out, and Officer Richard Peyton stepped into the room, his gun raised. "Hands in the air!" he shouted. Behind him were half a dozen more police with weapons and body armor.

Jean raised her hands. Chance started screaming again, frightened by the noise. "I just need to pick up my baby," Jean said.

"Don't let her do it," I said.

"Stop where you are," Peyton warned her, taking a step forward. "Don't move."

"She's the real murderer," I said. "She's trying to kill that child."

One of the other policemen was training his gun on me. "All of you, hands on your head. Lie down on the floor," he barked.

"Watch out," I said. "She can—"

Jean attacked. Peyton's gun flew out of his hand and his uniform burst into flame. Behind him, the other policemen were burning, too, but they were well trained. They didn't know where the attack was coming from, but they didn't panic or run away. They charged into the room, trying to control the apparent aggressors. Jean reached for Chance, and I knew if she touched her, she would teleport them both away and we would never find them. I reached for her, but it was ultimately Nick who took her down. He snatched a lab coat off a hook on the wall and rushed her, holding it high, blocking her vision. He wrapped the coat around her head, knocking her to the ground, preventing her from using the visual interface that controlled the Higgs projector. I reached her a moment later and tore the projector out of her hands.

Without it, Jean was just a person. She lay still under the lab coat, crying bitterly. I synched my lenses to her projector and saw immediately that it had a much improved interface, with more subroutines available and a more natural way of selecting and executing them. She must have been the intellect behind the software, not Brian, and she must have kept writing code even after he died. I imagined how furious she must have been when she killed him, only to find that he didn't have the projector on him, and she couldn't find it among his things.

I heard the voice in my head again: *Turn off all the power.*

Was my double actually communicating with me directly? *The power to what?* I thought.

To the whole collider, came the reply. *All of it. Hurry.*

I felt a sudden rush of panic, and then I could see everything my double was seeing as if I were there. I saw my family and Marek and the concrete sub-basement and the crisscrossing wires. Then I saw the reason for my double's panic: the varcolac had appeared next to Claire.

She screamed in utter panic and scrambled backward away from it. My double shouted and waved his hands and cursed at the thing, and I shouted and waved and cursed along with him. The varcolac lifted her with one hand and held her over the wires, where she flailed and screamed and smoked in the jagged lightning arcs.

The vision disappeared. Nick was shaking me. "What's wrong with you?" he asked.

I blinked and shook my head. "I have to go," I said. "Claire's in trouble."

"I don't think so," Peyton said. "I think you're innocent in all this, but I'm still going to have to take you in."

"I understand," I said. "But I'm sorry. I really have to go."

I flicked my eyes, executing the Teleport subroutine from Jean's projector, and disappeared.

In theory, shutting down the power to the NJSC wouldn't be all that difficult. There was an elaborate safety code that included the means to cut off power to any local region, or to the entire accelerator at once. An electrical fire in the wrong place could have devastating consequences. There were radioactive materials on site, flammables, and coolants that, if they outgassed, could kill anyone who didn't get out in time. There were blast doors and corridors designed intentionally as labyrinths to put as many walls as possible between people and potential accidents.

I materialized in the accelerator tunnel at a mile marker, right in front of a green-painted call station. I lifted the phone and punched the red button intended for emergencies. It was answered immediately by a professional-sounding female voice. "Fire in the tunnels!" I shouted, trying to sound out of breath. "It's spreading fast. Shut down the particle beams; shut down everything. This is a full-site shutdown emergency. Repeat, a full-site shutdown."

The voice on the other end acknowledged me, her voice raised in intensity but still calm. "I have you at mile marker twenty," she said. "We see no fire alarm indicators; are you certain?"

"The smoke is filling up the tunnel pretty fast here," I shouted. "I have to go. We're going to need some EMTs down here."

"How many people are with you?" I could hear the frown in her voice; she probably knew there shouldn't be any people in that part of the line.

"Just me and Frank," I said. "He's hurt pretty bad. Shut it down, will you? Follow the protocol!"

The safety rules didn't give her a choice. Anyone on site had the authority to call for a shutdown, and they couldn't decide at the control center to ignore it. It wasn't something that had ever been abused in the past.

"Hang tight," she said. "Power shutdown is in effect. Help is on its way."

CHAPTER 39
UP-SPIN

The lights went out. One moment, the varcolac was holding Claire over the wires; the next, the room was plunged into complete darkness. Jacob had done it!

"Run!" I shouted. I didn't know if the varcolac was still there, but I didn't want to wait around to find out. I raced toward where I thought Claire had been and nearly tripped over her where she lay, slumped on the floor. I threw her over my shoulder and groped blindly toward the exit, hoping that everyone else was headed the same way. A second later, an arc of electricity stabbed through the darkness into my body, and once again I was thrown back onto the floor.

The lights came back on, more feebly this time, but enough to see that no one had made it out.

"It must control the backup generators," Marek said. He, too, was lying on the floor, and I assumed he'd found out that our electric cages were operational again in much the same way I had. I sat up and cradled Claire in my arms.

The varcolac cocked its head, sniffed the air, and then vanished. I closed my eyes and could see where the other Jacob was in the tunnel. *Get out of there*, I thought. *I think it's coming for you.*

Claire moaned and opened her eyes. I stroked her hair and kissed her forehead. I could see places where her skin was burned in lightning fork patterns.

Alex was crying softly. "This is all my fault," she said.

"No," Elena said. "No, it's not."

"I ran," Alex said. "At the house. I was a coward; I just ran away and left you and Claire and Sean to die. If I'd stayed, if I'd fought . . ."

"If you'd stayed, you would have been killed with the rest," I said.

"You couldn't have done anything. I couldn't have done anything if I'd been there, either." The words prompted a pang in my own conscience, however. If I had been there with my family instead of off on a wild goose chase to find Brian, what might have been different?

"I could have warned them. Maybe they could have gotten away, too," Alex said.

"Look around you. They're here. They're alive." At least for the moment, I didn't say.

"I don't want to be a coward," Alex said.

"You found Lily Lin. You found the viewfeed that proved that Mom and Claire and Sean and Alessandra were still alive," I said.

"That was skill with a network, not courage," Alex said. "Next time, I don't want to be the one who runs away."

"Listen, if you get a chance, you run," I said. "Don't sacrifice yourself out of some stupid idea of heroism. You're no good to anyone dead."

I wanted to say more, but I was interrupted by the reappearance of the varcolac. In one of its hands, held as easily as if he weighed nothing, was Jacob, limp and unconscious. In its other hand was the only remaining Higgs projector.

It dropped Jacob on the floor. The projector—the last copy of it available on Earth, as far as I knew—flared with light and disintegrated. The varcolac stepped across the wires without effect and stopped in Sean's square. Sean looked up at it in silent horror.

Dread gripped my throat. Why was it doing this? Was it malicious or just curious? Did it know it was hurting them? Did it care? Sean was fragile; he always had been. I didn't know if he could withstand a prolonged electric shock. If I couldn't stop this now, there was a very good chance that Sean would die.

The varcolac grabbed him by the collar, ignoring his struggles, and rotated like a steel crane toward the wires. The lightning arced into Sean's body, and he screamed and danced and jerked.

I stood paralyzed, overcome with terror and panic. Claire and Alessandra were crying; Elena was shouting Sean's name. Marek had his hands balled in fists, as helpless as I was. Alex was yanking again on the drain cover in her square.

There was no time for cleverness, no way to climb up or around, no way to distract the varcolac from its task. I had heard that a dog could ram its way through an invisible fence if it was determined enough. I knew it was a bad analogy—a dog's electric fence was intended to keep him out by small shocks of pain, not throw him back by sheer voltage. Even so, it was the only chance I had. If I killed myself trying, we could hardly be any worse off.

Starting from the far side of my square, I ran at the fence, head down, barreling forward with all the speed and strength I could muster. I shouted an animal cry of determination and rage and plowed into the barrier with every intention of running straight through it and tackling Sean away from the wires and the varcolac.

I didn't make it. By sheer inertia, I pushed a few inches farther than I had before, but I was still hurled back into my square, the shock snapping my head back with skull-cracking force against the concrete. Pain flooded my mind, I saw the galaxies of lights again, and suddenly my vision split and I was two people at once. My memories flashed through my mind. I lashed out with a two-punch combination to the policeman's face at the same time that I peacefully accepted the handcuffs. I saw the back of the police car and the questioning at the station and my first night in jail; at the same time, I drove into Philadelphia to find Colin with Marek and Alex and slept in Colin's safe house. It was finally happening. The probability wave was collapsing. Jacob and I were merging back together.

The memories clashed and vied for ascendancy. At times, I slipped into one viewpoint and thought of that one as the real me and the other as the imposter. I tried to claw my way up, back out into consciousness, but my identity was fractured and my mind overwhelmed. I couldn't let go of either Jacob. They were both me.

The later visions seemed to stretch farther apart, like having one foot on land and one in a canoe as it drifts away from shore. We no longer fit in a single mind, but the wave was collapsing. There could be only one Jacob Kelley.

We were different, but there was much we had in common. We both loved Elena and Claire and Sean and Alessandra. Sean was suffering, dying. We had to help him. I stopped fighting, and just let it happen. I felt an internal click, as of two machined parts coming together, and without understanding quite what I had gained or lost, I knew I was one person again.

I opened my eyes. Sean was still screaming, the others yelling and crying. The square where my double had been was now empty. The air was filled with acrid smoke and the smell of burning flesh. Sean! I had to try again to reach him.

I pushed myself up, but my body betrayed me, muscles spasming and dropping me back to the floor. How long had Sean been held in the wires? My sense of time was completely lost. Through the haze, I saw Alex yanking off her socks and shoes. There was a small amount of water puddled in the gaps around the drain, and she splashed her hands in it, followed by her feet. I tried again to stand, and this time I managed a shaky vertical. Alex planted her feet on the grate and knelt in front of it, holding her hands forward as if she was going to push something. What was she doing?

I figured it out just as she uncoiled like a spring, kicking forward hard with her legs and straightening her body with her arms outstretched toward the wire bundle. "No!" I shouted, but it was too late. The force of her kick was hard enough that she reached the bundle and grasped it just as electricity jolted through her wet hands, down the length of her body, and across her wet feet to the grounded drain pipe.

It worked perfectly. I watched, horrified, as an unspeakable number of volts arced through her body in a blazing flash, and then everything went dark.

Or not quite dark. The varcolac glowed. It dropped Sean, who slumped to the floor. I ran and scooped Sean up. The electric fences were no longer operational. Light streamed from the varcolac in every direction, and then it seemed to dissolve, disintegrating into photons just as the steel pipe had done in the bunker so long ago. When it dwindled to a single point in space, there was a pulse of sound, like a deep bass drum.

"Run!" I shouted. I yanked Claire and Elena up and pushed everyone toward the open door. "Get out of here!"

The point exploded. The air shimmered, and the cinder block walls cracked. The ceiling crumbled, dropping pieces of masonry into the room.

"Wait!" Alessandra said. She stood rooted, staring at her double. Alex's body was stretched motionless across the floor, her skin and clothes blackened. "Is she . . . did she . . . ?"

"Go!" I said. I pushed her out the door, and looked back at Alex. Everything in me screamed to go back for her. I wanted to believe she could still be alive, even though I knew it was impossible. But I couldn't carry both her and Sean, and to try would be to endanger Sean. He was alive. I had to save him. Crying, I pushed out of the door after the others, just as the ceiling collapsed.

"Keep running!" I said. We ran up two flights of stairs and burst out into the accelerator tunnel. The varcolac was gone, but that didn't mean we were safe. The explosion had rocked the tunnel foundation and fired who knew what kinds of exotic particles through us and all the collider equipment. Cracks snaked across the tunnel roof and along the floor.

We ran, Claire in the lead, followed by Alessandra and then Marek and Elena. Carrying Sean, I fell behind, but not out of earshot. "Hide in the bunker!" I shouted.

We could see the entrance to the CATHIE bunker just ahead, where only hours before the varcolacs had surrounded us. I hoped it would be better protection than the open tunnel, where chunks of rock were already falling from the crumbling ceiling.

Before we could reach it, a large chunk of concrete landed on the back of Marek's leg, and he went down. "Go," he said. "It's just my ankle. I'm right behind you."

"I'll come back for you," I said.

I ran past him with Sean and ducked into the bunker, where the others were already gathered. I placed Sean in Elena's open arms, and then stopped, staring at them. All four of my family members had begun to shimmer, flickering back and forth between one image and another. Behind Elena and Claire and Sean, I saw their bodies as I had found them in the house, twisted and lifeless. Behind Alessandra's face, I could see Alex as she was now, blackened and burned by electricity. What was happening to them? Was this how I had looked when my probability wave had collapsed? Each of them wavered between themselves and their double, only in their case, each of their doubles was dead.

But hadn't Elena and Claire and Sean had already resolved to these versions of themselves? Their bodies had disappeared. Yet here they were, flickering between the two possible paths their lives had taken. Their quantum state must have been linked to the varcolac's, a kind of entanglement that forced all states linked to its existence to reach a final resolution, one way or another, now that it was gone. From a quantum perspective, it was simply a matter of probability. A coin toss whether they would live or die.

I stared at them, unable to move. There was nothing I could do to change what was going to happen. But I could help Marek. With a cry, I tore my gaze away and raced back into the corridor. Marek had pulled his leg free, but he couldn't put any weight on it. I draped one of his arms over my shoulder and supported him like a crutch. Together, we hobbled back toward the bunker.

We had only taken a few steps when the ceiling came down on top of us.

CHAPTER 40

We were lucky. Back near the power conduits, the entire ceiling had collapsed, filling the tunnel with rock and crushing the accelerator equipment and anything else in its way. Where Marek and I were, the damage was less, though we were still half-buried with falling debris. In front of us, the door to the CATHIE bunker was no longer visible. The entrance was blocked with collapsed masonry.

I called to my family, who were either dead or trapped inside, but I heard no answer. I had sent them there for their safety, figuring the bunker was structurally isolated and thus more likely to withstand the tremors, but I hadn't considered the volume of air. There was ventilation all through the tunnel and experiment bunkers, of course, but if it had been compromised by the collapse, there would be four people inside with not very much oxygen to go around. If they were even still breathing.

There would be a rescue crew, eventually, but we couldn't afford to wait. I started picking up rocks from near the door and hurling them aside as fast as I could. I was haunted by the sight of their flickering images, wavering between life and death, like a macabre slot machine with more at stake than just a few coins.

In the early part of the twentieth century, when the quantum nature of subatomic particles was just beginning to be perceived, there was a dispute among scientists, some of whom found the notion of collapsing quantum waveforms to be too ridiculous to be true. One of the leading scientists of the day, Erwin Schrödinger, wrote a letter to Albert Einstein and others with a reductio ad absurdum argument, describing a thought experiment involving a cat in a box, meant to demonstrate that the probability wave concept was nonsense. In subsequent years, Schrödinger's cat became even more well known than the scientist himself.

According to Schrödinger's experiment, a cat was enclosed in a steel chamber along with a flask of hydrocyanic acid and a Geiger counter. In the Geiger counter was a tiny amount of a radioactive material, small enough that in the course of an hour, one of the atoms of that material might or might not decay, with equal probability. If the atom did decay, the Geiger counter would detect the emission, prompting a hammer to fall and shatter the flask, releasing cyanide gas that would kill the cat. If no atom decayed, no hammer would fall, and the cat would live.

The chance of radioactive decay was not a simple chance in the larger world, like flipping a coin, but a fundamental, subatomic, quantum probability. It meant that if the box were left closed for an hour, the atom would exist simultaneously in both states, decayed and not decayed, in a probability wave that had not yet collapsed. The cat, as a result, would be split: both alive and dead at the same time, entangled in the same probability wave that governed the atom. Until you opened the box.

Schrödinger's thought experiment, ludicrous or not, was exactly the situation my family was now in. Both alive and dead, their probability waves would be indeterminate until I opened the door. The thought crossed my mind that I should stop digging, that it was better to be caught in a state between life and death than to be completely and irreconcilably dead. But that was no argument. The air inside would only last so long, and then there would be no living possibilities.

Eventually, a rescue crew arrived, and the work went much faster. The door was uncovered, the men shouted for anyone inside to stand back, and they smashed it open with a fire axe. A thin swirl of rock dust drifted out of the open doorway. I waited, holding my breath.

Elena emerged, coughing but smiling. "We're all here," she said. "We're all okay."

She ran to me, stumbling, and we had our reunion at last, colliding into an embrace despite our injuries and holding on to one another like we would never let go. The children came out next, Claire and Alessandra and Sean, bruised and burned but alive, completely alive. I hugged them each in turn, though as I reached Sean, I could tell that he was about to collapse. His skin was badly burned, and he was just starting to feel the pain, which I knew would get a lot worse before it got better. I held Alessandra close, thinking of Alex lying dead under tons of rock, and knowing that even if Alessandra remembered none of the last few months, she was still the same person I had come to love and admire.

The medics arrived with kits and stretchers. They took Sean and Elena and Marek away, loading their stretchers onto golf carts to take them to the elevators, and from there to waiting ambulances and to the hospital. Claire and Alessandra, unharmed, were left behind with me.

I hugged them both again. "I'm so glad you're safe," I said.

Claire gave me a tired smile. Somehow, even filthy with dust, she was beautiful. "Will the others be okay?"

"I think they will. Sean might be in for a long recovery, but he'll make it."

"I don't understand," Alessandra said. "What happened to Alex? What did she do?"

I explained as best I could about the final sacrifice she had made that had saved us all. I told Alessandra that Alex was dead, but not really dead, because everything Alex had been was part of who Alessandra was. They were the same, both of them, and I praised her for her quick intelligence and willingness to sacrifice herself for her family.

"But that wasn't me," Alessandra said.

I knew how it sounded, me heaping more praise and affection on a dead girl than I had ever shown to her. It would take time to turn that around. Time for me to demonstrate that I understood her better now, and loved her, not to the extent that she could be like Claire, but for herself.

"It was you," I said. "It really was. You just don't remember it."

Though it was strange that she wouldn't remember any of the last few months. I stopped to consider my own memories. I couldn't bring to mind everything about what it was like to live in jail, but I could remember the horror of my first night there. I could remember all the time I had spent with Alex, but at the same time, I could remember enduring the trial from the perspective of the accused. Some of my memories had blown away into the clouds of what might have been, but some, from both sides, were as clear as daylight. Why couldn't Alessandra remember some of those same things? Had the Alex I had known been lost entirely? Did this version of her really remember nothing?

Aid workers brought us blankets and bottles of water. A professional team arrived who regularly dealt with collapsed buildings and cave-ins and knew how to remove debris without risking further collapse.

"How many were in your party?" one of the professionals asked me.

"Six," I said. "Myself, my wife, three children, and my friend Marek Svoboda. My wife and son were taken to the hospital, and these are my two girls."

"We found another body in a chamber back that way." He pointed. "We haven't cleared enough to reach her yet, but she's female, a child about the age of yours. You don't know who she might be?"

I frowned. Alex shouldn't have left a body behind. It should have disappeared when her waveform resolved, just as the other Jacob's had. The truth hit me like a bath of icy water. When my two minds were coming together, and I was glimpsing flashes of both our memories, there was a moment when I felt like I might have resisted, might have held back or even prevented the collapse. It was an odd thought, scientifically, but wave collapse had always shared a strange connection to consciousness. If Alex had resisted collapse, however, then that meant . . .

"That's my daughter, too," I said. "And she's still alive."

CHAPTER 41

"A little higher on the left," I said. Alessandra lifted the left side of the Happy Birthday banner fractionally. "Perfect. Now climb down and help me with these balloons."

The summer sun streamed through the windows, giving the dining room a bright, cheery air. Alessandra and I untangled the strings of a dozen latex balloons and tied them to the chair backs in pairs: two reds, two blues, two yellows, two greens. Claire walked through with a pile of presents, radiant herself in an orange sundress and ribbons in her blonde hair.

"Tell Sean to come down, will you?" I said. "He can help, too."

Sean charged into the room at top speed and crashed into the opposite wall to stop his momentum. He had come home from the hospital just two weeks ago, but he was gaining in strength and energy every day. The plastic surgery had made the skin grafts on his face almost undetectable, and the doctors said that, given how young he was, the remaining scars would fade in time.

"Look what I made!" Sean said. He had taped five sheets of paper together and scrawled his own banner that read, "WELCUM HOME!" He had decorated it with pictures of fighter jets and dinosaurs, which was what he used to decorate everything.

"Great," I said. "We'll hang it up under the other one."

It had long been a tradition in our house that no birthday was complete without noisemakers, so I distributed horns and whistles to everyone's places around the dining room table. The flowered tablecloth was bright and festive, with colors that matched the fresh blooms in a vase at the center. Everything was ready.

Alessandra threw her arms around me and gave me a kiss. "Thanks, Dad," she said.

The doorbell rang. "It's them!" Sean shouted and galloped for the front door. I heard him wrench it open, and a brief pang of dread hit me, remembering Elena opening the door for the varcolac. But that nightmare was behind us now, and slowly but surely we were healing from it. Today was a celebration of that.

"It's not them!" Sean shouted at the top of his lungs. "It's only Uncle Marek!"

I went to greet Marek with a handshake so firm it would have crippled another man, and we exchanged looks of satisfaction. There was no need to thank him or say what I was feeling. It was understood. Colin arrived a few minutes later, and the room began to bustle with laughter and conversation.

Our van pulled into the driveway with Elena at the wheel. "They're here, everybody!" I said.

The conversation hushed, and we watched from the window as Elena unfolded a wheelchair from the back and helped Alex transfer into it. Elena took the handles, ready to push, but Alex waved her off. She used the hand controls, and after one bump into the rail, managed to maneuver up the newly installed ramp. Elena held the door open while Alex motored into the house.

"Surprise!"

The clamor startled her at first, but then she looked around at everyone and smiled. Her new skin was still pink—not a graft like Sean's, but a nearly complete replacement. Her hair had only just started to grow back, though it was coming in unevenly, some clumps growing better than others. Almost every system in her body that could go wrong had gone wrong, and she had spent months in the hospital fighting infections that had nearly claimed her life half a dozen times.

But here she was, alive and improving dramatically each day. The most painful parts were behind her, and now, at long last, she was home. Alessandra ran up with tears in her eyes. "Welcome home," she said and gave her sister a careful hug.

The varcolac had not reappeared, and for all we could tell, both Alex and Alessandra were here to stay. Alessandra had visited the hospital every day, and the two were now as tight as any pair of twins—tighter, even, since they shared so much history that they seemed to read each other's minds. I was still sorting through the task of explaining to the government and our medical insurance how I suddenly had three daughters where I had previously only reported two.

We headed for the dining room, where we had cheesesteaks for lunch (Alex and Alessandra's favorite) and shared stories about the days when the world had gone mad, some of which still hadn't been heard by everyone in the room. For dessert, Elena had made a pair of birthday cakes, one a reverse image of the other. We sang, the girls blew out their candles, and Elena passed around generous slices with scoops of vanilla ice cream.

After dinner, there were presents. Alessandra picked up a blue-striped box and started tugging at the bow, but I waved her down. "Open that one last," I said.

They took turns opening the other presents: a pair of necklaces from Claire, tickets to a Phillies game from Colin, and a beautiful pair of hand-carved, Romanian crosses from Marek. Finally, I handed them the blue-striped package.

They tore off the wrapping together and shrieked as they saw the familiar *Google* letters with the outline of an apple in place of the red *o*. They knew what it was before they even opened it.

The box was much larger than the actual gift, stuffed as it was with cushioning bubbles and elaborate, decorative packaging. Inside were two new pairs of eyejack lenses, complete with Google Apple's new stereo technology. This allowed a pair of viewers to record viewfeeds of the same event from different angles, and the software would stitch the feeds together into a three-dimensional immersion view. Alex and Alessandra threw the directions out with the wrapping paper, but they soon had their new toys up and running.

Elena and I watched as the two of them circled Claire, recording her as she tickled Sean to the point of tears.

"Hey, don't make him wet his pants," Elena called.

I put my arm around her and touched my head to hers. "It's a great family you have there," I said.

"I always knew she needed a friend," Elena said. "It's perfect, really, how it turned out." Her forehead creased as she said this, and I knew the statement was intended to convince herself as much as me. She was remembering the horror, and worrying how it would affect our kids' lives.

Alessandra distracted Marek while Alex slipped in and stole his second slice of chocolate cake. They put bites in each other's mouths and slapped hands in a high five. I knew all of the footage they were taking was being simultaneously posted on their joint viewfeed site, which was growing rapidly in popularity, given both the general interest in Alex's recovery from her injuries and the uniqueness of Lifer twins.

"They'll be fine," I said, giving Elena another squeeze.

Later that evening, when our guests were gone and the kids were finally settled in their rooms, Elena and I sat up in bed, holding hands and talking.

"It's still hard for me to put it out of my mind," she confessed. "You were exonerated months ago now, but I still keep expecting the police to show up at our door and drag you away."

"The judge's dismissal was final," I said. It had been a grueling private hearing, lasting hours, but Officer Peyton had finally convinced Judge Roswell that the police no longer considered me guilty of the crime and had arrested someone else instead. He told her that, in light of the arrest of Jean Massey, the police were ready to drop all charges against me. Considering how seldom the police admitted to a mistake of that magnitude, the judge listened carefully and ultimately dismissed the case. The jury, which had reached the end of its deliberations with a verdict, had been sent home without the opportunity to deliver it.

"I know," Elena said. "But the whole thing was so unexpected to begin with. I still dream of the varcolac and that empty face with no eyes. I know you say it won't be back, but you can't possibly be as certain of that as you try to appear around me."

"I don't believe it can get back on its own," I said. "And Brian and Jean's research has been destroyed. But the fact that it's possible means that, yes, some other quantum researcher at some other time could unwittingly open that door again." I squeezed her hand. "In the meantime, we have four beautiful and healthy children."

"Not quite healthy," Elena said.

"Getting healthier all the time." I laughed. "And there are four of them! Who would ever have thought it."

This coaxed a smile from her. "They are perfect together, aren't they? Did you see how they ran Marek in circles?"

Our laughter was cut short by the ringing of the phone. It was past ten o'clock. I could see Elena stiffen again. She looked at the screen. "It's Terry Sheppard," she said, the worry back in her voice.

I frowned and took the call. "Hey, Terry," I said. "What's going on?"

"Jacob, I have someone here who wants to talk to you," Terry said.

There was a rustle as the phone changed hands.

"Mr. Kelley?"

I didn't recognize the voice. "Yes? Who is this?"

"My name is Anna Majors."

"I'm sorry, do I know you?"

"I was juror number six."

Elena must have seen the look on my face, because she gave me a concerned look and mouthed, "Who is it?"

"Hello?" said the voice on the phone.

"Yes, I'm still here," I said. "What can I do for you, Ms. Majors?"

"I've been watching the news. I saw how that woman, Jean Massey, was convicted of Mr. Vanderhall's murder."

"Yes," I said warily. "Ma'am, I can assure you that the verdict was the right one." I had been a significant witness in the case, of course, and Jean's conviction finally closed the door on that whole affair. If I never walked into a Philadelphia courthouse again in my life, I would die a happy man.

"I don't doubt the verdict," Anna Majors said. "I just thought you might like to know *our* verdict, the one we were never allowed to read. We found you not guilty."

"Seriously? I thought for sure . . ."

"Yes, I'm serious. At the time, I thought you might very well have committed the murder—I apologize—but as a group, we felt that the story and evidence just wasn't clear enough to prove it. Not everyone agreed, at first, and it took a lot of argument, but that's what we all came to. Now, since they've caught the real murderer, I know you didn't do it, and I'm glad we came to that conclusion, even though it didn't count for anything. Anyway, I thought you might like to know."

I knew I was grinning, and Elena was giving me more and more curious looks. "Thank you very much, Ms. Majors. I do very much appreciate that you called. It's very good to know."

I clicked off. "What was that?" Elena asked.

I explained what Anna Majors had said, unable to keep from smiling. It didn't really matter in any practical way, but somehow knowing that, even with the limited information they had, a group of my peers had found me innocent gave me a great sense of peace. "It's the perfect ending to a perfect day," I said.

Elena grinned slyly at me. The tension was gone from her body. She crossed her arms in front of her and gently took a hold of the bottom of her T-shirt, twitching the ends up slightly. "Really?" she said. "The perfect ending?"

My smile grew even bigger. "Maybe not quite perfect yet," I said.

Then we stopped talking for a while.

ACKNOWLEDGMENTS

A great thanks to Eleanor Wood for loving this book and finding it a home. To Lou Anders, for making me so much a part of its production, and all the great people at Pyr and Prometheus for their enthusiasm and loving attention to this story. To the many people who read early drafts and pointed out its flaws: Mike Shultz, David Cantine, Chad and Jill Wilson, Mike Yeager, Roger Savage, Joe Reed, and Bob Walton. And to Karen, Ruth, Miriam, Naomi, Caleb, Lydia, Magdalen, and Silas, for making my life a delight.

ABOUT THE AUTHOR

Photo by Chuck Zovko

D avid Walton is the father of seven children, none of whom sprang into being via quantum superposition. He lives a double life as a Lockheed Martin engineer with a top secret government security clearance, which means he's not allowed to tell you about the Higgs projector he's developing. (Don't worry, he's very careful.) He's also the author of the Quintessence trilogy and the award-winning novel *Terminal Mind*. He would love to hear from you at davidwaltonfiction@gmail.com.